HAWK
CITY OF THE
DEAD

JAMES PATTERSON
AND MINDY McGINNIS

JIMMY PATTERSON BOOKS
LITTLE, BROWN AND COMPANY
New York Boston

JIMMY PATTERSON BOOKS
FOR YOUNG ADULT READERS
BY JAMES PATTERSON

Confessions

Confessions of a Murder Suspect
Confessions: The Private School Murders
Confessions: The Paris Mysteries
Confessions: The Murder of an Angel

Crazy House

Crazy House
The Fall of Crazy House

Maximum Ride

The Angel Experiment
School's Out—Forever
Saving the World and Other Extreme Sports
The Final Warning
MAX
FANG
ANGEL
Nevermore
Maximum Ride Forever
Hawk
Hawk: City of the Dead

Witch & Wizard

Witch & Wizard

The Gift

The Fire

The Kiss

The Lost

Cradle and All

First Love

Homeroom Diaries

Med Head

Sophia, Princess Among Beasts

The Injustice

The Girl in the Castle

The Runaway's Diary

For exclusives, trailers, and other information,
visit JamesPatterson.com.

Copyright © 2021 by James Patterson
Excerpt from *The Girl in the Castle* copyright © 2022 by James Patterson

Cover design by Derek Thornton/Notch Design. Cover art: figure © faestock/Shutterstock.com; feathers © CyberKat/Shutterstock.com; city © Zastolskiy Victor/Shuntterstock.com. Cover © 2021 Hachette Book Group, Inc.

JIMMY Patterson Books / Little, Brown and Company
Hachette Book Group
1290 Avenue of the Americas, New York, NY 10104
JamesPatterson.com

Originally published in hardcover and ebook as *City of the Dead* by Little, Brown and Company in November 2021
First Trade Paperback Edition: January 2023

JIMMY Patterson Books is an imprint of Little, Brown and Company, a division of Hachette Book Group, Inc. The Little, Brown name and logo are trademarks of Hachette Book Group, Inc. The JIMMY Patterson Books® name and logo are trademarks of JBP Business, LLC.

The publisher is not responsible for websites (or their content) that are not owned by the publisher.

ISBNs: 978-0-316-50069-2 (trade paperback), 978-0-316-55868-6 (ebook)

Little, Brown and Company books may be purchased in bulk for business, educational, or promotional use. For information, please contact your local bookseller or Hachette Book Group Special Markets Department at: special.markets@hbgusa.com.

The Library of Congress has cataloged the hardcover edition as follows:
Names: Patterson, James, 1947– author. | McGinnis, Mindy, author. Title: City of the Dead / James Patterson and Mindy McGinnis. Description: First edition. | New York : Jimmy Patterson Books, Little, Brown and Company, 2021. | Audience: Ages 14–18. | Audience: Grades 10–12. | Summary: Hawk accepts her mother Max's help to prevent vengeful hybrids, amoral scientists, traitorous politicians, and a deadly virus from overwhelming her beloved, polluted city.
Identifiers: LCCN 2021038103 (print) | LCCN 2021038104 (ebook) | ISBN 9780316500159 (hardcover) | ISBN 9780316500692 (paperback) | ISBN 9780316500326 (epub) | ISBN 9780316398633 (epub)
Subjects: CYAC: Genetic engineering—Fiction. | Survival—Fiction. | Mother and child—Fiction. | Science fiction. | LCGFT: Novels. | Science fiction.
Classification: LCC PZ7.P27653 Ci 2021 (print) | LCC PZ7.P27653 (ebook) | DDC [Fic]—dc23
LC record available at https://lccn.loc.gov/2021038103
LC ebook record available at https://lccn.loc.gov/2021038104

Printing 1, 2022

LSC-C

Printed in the United States of America

HAWK
CITY OF THE
DEAD

PROLOGUE

Who goes back to the city that tried to kill her? An idiot, that's who. But this idiot has wings, and I've spent most of my life learning how to fight. I guess that's supposed to be some sort of primal thing—fight or flight. There aren't a lot of people who learn how to do both at the same time. I'm one of them.

But I'm still an idiot.

Last time I saw Max—my mom—she told me that there will always be a war somewhere, and wherever that was, she and the Flock would be there to fight it. Given that she had two bullet holes in her at the time, the speech was pretty darn moving. I told her I'd be right there next to her, but that had lasted about as long as a pretty sunset... which in the City of the Dead means *not long*.

The pollution is better than it used to be, because the new Hope for Opes centers shut down the dope factories. But I still have to fly pretty high to get to clean air. That's where I am now—up. It's the only place I can get away from the Council, the people who are running the city now that McCallum and the Six Families are gone. Max and Fang—my dad—had me stay behind with my own little flock, kids from the Children's Home that I'd grown up with and looked out for. Calypso, Rain, and Moke.

But sometimes I even gotta get away from them, so I glide over here to the Marble Tower and watch the sunset, the warm rays getting choked out by the still-lingering smog. This is pretty much my own quiet time, and I can get kinda pissy if the Council needs me, or even my own group of orphan kids. The only person allowed up here with me is my trained raptor, Ridley.

Her head turns, eyes unblinking as her talons dig into my shoulder. She sees something she doesn't like, which means I probably won't like it, either. I follow her gaze, squinting in the dusk to see a fast-moving shadow tracing the edge of the Fallow Forest, which is just weird. Nobody goes in there. That place is overgrown and impossible to move through . . . plus I've heard more than a few scary stories about it. Not exactly bedtime stories, either, because I didn't have a mom or dad to tell me those. More like nightmare stories about things that live in there.

Things like I'm seeing right now. I shift and Ridley moves with me, both of us extending our wings as we take off, cutting the distance between us and the shadow. In the last of the evening light I can see that it's a creature on all fours, back hunched, a tail zigzagging in the grass behind it. I dive for a closer look, and it stands up on its back two legs—like a human. I hit the skids, letting an updraft grab my wings as Ridley lets out a distressed *caw,* right into my ear. She knows as well as I do—nothing and nobody goes into that dark, overgrown wreck of a woods. Nothing human, anyway.

Yep, like I said, I'm an idiot for agreeing to come back here.

But maybe Max and Fang are idiots, too. Because they didn't have to leave the City of the Dead to find the next war.

Looks like there's a new one brewing right below me.

CHAPTER 1

I've never been much of a morning person, and seeing the Council first thing doesn't improve my mood. The Council was formed after McCallum was overthrown and the thug families of the Six went down with him. I know that bullets and bragging are no way to run a city, but I don't think that boring meetings at six in the morning are the way to go, either.

I'm yawning and have a knuckle in my eye when somebody says my name. I look up to find that every adult in the room is looking at me—and I don't know what the question was. Or even who asked it.

"Um..." I play for time, scanning faces, hoping one of them seems friendly.

They don't. Not a single person is glad I'm here. I bet they're all wishing I was Maximum Ride, the hybrid hero, sitting in this chair. Not her daughter, a gangly fifteen-year-old who was left behind to speak on her behalf... even though I never know what to say.

"Yes," I finally decide on a word to use. I'm trying to keep it positive.

"Yes," a woman with steely-gray hair repeats, looking over her glasses at me. "The question was, which vehicles should we be relying on? Gasoline, diesel, or electric-powered. And your answer is…yes?"

"Yes to all," I say, determined to stand my ground even though I don't know what I've put my foot in. "I mean, it's kind of dumb to want my feedback on that. I just fly everywhere." I spread out my wings to illustrate, and one of the men rolls his eyes before shuffling his papers.

"*Kind of dumb* or not," he says, "Langford is required to ask for your input, as you speak for the hybrid population."

Langford, that's the woman's name. I can never remember because I just mentally refer to them in my head by the nicknames I made up. Bad Haircut. Worse Breath. Really Big Gut. Of course, for all I know they might think of me as Bird Girl, so maybe I should shut it.

"I saw something go into the forest last night," I say. Everybody looks up, twelve pairs of eyes just boring into me. So much for shutting it. Oh, well. Go hard or go home. "It wasn't human," I add.

"Wasn't human?" Langford asks. "Could you be more specific?"

"Well…" I stretch my legs out, resting my black boots on the table. The man next to me pulls one of his papers out from underneath them. "I'm here to speak on behalf of the hybrids, right? Well, I think that's what I saw last night. Another type of hybrid."

There's a minor uproar. The guy beside me immediately launches into an argument with the woman to his right, saying that there's no proof that there are more hybrids. "She's just a science experiment gone wrong," he says, hooking his thumb back over his shoulder in my direction.

"We don't know that," another woman, one with long blond hair, argues back. "The scientific exploration that created Maximum Ride and others like her was a secret, and could have been carried out in any number of places. We simply don't know what's out there."

I'd rather be referred to as an *exploration* than an *experiment,* but I don't have time to share my preferences. At the head of the table, Langford rises to her feet and slams down her sheaf of papers, bringing all the voices in the room to a screeching halt.

"Is this what happens when I don't bring coffee?" she asks, and the tension in the room evaporates into polite laughter.

"Now," she glances down at her notes. "I think we've agreed solar power is our best bet for the moment, but that some of the panels need repair. Holden, that's your area."

The guy I think of as Worse Breath nods. *Holden,* I remind myself. His name is Holden. Langford refers to her papers again.

"And as far as weapons resources go, we'll need to contact former members of the Six Families and see if any of them would be willing to share."

I snort. I don't mean to, but it slips out. I can't imagine my old friend Pietro, or any of the former bosses of the city, letting anyone know where their weapons cache is. Especially not the Council.

Langford ignores my snort and clears her throat. "As for the question of, ah...a monster in the woods..."

Laughter erupts again, not as nice this time.

"Well...I think that speaks for all of us," Langford says, tossing me an apologetic look.

A familiar burn starts in my gut, making its way up to my throat, where I know some really nasty words are going to come out if I don't get ahold of myself. I'm fuming as the Council members get up and start streaming out the door. Max and Fang left me behind again, just for this. To be mocked by a bunch of people who couldn't win a knife fight if they had a gun. Nobody in here probably knows the first thing about pressure points, or how to choke someone out, either.

Why am I even here, in a boardroom at the top of a huge building? I belong down on the streets, getting my hands dirty and my face dirtier. My mom and dad made a mistake, asking me to be their stand-in for the Council. Nobody here takes me seriously. And no one is willing to listen.

"Hawk?" I look up from sulking to see that Langford has hung back. "Has anyone ever told you that you catch more flies with honey than vinegar?"

"Who the hell wants to catch flies when you can swat them?" I ask, and she gives me a smile.

"I'll see you at the next meeting, Hawk," she says, smacking my boots off the table as she leaves.

"If I bother to show up," I say under my breath, but then I spot a yellow square of paper on my boot. Langford must have stuck it there.

I'm about to crumple it up and leave it for trash when I see there's writing on it.

You're not wrong. There's something in the woods. I've seen it, too.

CHAPTER 2

Something is tickling my face and I swat it away.

"Not now, Ridley," I mumble, rolling back into my pillow. But the feather follows me, this time inching its way right up my nostrils.

"Hey!" I swat at it. Only after I manage to thump myself in the face do I hear a familiar laugh.

"Nice," I say, sitting up to see my mom perched at the foot of my bed, her wings unfurled. "There are better ways to wake someone up from a nap."

Maximum Ride fluffs herself, a few stray feathers falling. "Well, I could just smack you around a little bit," she says. "It's not nice, but it's effective."

"Ha," I scoff, sitting up and pulling my sticky T-shirt away from my skin. I'd come back from the meeting in a crap mood and fallen asleep in my clothes. "Effective like the Council, you mean? I don't know why you want me there. I'm just expected to sit and be quiet in the meetings. No one ever listens to what I have to say."

"And what's your tone like?" Max asks. "Do you

have a weapon and are you threatening anyone when you speak?"

"Um..." I actually have to think about that one. There was an incident involving a switchblade and Holden that I'd rather not tell her about. But judging by the way her eyebrows go up, I'm guessing she already knows.

"Hawk," she sighs, coming to sit on the bed next to me. "I know you don't like being left behind—"

"Again," I cut her off. "Being left behind, *again*."

She goes on, ignoring me—just like everyone else.

"I talked it over with your dad, and Fang and I agree that having you with us right now is just too dangerous."

I pull a pillow onto my lap and wrap my arms around it. "What are you guys even doing?" I ask.

"We're trying to reform the prison that McCallum had me held in," she says, her eyes going dark at the memory.

"So why can't I be there, helping you?" I ask, but she shakes her head.

"No dice," she says. "It's not a friendly place, and I don't just mean the guards. There were so many factions fighting for control within the prison population, too. Right now, we're still trying to sort out who we can trust and who we can't." She pauses for a second, considering. "Also sorting out the death threats and trying to decide which ones actually mean it."

"You're getting death threats?" I ask. "But you're Maximum Ride! Everyone loves you!"

She pulls a face at that. "Not necessarily. McCallum did a good job of smearing my reputation—and your dad's—before we put him down. It'll take years to get everyone to believe we actually are the good guys."

I can't argue. Still, at least in a prison the bad guys are behind bars. As a kid, I lived on the streets without any kind of protection for a long time.

"I can take it," I say, shoving my chin out. "Let me come with you."

But Max just shakes her head and gets up, tucking her wings back in as she paces my room. There's plenty of space to do it in; the Council set aside the best suites near the top of this fancy hotel for themselves as soon as they came to power. As a representative, I got one, too. It's just about the only reason I keep showing up to meetings.

"Hawk, look at what you have here," she says, her thoughts following mine. "A warm bed, running water, clean sheets...and a great view." She goes to the window, her wings reflexively opening again at the sight of all that sky. They spread wide, lustrous and large. Maximum Ride is a breathtaking sight...but also kind of a punch in the gut when she's your mom. How am I supposed to live up to having superheroes as parents?

"Yeah, I'm spoiled," I say, looking past her wings to the view. "But I'm also bored."

"Bored isn't the worst thing," she says, turning back to me.

"What is?" I shoot back.

"Dead," she says.

I groan and fall back onto the bed. "Really? You're going to pull the parental concern card, after leaving me alone on the streets when I was five years old?"

"We've talked about that," she says, her voice hardening. "Fang and I thought someone was coming for you. We didn't mean for you to be alone."

"For ten years," I mutter.

"When are you going to stop punishing me for that!" she yells.

"When you stop treating me like a child!" I yell back.

She sighs and walks over to my bed, her voice soft again. "Hawk, you *are* a child. You're my child. And I'm going to make up for all the protection I didn't give you then by taking care of you now. This is the place for you, here," she says, spreading her arms.

"I know you think the Council is boring, but you are fulfilling an important role...."

I put a pillow over my face to block her out. Her words are different, but it's the same conversation we've been having ever since McCallum fell from power. Both Max and Fang want to make the world a better place, and they'll go wherever they need to be in order to make that happen. Someday, I'll be by their side. But right now isn't *someday*, which boils down to this—I'm being left behind again. My mom is basically still saying the same thing she did the day they left.

You're not ready yet.

I was ready enough to fend for myself for ten years on the streets. Ready enough to take on members of the Chang family with only my fists. Ready to drop-kick McCallum and face down the head of the Pater family. But...none of that matters to Maximum Ride. She's still going to treat me as if I were an overfed baby, just like the Council does.

Except for Langford...the woman who slipped me the note. Her voice drones on, but my mind wanders to Langford's words instead.

You're not wrong. There's something in the woods. I've seen it, too.

Sounds like there's someone who thinks I'm up to a challenge.

And I'm going to prove her right.

I go to the roof with Max to see her off. She's returning to the prison, where I'm sure she'll save the day and win the battle and do all the other things she doesn't think I can. She leans in for a hug, and I reluctantly give her one. But I'm stiff in her arms and Ridley takes a poop at exactly the wrong time, so it's a less-than-affectionate farewell.

I wait until my mom is a speck on the horizon and Ridley is firmly settled on my shoulder before going to see Langford. As acting head of the Council, she has an open-door policy, but I don't think she's quite expecting me when I knock.

"Hawk," she says, politely reframing her confusion into a welcome smile. "Come in!"

I follow her into her quarters, which I can't help but notice are nicer than mine. I grew up poor as dirt, which means that I know the value of things. I learned quick, mostly because that way I knew what to steal. Everything in her suite is high-quality, right down to the hardware. I bet I could get five bucks for just one of the drawer pulls.

She motions me to sit down on a white leather sofa. I do, fluffing my wings out and hoping that Ridley doesn't take another crap. Despite her smile, I don't know how welcome I actually am here. A steaming drip of doo-doo on her spotless furniture won't help.

"So, what did you want to see me about?" she asks.

Really? She's going to pull that line? Does she think I came here to debate the finer points of the democratic system? Last time we saw each other she stuck a cryptic Post-it to my boot. I level her with a glare, and she holds the politely inquisitive look for about thirty seconds before crumbling.

"My note," she says. It's not a question. It's a statement.

"What did you see?" I ask.

Langford leans forward, her knees bumping against the glass table that sits between us.

"I jog every evening. Sometimes I just have to leave this place behind," she lowers her voice like she's sharing a secret. "I know you understand. I've seen you flying sometimes when I'm out."

I nod, and she smiles, leaning back in her chair. "I think we're both feeling a little cooped up."

"You saw something while you were running?" I ask, and she drops the smile.

"Yes, I..." She hesitates, her eyebrows coming together as if she either can't remember, or couldn't understand what she saw.

"It was difficult to make out," she says. "At first, I thought I'd just imagined it, but then there was a flicker of movement. If it hadn't bolted for the forest, I would have never spotted it again."

"I know what you mean," I say. "I've got a bird's-eye view when I'm up there. Everything is small, but movement will catch my attention."

"What did it look like to you?" she asks. "I know what I saw, but I want to make sure we're talking about the same thing."

I close my eyes, remembering. "It was mostly like you said, shadow and motion. I did see a tail, for sure."

"Me, too!" she reaches out and taps my knee. I jump, and my eyes fly open. Ridley lets out a resentful screech but otherwise behaves herself.

"I'm sorry," she says. "I should have realized that you might not be comfortable with touch. I know you spent your childhood on the streets." She shakes her head. "Such a shame. A remarkable girl like you, left to fend for herself."

"I did okay," I say.

"And took care of a few other orphaned children, too. Am I right?" she asks, eyes wide.

"Yep. Calypso, Rain, Moke, and..." *Clete*. But I don't say his name. I'm not ready to talk about him with her. Or anybody.

"Astonishing." Langford shakes her head. "I can't speak for the whole Council, but I for one am glad to have you among us. Your instincts are clearly top-notch."

"Yep," I say again, squirming a little. I'm not used to people being nice to me. I mean, everything she is saying is totally true. I did survive the streets of the City of the Dead, and kept the others safe as well. I've always been proud of that. I've just never had anyone else be proud of me, too.

I feel a little warmth in my gut again, but this time it doesn't spread up to my throat and come out of my mouth in a stream of bad words and anger. Instead it stops halfway, somewhere around my heart.

She gets up and moves over to the minibar, where she pours herself a drink, holding a cut-glass decanter toward me with a question on her face. I wave it off. I've seen enough Opes on the streets to know better. Dope might have put a lot of them there, but I'm guessing more than a few started with the bottle.

She sips her drink and looks at me over the rim. "Shadow and motion," she repeats. "And a tail."

"It stood up, too," I tell her. "It was running on all fours, but I think it sensed me or something. It came up onto its hind legs, like a person."

She nods. "It's the same thing I saw. There's something living in our forest, right here in the middle of the city. We don't know what it is. We don't know where it came from. We don't know what it wants. I'm the head of the Council, and I want those questions answered. And I think you're the person who can do that for me."

I stand up, the warmth in my chest spreading.

"You bet your earrings I can," I say, and her hands go to cover them protectively, then laughs at the gesture.

"These are real diamonds. You've got a good eye."

"I've got two," I say. "So when do I start?"

"As soon as possible," she says, all business again. "I want to know all the intelligence you can gather. Report back to me—and only me. Some Council members..."

"Don't like me much?" I supply.

"I was going to say, 'aren't as open-minded as I am,'" she says. "But who am I to improve upon your words?"

"I'll start first thing if you let me skip the morning meeting," I say.

"Done," she says so quickly I think maybe I should've asked to skip a whole week of morning meetings. I head for the door, Ridley bobbing on my shoulder, restless and ready for the Marble Tower and a little alone time.

"Oh, and Hawk?"

I turn to find Langford right on my tail, a piece of paper and a pen in her hand.

"If you're going to miss out on the meeting tomorrow, I'll need your signature on this ahead of time."

"Sure thing," I say, scribbling out my name. There are twelve other signature lines, all of them for designated Council members. And me. A kid with wings in a room full of politicians.

"Thank you," she says, her hand resting on the door. "You're such a valuable member of the city. I can't wait to see what you'll become."

And for the first time in my life, I can't, either.

CHAPTER 4

There's nothing like flying, and I love having the skies to myself. Sometimes I don't know how regular people can stand it, constantly bumping into each other, sharing space, following in one another's tracks. Up here, it's just me and Ridley. We're the biggest things in the air, and all the other birds give us a wide berth. I glance over my shoulder, and the hawk's unblinking gaze finds mine. We bank together, her following in my downdraft as we wheel over the forest.

It's late evening, the last red rays of the sun flickering through some low-hanging clouds. Max would say it's beautiful, but I've got my eyes trained downward, not on the heavens. I don't give my mother another thought as we fly lower. I've tried time and time again to prove myself to Maximum Ride, but it was never enough. Now Langford has given me a job. And I'm not going to fail at it.

Except, I kind of am.

I punch a fist into my palm in frustration as we take another pass. Ridley follows, but I swear there's a question on her face. We're covering the same ground, over and over, and so far all I've seen is the tops of trees.

It's pretty to look at, for sure. There's an unbroken carpet of green beneath us, and while it looks as soft and puffy as a cloud, I know that it's made up of limbs and branches that would clock me a good one if I did a nosedive. For the record, clouds aren't that great to fly through, either. You come out wet and cold and it takes some time to figure out which way you're pointed.

I got lost in a cloud bank once when I was about ten. Flew right out of the city and over a lake so big at first I thought it had to be the ocean, and that I was straight-up screwed. My wings had just about given out on me before I found the shoreline, and I've never been more relieved than when my feet touched the ground. I slept wild that night, and was so happy to see the sun in the morning that I considered staying out there forever. The air was clean, the water was cool, and the sun was the brightest thing I'd ever seen...other than Calypso's eyes. I had my little band of orphans even then, and it was them that drew me back to the city.

I guess they're like my own little flock.

I turn again, Ridley still in my wake. If the orphans are my flock then she was the first member. It's always been the two of us sharing the winds and riding the storms out together—both in the skies and on the ground.

"One more pass," I call to her, hoping that there isn't desperation in my voice.

I scan the trees again, eyes focused for movement, a

shadow, anything that might resemble what I saw before. But there's nothing, only leaves trembling in the breeze. I dive lower, close enough to see spaces in the canopy. But there's nothing in them, just the forest floor—dark, dank, and overgrown.

"Crap turds," I say under my breath. Moke had given me a lecture about watching my language after Calypso had dropped the f-bomb last week. I promised him I'd try to do better, and mostly I manage okay.

Like right now, I really, really want to say some bad words. Frustration is welling up inside of me as I stare down at this unbroken sea of rippling green. Sure, it's pretty. But it's hiding a monster, one that I've been tasked with catching.

Ridley must feel my anger. She glides up beside me, cocking her head in a question, like she's asking, *Are we done here?*

"Yeah, I think maybe—"

I don't get a chance to finish.

There's a *crack* from below and Ridley evaporates into a red mist.

CHAPTER 5

I pump my wings once, twice, elevating myself out of gun-shot range.

Below me, Ridley's feathers float lazily down toward the forest, leaving a trail right toward the person that shot her.

"You son of a—"

I dive. I don't care about the bullets or the gun they came from. Ridley is the dearest thing I have, my oldest friend. She was with me before my orphans, before the Flock, and for damn sure before my mom and dad. I'm spitting angry, cursing as I fall like a meteorite, clutching Ridley's feathers in my fingers as I speed through them toward whoever—or whatever—shot her.

But my temper can't penetrate the canopy, and I doubt my words can even be heard beneath those leaves. I make it about five feet past the tip of a huge pine and have coni-fer needles in my teeth before I have to come back up. I spit them out and circle back, surveying the forest for a break, for a place that I can penetrate and find Ridley... or at least her body.

It's a terrible thought, and I screech with anger as I dive again, this time aiming for a gap in a maple's branches that I think I might be able to squeeze through. I get about as far as I did with the pine, but for the first time in my life my wings are not a benefit; I can't get through the trees with them spread out, and I don't know how far I'll have to fall if I lose my grip. I can't even see the ground, but the air still feels thin. I'm pretty high up. High enough to ring my own bell if I fall.

I rise again, losing all feeling of where we were when Ridley was shot. I fly in a crisscross pattern, on the alert for any more of her stray feathers, but I don't see anything, and the forest is deadly quiet. I know this sound, it's the same kind of silence that slinks through the streets after a scream that's been cut short. In the wild or in the city, there's always a moment where everything that's still alive takes a breath to be thankful, because they know something else just died.

And it wasn't them... this time.

No, but it was Ridley. And I am not going back to the City of the Dead empty-handed. I came out here looking for answers. I won't limp home minus a friend.

I spot a break in the canopy and go for it. I'm screaming as I crash through the first few branches. They're small, but that doesn't mean they're weak. They whip back at me and slash at my skin, raising welts on my wrists as I try to protect my face.

I pump my wings again, pressing downward, pulling apart crossed limbs as I go, hoping for access. Still, I can't see the forest floor, and what light was left above me is fading. It gets dark fast under a canopy this thick, and I've hardly made any headway before I can't make out much more than shadows. Frustrated, I spot a thick branch and settle my boots onto it, leaning down into a crouch. I need to catch my breath, need to think about the fact that I won't be able to spot Ridley's body even if I do make it to the forest floor. And I won't be able to see anything else, either... anything with a tail that walks on two legs.

I glance downward, hoping to get some sort of feel for how far below the ground is. Instead, I see a pair of eyes looking back at me through the leaves.

"Holy hell!" I shout, jumping to my feet. The branch gives out underneath me with a *snap,* and my wings open reflexively to break my fall. But there's not enough room for their entire span, and there's a sharp pain in my left wing. I cry out and push harder with my right wing, easing upward just as I glance down to see the eyes blink, once, twice, and then they're gone.

I bolt for the open sky, breaking out in the fading twilight like a swimmer in need of air, my left wing flopping, half-useless. I gasp and catch my breath, aware that I've got nothing to give but threats.

But I've always been good at those.

"I saw you," I yell at the trees, shaking my fist and the last of Ridley's feathers clutched there. "And when I come back, these feathers will be your last meal, 'cause I'm going to shove them down your throat 'til you choke."

But I'm the one that chokes, my voice breaking on the last word as I wheel toward the city, tears falling from my cheeks.

And I swear the sound of laughter follows me.

CHAPTER 6

It's impossible to straighten up and fly right with a damaged wing.

I keep pulling to one side, my healthy wing becoming tired more quickly than usual because it's doing twice the work. My tears are still falling, but a rising wind blows them away. I've got to find cover, quick, and somewhere I can get patched up, too. I make a decision and head toward the Pater estate, where I know I'll find Pietro.

He's an old friend...if you can call people that you've kissed a *friend*. But we never exactly talked about it.

After the fall of the Six Families, Pietro became the head of the Paters, and has done everything he can to wash the stain of violence from his family name. Their estate is now a Hope for Opes center; a place where strung-out people can get clean. They've got medical supplies there and a staff of trained doctors—all on the Pater dime. I'm sure someone there can check out my wing, and even better, not ask questions like they would at the city hospital. I don't exactly want Langford to know how badly I screwed up the one thing she asked me to do.

I land on the roof, my injured wing folded awkwardly at my side as I make my way to a trapdoor that I know will let me drop down into an upper hallway. I land on the floor badly, scaring the living daylights out of a nurse pushing a trolley loaded with clean linen. Unfortunately, some of my blood seems to have landed on her white sheets. She looks from the bright-red drops to me, her mouth a straight line of disapproval.

"Sorry," I say, and then add awkwardly, "I'll pay for that."

It's a stupid thing to say, mostly because I don't have any money. The nurse looks me up and down like she probably already knows that.

"Pietro?" I ask, and her eyes widen a little. "He's my friend," I explain.

"All right," she says, but there's more than a little doubt in her voice. She motions for me to follow her and I do, highly aware that I'm leaving behind a trail of mud, leaves, and pine needles. We pass a few patients in the hallways, all of them going through varying degrees of detoxing. Some are bright-eyed and give my wings a curious glance. Others carry blank stares, windows into a foggy world of semi-consciousness that not even a winged girl can impress upon.

I follow the nurse to the second floor, where she motions me forward with a nod. Pietro stands at the end of the hallway, talking in a group of people. I see him, and

27

blood instantly runs to my face, but it's not only because I'm remembering our kiss.

I'm also jealous.

The adults are listening to Pietro, nodding along with his words. And they're not just adults—these are doctors. Their white coats remind me of the spray of blood I left behind on the nurse's sheets, and I'm embarrassed all over again. Here I am, just a street kid, leaving a literal trail of dirt behind me as I wander into a rich guy's house. And not just any rich guy...one who talks and gets people to listen.

I remember this morning's Council meeting, where everything I said was dismissed with a laugh, and my blush deepens. Of course, that's the exact moment that Pietro notices me.

"Hawk!" He waves, making apologies to the doctors and walking toward me, his face instantly changing from happiness to concern at the sight of my awkwardly hanging wing. He told me once they were beautiful, and I can't help but wonder if he still feels the same way. "What happened to you?"

"I was in the forest," I say. "And Ridley..."

Great. Now my throat is closing up and I'm about to cry. On top of being dirty and hurt and in everybody's way, I'm also going to look weak.

"C'mon," Pietro says, grabbing me by the elbow and leading me into a patient room. He closes the door, and I sit on the paper-covered table, no longer concerned about what I look like. I only care about how I feel.

Which is shitty.

I cry, and he feeds me tissues like it's his job, finally wrapping his arm around my shoulder and pulling me into his body for an awkward sideways hug, my injured wing bent between us.

"Ouch," I say, voice thick with tears.

"Sorry." He pulls back and begins to examine my wing, as if he were a doctor himself. I cautiously allow it, fanning out my feathers so that he can find the wound. He pulls away bloodied feathers until he finds the cause.

"Not too bad, think I can patch you up myself," he says, turning to a small cupboard in the corner. He's all business now, and I try to be as well, straightening up my spine and wiping my face clean.

"It's really just a scratch," he continues. "You want to tell me how you got it?"

I'm drained. All emotion spent and gone. I don't have the energy to keep secrets right now. "There's something in the forest," I say. "Langford wants me to find out what it is."

"And what do you want?" Pietro asks, approaching me with a cotton ball and a squeeze bottle.

"I want to find out what it is, and then I want to kill it," I say through clenched teeth. "Whatever it is, it killed Ridley."

"I'm sorry," he says. "I'm sorry about Ridley...and that this is going to sting."

I nod, appreciating the warning, and then grind my teeth even more tightly together. He's quick and efficient, like he's been learning a lot from the doctors, while all I've been doing is showing up late to Council meetings and putting my boots on the table. Oh, and getting another one of my friends killed.

Damn it. First Clete, now Ridley. I'm not just ineffective and an idiot. I'm also a dangerous person to know. It's that thought in my mind as I pull away from him and hop onto my feet, spine ramrod straight.

"Thank you," I say tightly, nodding to Pietro. I head for the door, but he stops me with a hand on my shoulder.

"Listen, Hawk," he says. "I want you to be more careful."

I spin, all my anger coming out and landing on him. "Okay, thanks, *Mom*."

"I'm serious," he snipes back. "I know you're on the inner circle now, but the Council doesn't know everything."

"Inner circle?" I scoff. "Oh yeah, right. I'm a critical member, mostly there to provide comic relief when I try to tell them about the hybrid in the forest."

"A hybrid?" His irritation with me is forgotten. He's all ears. "What did you see?"

"It's hard to explain," I say, cautious. "It moved quick and I didn't get a good look. It was mostly shadow, but there was definitely a tail and..." I remember the eyes I saw right before I escaped from the forest. "And eyes," I say.

"A tail and eyes." Pietro makes a fake salute. "Roger that, I'll be on the lookout." I punch him in the shoulder and he shakes it off, but I definitely caught him wincing.

"Look, seriously," he says, straightening up again.

"Would you mind bringing something up for me in the next Council meeting?"

I sigh, and not just because it's a reminder that I do, in fact, have to be at the next meeting. It's also because I remember a time when Pietro and I used to talk like normal kids, complaining about our parents. Now he's helping recovering addicts and I'm a liaison for hybrids. It's like we both grew up too fast. But that doesn't change the fact that it happened.

"Yeah, sure," I say. "What do you want me to talk to them about?"

"Well, first of all, I'm not kidding when I tell you to be careful, and I don't just mean whatever is in the forest, either," he says. "I'd like permission from the Council to start training a militia." He holds his hand up as soon as he sees me about to shoot him down. "I know the Six didn't exactly do things right, but they did serve a purpose."

"Yeah, like keeping bullets in business," I snort.

"True," he agrees, not missing a beat. "But a lot of those bullets were being shot at the Marauders."

"The who, now?" I ask. I know all the gangs on the street, but I've never heard of anyone calling themselves the Marauders.

"Outsiders," he says. "The City of the Dead might be a dump, but it's also a gold mine, in its way. This place used to be one of the biggest cities in the world, and it's loaded with guns, ammunition, and even old tech that can still be useful."

I fold my arms, listening. "And somebody wants a piece of that action?"

31

"Everybody wants it," Pietro says. "But only a few groups outside of the city have the know-how to get it. The Marauders are sneaky, a real fly-by-night outfit. They use darkness as cover to get in, get what they need, and get out."

"What do they need?" I ask.

"Used to be just guns and ammo, something to shoot back at us, I guess. But lately..." He drops his voice, even though the door is still closed. "Some of my boys are still on the streets, unofficially speaking. And they say the Marauders are after batteries."

I splutter a laugh. "Uh-oh! Batteries! What will we do when our CD players die?"

It's a dumb thing to say, mostly because CDs are a thing of the past. But Pietro isn't smiling.

"This is serious, Hawk. If you'd think about it for a second, you'd see the danger."

Think about it for a second.... It's like something Max or Fang would say to me.

"Yeah, danger," I say, pulling open the door. "That's just not something I have a nose for, you know? Like all the times I've been shot, or stabbed, or chased. I have no idea what danger looks like. Draw me a picture, why don't you? That way I can spot it next time."

I slam the door behind me, but not before Pietro's words reach my ears.

"What do they need batteries for? What kind of machine are they trying to power? And what do they plan on doing with it?"

CHAPTER 7

The Marauders and their machine are the last thing on my mind the next day. The morning Council meeting went as planned—meaning that I sat still and shut my mouth. Langford didn't meet my eyes the whole time, but that could have been because I avoided her gaze. I've got nothing to show for my trip to the forest yesterday, nothing but missing the weight of Ridley on my shoulder.

Tears prick my eyes at the thought as I glide over the city, searching for Calypso. I know the little girl will be somewhere near our old stomping grounds. I might have been designated a nice room in a fancy hotel, but the rest of the orphans were still exactly that. My feet hit the cracked pavement in front of the old Children's Home, and I scan the windows, ready to see the faces I love best in this world.

Calypso is there, waving happily, and Moke is next to her, pointing to the side entrance. I make my way around to it, kicking aside trash as I go. I might live in a nicer place now, but it doesn't mean I don't miss this one. I understand why Calypso and Moke chose to stay here. Sometimes home isn't pretty, but it's still home.

"Hawk!" Calypso crashes into my arms, and I'm knocked a few steps back, almost tumbling down the stairs I just came up.

"Hey, girl," I say, ruffling her hair. Like me, my orphans are hybrids. Moke has blue-tinted skin, for some reason we've never been able to figure out. Calypso has very slim antennas. They extend from her back, smooth as silk, but strong and flexible.

It's those antennas I'm relying on today. She's told me before that she's pretty sure her DNA is mixed with some sort of insect. She can smell through her antennas, pick up a scent like a bloodhound. I'm hoping that whatever is in the forest stinks as bad as an Ope gone cold on the sidewalk, because I'm ready to chase it down.

"Want to come out with me?" I ask her. "Give Moke here a little break? He looks like he could use it."

Moke nods at me ever so slightly, and I realize it's true. I don't think I've ever seen my old friend look tired, but right now he seems worn out.

"Yeah, sure. I'll go," she says, practically hopping at the idea. Moke waves as we leave the complex behind, Calypso happily holding my hand as we weave through the city toward the forest.

"Where's Ridley?" she asks, and my throat gets real tight, almost not allowing my next words out.

"I lost her in the forest yesterday," I explain, which isn't entirely a lie. "I was hoping you might be able sniff her out."

"Lost her?" She releases my hand as we near the forest. "But Ridley never leaves your side."

"No," I say quietly. "No, she doesn't. All day I've caught myself looking over my shoulder to say something her, or just rub noses. I can't—"

She cuts me off, one hand gripping my wrist, eyes wide. "Don't move," she says, and I don't. The girl is spooked. Goose bumps have broken out all over her skin, her antennas wiggling furiously, face crunched together in concentration.

"Something's not right," she says. "I smell something... weird."

"How do you mean?" I ask. "What does it smell like?"

Her nose wrinkles, even though the antennas are doing the work. "Fish, maybe?" she says, then shakes her head. "I don't know, exactly. I can smell Ridley, just a little, and..." She gasps, her hand going to her mouth. "Blood! Ridley's hurt!"

I'm not surprised she can smell the hawk's blood. There was plenty of it.

"What else?" I ask, pushing harder.

"It's... human, but not quite. Like us," she confirms.

"But also a fish?" I ask, disbelieving. I saw this thing walking on dry land. Even if it is a hybrid, I don't think it was crossed with a fish.

"No." She squeezes her eyes shut, letting her antennas lead. I follow her footsteps to the edge of the forest, where dark branches reach for us like fingers. "But something cold-blooded, I think."

She opens her eyes. "And it's got three toes."

I gape, astonished at her ability. "You can smell how many toes it has?"

"No," she says, pointing. "I was looking at that."

I follow her gaze, where a footprint is stamped deeply in the wet soil.

"Stay here," I say stiffly, and go closer. Calypso was right. There are three toes…and a claw springing from each one.

CHAPTER 8

"Claws?" Langford repeats, staring back at me.

"Yeah," I say, relaxing my head back against her couch. "Big enough to leave a track."

She swallows her drink—which came out of the cut-glass decanter again, even though it's still morning. When I told her I wanted to speak to her after the meeting, her eyes went cold and still. I knew she wasn't expecting me to tell her anything good, but I don't think she was expecting claws.

"Interesting." She rolls her glass in her hand, the amber liquid inside following the motion. "Anything else?"

"Calypso said it smelled cold-blooded," I say. "I don't know exactly how she can tell cold-blooded from hot-blooded, but she said to trust her."

"Warm-blooded," Langford corrects me, then laughs when she sees how I stiffen. "Although I guess there are certainly some hot-blooded folks who walk among us, too. Right here in this room, even."

I relax a little, and she smiles at me over the rim of the

glass. "Thank you, Hawk. Obviously, I picked the right person to send into the forest."

"Yeah, so what are we gonna do?" I ask.

The liquid stops swirling. "Excuse me?"

"What are we gonna do?" I repeat. "My raptor was killed. And all I've got to show for it is a footprint."

Langford shakes her head. "I think you're misunderstanding what the goal is here. I wanted you to gather information. You have."

"Yeah," I agree. "So now what?"

She sighs and leans forward, setting her glass aside like she thinks sobriety is going to be necessary to handle this conversation. "Look, I understand that you're a...person of action. But there are safety concerns at work that you haven't considered."

"No, I haven't," I say. "Just like I wasn't worried about my safety, or Ridley's. I did what had to be done, and now what? We're just going to *gather information*?"

"I'm sorry about your bird. Truly, I am," she says. "But what is it that you would have me do? Issue a public notice? If the general populace knows there is an unknown creature in the forest, they'll either panic or try to kill it. Neither option is good for a city trying to rebuild and function in peace."

I stand up and stalk over to the windows. I thought she was going to give me a chance to prove myself. Instead she's spewing the same sort of talk as my mom—*be careful, stop being angry, use nicer words.*

Okay, Moke was the one who told me stop swearing,

but still. The feeling is the same. I'm doing something wrong. Asking for too much, or giving too little.

"We need this city to remain calm and safe," she says, and I feel a spike of anger in my veins. This city has never been calm and safe. It might look that way from up here, but when you get down to street level, you get dirty, fast. I knew that when I was just a kid, and I know that now.

"The Marauders have been raiding the city," I say, low and quiet, waiting for a reaction. Behind me, Langford falls silent. I turn to face her. "They're looking for batteries to power something. And we don't know what it is. Does that sound calm and safe to you?"

She clears her throat and gets up from her chair, leaving her drink behind. "I think this sounds like something you should have told me sooner."

"Sorry, I was busy getting my friend killed," I say. "Because you asked me to."

"And I may have to ask more of you in the future," she says, crossing the distance between us. "You have the courage and the power to act. I admire and respect that quality. But you have to let me decide when, and to what measure."

We hold gazes for a second, and she looks away first.

"What can you tell me about the Marauders?" she asks.

I repeat Pietro's words of warning and pass along his request to form a militia.

"Well, let's not use the word *militia*," she says, smiling brightly, drink back in hand. "At least, not in the Council meeting. In fact, it's probably best not to mention it yet.

I'll speak to members who I know will be friendly to the idea, just to ensure the vote goes our way when it comes up. Pietro should feel free to begin training, of course. But you didn't hear that from me."

She tips me a wink and reaches for my wings, fingers brushing against my feathers. I stutter-step backward, but she pretends not to notice.

"You know, not everyone appreciates the beauty of hybrids. I can see it. But I know others…well…" She looks away, out at the city skyline. "I don't like telling you this, but it might be smart to keep something of a lower profile in the coming days."

Lower is something I've never liked. The skies are where I belong. "What do you mean?" I ask. "Why?"

Langford sighs and turns her gaze out the window. "McCallum worked hard to sow distrust among the people of the city. He was very successful at convincing some citizens that hybrids are the enemy."

"Enemy?" I repeat. "He's the bad guy! He's the one that got half the city hooked on dope and the other half practically starving or killing each other!"

"Of course," she agrees. "But it's an old trick. Convince the people that someone else is at fault, then nobody blames you. Unfortunately, some in the city have turned against hybrids. Some people even call you an abomination."

"I've been called worse," I say.

"I'm sorry to hear that," she says. "Like what?"

"I can't say," I tell her. "I'm supposed to stop swearing."

She smiles wryly and walks me to the door. When

we reach it she pauses, hand on the frame. "I know you want action, Hawk. And I hear you. You asked me—*now what?* I'll tell you. Find out where Pietro has the Pater weapons stashed, and I promise we'll point them at the forest first."

CHAPTER 9

I head right over to let Pietro know he can start training his militia—but not to call it that. I haven't flown since I dodged the bullet above the forest, and while there is a dull ache in the wing, it's minor. Max always said that babying an injury makes it heal more slowly. I don't know if that's true, but I can't picture Max babying anything... even a baby. But I do miss the cleaner air, so I decide to give it a shot.

Pietro was right; my injured wing hurts, but it's more of a scratch than anything. I've been holding it awkwardly and being super careful with it, which has made my shoulder sore and caused more pain than the bullet I caught. Up in the sky, I pump both my wings, reassured by the loosening in my muscles.

"I'm back!" I shout at the city below me, but at the same moment I turn my head to say something to Ridley. Except she's not there. My happiness dies on my lips, and so does some of my mood. I glide down lower, keeping an eye out for anyone I might know.

I've got a couple of different air patterns I take around the city and quite a few friendly faces along each of them. My cushy rooms might be the best benefit of being on the Council, but having people wave me down to ask my opinion—or for a favor—is nice, too. Makes a girl feel appreciated.

But that's not happening today.

I wheel around past the nicer section of town, where a line for bread snakes out the bakery door. A few of the customers glance up, but most of them look quickly away, and one young mother even snatches her daughter's hand when she lifts it to wave at me.

Weird.

I turn east, cruising low, and pass over an upper-end apartment building where I can usually spot a few people hanging out on the balconies. One woman shades her eyes with the novel she's reading, sees me, and ducks inside like she's afraid I'm about to drop a bomb on her. Another man hangs over the railing, yelling something. I'm far enough away that I can't hear him, but the way he's shaking his fist, I'd say it's probably not a compliment.

What the hell? Was Langford right? Do some humans hate hybrids?

I cut my pleasure cruise short and head toward the Pater estate. I've got to pass over some rough parts of town to get there, but that's nothing new to me. I lived there most of my life.

I'm wheeling over an ugly old factory when I hear the snap of a bullet and instantly dive for the ground. I've heard enough lead fly through the air to know when it's close, and when it's not. A stray shot above these streets wouldn't be unheard of, but that one was meant for me.

I spot my shooter in an alley and dive for him. He gets another shot off, but it goes wild, and I hit him square in the chest with my boots. He goes down, and so do I, both of us rolling through trash. I come up first and snap-kick his knee, which sends him down again, but he keeps a grip on the gun. It's the old kind, a revolver with a spinning cylinder. He's only got six shots and he already missed two. I rise above the ground, watching him struggle to gain his footing in a pile of garbage.

"Hey," I call. "You've got four more shots. Want me to stick around?"

"You nasty—"

"Guess so!" I say and clip him with my boot again, this time in the teeth. He keeps his legs under him though, and the next shot doesn't go wild. It zips past my skull, tracing a path through my hair right above my ear. Blood sprinkles down on him like rain, and he dances in it.

"I got you!" he yells. "I got you, you dirty hybrid!"

There's blood running down my face, into my mouth and my eyes. I can't see, and that means I can't fight. I pump my wings furiously, but I'm flying blind, and the alley is tight. My back crashes against a brick wall and I slide down to the ground, dazed.

He drags me up by my wings, which hurts like hell. I wipe blood from my face and smack the pistol aside just before the fourth shot goes off, pinging off the wall behind me. I grab his wrist and pull his gun arm toward me, twisting at the same time. There's a wet *pop*, and his face goes white. The gun hits the ground with a clatter and I scoop it up, tucking it into my jeans.

He's crawling away from me now, using his good elbow to drag himself forward. I leap over him, my boots hitting the ground in front of his face. He looks up at me and spits.

"What the hell is wrong with you?" I scream at him. "Why would you take a shot at me like that when I'm just minding my own business?"

"Above my city," he screeches, face going red with anger. "A city that belongs to people. Not someone like you."

"I grew up here, butt-breath," I say. "I belong here."

He shakes his head furiously as more of my blood drips down on him. "No, you don't! You belong in a lab. Or in hell with the other demons!"

"Oh, I'm a demon now?" I ask, kind of liking the idea.

At the mouth of the alley, there's a crowd forming, which is not good. The shots must have attracted attention, and in this part of the city that means anybody who heard is coming to see who lost...and what they left behind.

"Good talk, but I gotta go. I'm going to keep this to remember you by," I tell the man, patting the gun as I rise up, blood still dotting the pavement from the wound in my head.

I keep the smirk on my face until I'm high enough he won't see it fall away. I won that fight, no doubt, but there was no reason for it to have happened in the first place. He took a shot at me when I was gliding and posed no threat to him.

He took a shot at me because I'm a hybrid.

CHAPTER 10

I fly about ten blocks before it feels safe to be on the ground again. That guy rattled me, and I'm still bleeding. Woozy, I find a shadowed corner at the edge of an old storage unit and decide to rest before moving on to Pietro's. A trail of blood follows me, bright splatters on the old pavement. I rest my head against the building, wiping away blood and sweat from my face.

Distracted, I hear the footsteps a second too late. I leap to my feet and am reaching for my gun when a cold voice behind me says, "Don't move!"

I've been in a few tough spots, but I know when I'm beat. There was the click of a safety being thumbed off right before I was warned. This person is armed, and they have the drop on me. I raise my hands to either side of my wings, calculating how far away the guy is. I might be able to get a spin kick in . . . but I'm woozy, and spinning might be off my options list.

"Hawk?"

What the hell? I turn around, hands still in the air. "Pietro?"

His gun goes down, confusion on his face. "What the hell are you doing—never mind. You're hurt."

He comes forward, sliding under one of my arms. I lean into him, grateful for the support. "Let's get you inside," he says.

We make our way past the storage units, each one the size of a garage and bolted down tight. Pietro takes me into the office and eases me into a chair, then turns on a desk lamp to take a closer look at my head wound.

"It's just grazed," I say, running my fingers over it. "He missed."

"He kind of missed," he corrects me, snapping off the light and pushing it aside. "What did you do to deserve that?"

"Would you believe me if I said nothing?"

He cocks his head to the side, thinking. "Yes, actually," he decides. "This city is changing. McCallum might be gone, but he said a lot of nasty things about hybrids, and some of them stuck."

"I'll say," I wince, pulling a mat of blood-soaked hair free from my head. "What are you doing on this side of town, anyway?" I ask. "I was just coming over to let you know you can go ahead and start training your people."

"Yes!" Pietro jumps up so high it's like he's the one with wings, fist pumping the air. "Awesome! The Council said yes?"

"Well…" Technically, no. The Council hasn't said anything yet, but I don't want to derail his excitement.

"Then this is the perfect time to show you around," he says, grandly offering me a hand as I get up from the chair. "Madame, welcome to Pater Gun Storage."

"Oh!" I say, following him back outside. Rows and rows of units face each other, and he walks me down one aisle, guiding me with little touches on the elbow that aren't really necessary. "Are these all filled with weapons?" I ask, impressed.

"Well, technically this is called the Pater Garage, but there's not a car on the lot. We've got lots of guns and ammo, sure, but other stuff, too. I'm pretty sure there's a tank in 4F."

"A tank?" I repeat, unable to hide my shock. "Why would the Paters need a tank?"

He shrugs. "Because we heard the Chungs had one."

"Nice," I say, not sure if I'm mocking him. *This is impressive. There's enough weaponry here to power an army, not just a militia. Langford will fall all over me when I tell her, and I can barrel into the forest on a tank. That'll show whatever cold-blooded—*

"Hawk?" Pietro asks. "Did you hear me?"

"What? Huh?" I say, snapping out of it.

"I said you can't let anyone know where the stash is," he says, popping the bubble of my dream world where I avenge Ridley.

"Why?" I ask. "You can't possibly need everything here for yourself."

"No, but it's not about that. The Paters weren't known for being good people. But I'm coming at this from a different angle. I'm working to get guns off the streets, not flood them with more."

"Tell that to the guy who winged me with this," I say, pulling the revolver from my jeans.

"Old school!" he says, his face lighting up when he sees it. He turns it in his hands. "Needs cleaning, but I can show you how. And I should have ammo for it."

"So you're trying to keep guns off the streets, but you'll give one to me?" I ask, eyebrows raised.

"You probably need it more than anyone," he says, pulling me aside as he fumbles with a ring of keys. He opens the unit and we go inside. There's a table and chairs set up in front of a literal mountain of ammo.

"And besides, you're as dangerous without a gun as you are with one," he says, pulling out a chair for me.

"Thanks," I say, sitting down. "So glad I get to drop bullets from the sky as I continue my reign of terror as a demon."

"A what?" Pietro pauses his search among the ammo boxes, turning back to me.

"That's what that guy said, the one who shot me," I tell him. "I guess not everyone thinks my wings are beautiful."

A blush rises in his cheeks when I repeat his words, and he turns back to the bullets. "All the more reason to arm you," he says, pulling an ammo box from the stack. "Okay, I'm going to show you how to take this gun apart, clean it, and put it back together."

"They do more than go boom?" I ask, eyes wide with fake astonishment.

He pulls out a chair and sighs. "Don't make this harder than it has to be."

It takes me more than a few tries to get it right. Dismantling a gun is not easy, especially when you've got a head wound and a sore shoulder. But he is a good teacher, his fingers guiding mine when I do the wrong thing. His hand stays on mine once we've finished.

"There's something I want to talk to you about," he says. "Something important."

I glance down at our hands, a sinking feeling in my stomach. I don't know how to talk about this. I'm better at trading insults and teasing.

"I know why you got shot at today, and it's not just because you're a pain in the ass."

Okay, so I guess that's *not* what we're talking about. I take my hand away. "Yeah, I know. The guy has a problem with hybrids."

He shakes his head. "It's more than that. We don't just have Opes coming through our doors lately. My staff says there's a new sickness on the streets. One that kills quick. People are coming in with high fevers, ruptured eardrums, boils and blisters. I've treated some of them myself."

I'm so glad I'm not holding his hand anymore.

"What's this got to do with me?" I ask.

"This disease popped up fast, and spreads quickly," he continues. "The doctors are saying humans don't have any type of natural defenses against it. They think it must have jumped from another species."

"Oh...," I say, a sinking feeling in my stomach.

"A lot of people are blaming the hybrids," he says, following my thoughts. "It could get really dangerous out there for you guys, if this keeps spreading."

Spreading like the forest, dark fingers reaching out for people.

"It's always been dangerous for us," I say.

CHAPTER 11

I wake up to a persistent tapping on my window and roll over to see one of Max's messenger pigeons outside, wet and impatient. I groan and fall back onto my pillow, which only makes the bird keep tapping and the wound on my temple break open again.

"Hold on to your feathers," I snarl at the pigeon as I pad to the bathroom, grabbing a clean towel and pressing it to my forehead as I pull open the sliding door to the balcony. The city spreads out below me, a concrete maze that the rain won't ever quite be able to clean. The pigeon hops onto my wrist, and I pull the door shut again just as a gust of wind blows the rain against it in a sheet.

I pull the small container from the bird's foot and the pigeon flutters to the couch, perching on the edge, ready for a return message. Just like most people she meets, Max has this bird eating out of her hand. I fall back onto my bed and unroll the note.

Hey, Hawk! Hope everything is going well in the City of the Dead. We've had a few uprisings here at the prison, but nothing that some kind words couldn't fix. Also, some head-butting. (Your dad said I had to include that). And, if I'm being honest, Gazzy also had to show off some of his bomb-making skills in order to keep everything under control, so it's more like a war zone than anything else. We're very happy here. Keep that city under control, and let us know if you need help. Maybe ask the Council to consider renaming it? The City of the Dead doesn't have a great ring to it. Keep us in the loop!

Max

There was a time when getting a note from Maximum Ride would have made my entire day. Then I found out she was my mother, and I had to take the idea of this superhero that I'd idolized my whole life and mesh that with the person who had abandoned me on the streets—the person I'd vowed to never forgive.

This note is not helping. She and Fang are off on a reunion honeymoon, having the time of their lives, complete with bombs and head-butting. Meanwhile I've been left behind (again), because she thinks it's too dangerous for me to be where she is.

Dangerous. Whatever. I'll show her what's dangerous.

53

I flip the scroll over and find a pen.

Max—The forest has monsters in it. The Marauders are raiding the city. There's a plague going around that hybrids are being blamed for. The Council thinks I'm annoying. Also, Ridley died. But you guys have fun. I got this.

I put my less-than-comforting message inside the tiny canister and the pigeon hops to me, eager to be useful.

"Yep," I tell the bird as I attach my note. "Do everything she asks. Do it perfectly. See if it matters. She'll just come up with something else."

The bird cocks its head at me as if it were listening, then takes a crap on my leg. I sigh as I release it into the wind. At least my life is consistent. I can always expect to be shit on.

CHAPTER 12

I don't want to go, but I promised myself I would. I tuck my wings underneath a jacket and pull the hood over my face as I make my way to the Institute for the Blind. I tell myself that I'm hiding my wings and my face because of the rain, not because I don't want to be spotted as a hybrid.

I shouldn't have worried. Everyone on the street has their face down as the weather pelts us. I shake my hair out on the steps of the Institute, and I'm buzzed in. I approach the front desk, but don't need to introduce myself. The nurse glances up and recognizes me.

"Oh, Hawk. You must be here to see Rain for your weekly visit. Right on time!"

She smiles cheerfully, like being able to follow a calendar and a clock is an amazing display of skills. I pull some of my hair down to cover the wound from the bullet so that Rain won't ask me about it, then chide myself for forgetting.

Rain is blind. McCallum's scientists took her eyes out, and I couldn't do anything about it. Guilt sweeps over me as I follow the nurse down the familiar hall and to her door. This is where she lives now, all because I couldn't get to her in time. I straighten my shoulders when the nurse walks away, determined to at least sound like everything is okay.

"Rain!" I say as I walk into her room. "How are you doing?"

She turns from the window, looking directly at me even though I know she can't see.

"Hawk! Thanks for coming. You must be soaked to the skin."

She must have been able to feel the rain striking the window. "Yep," I say. "Little water never killed anybody."

"I don't think anything can kill you," she says, and I walk forward into her outstretched arms, leaning into the hug.

"Wish Max agreed," I say as I take a seat. Her hands flutter out, positioning herself in the room as she finds her own chair.

"Still babying you?" she asks.

I nod, then remember she can't see it. "Yep," I say again, and suddenly find myself at a loss for words. It's not the first time this has happened with her. It's hard to look at her eyelids stitched to her cheeks without blaming myself, the same way I blame myself for Clete's death.

"I don't know," I say. "Maybe Max is right not to trust me yet. I couldn't..."

I break off my words, not wanting to remind her of the bad times. Like she could ever forget.

"How is Calypso?" she asks brightly, effortlessly changing the subject.

I tell her about the forest, and how we think Calypso smelled out a new kind of hybrid there. I detail the footprint, watching Rain's forehead wrinkle in confusion. I don't tell her about Ridley, or mention how tired Moke looked when I saw him last. I try to keep my meetings with her positive, but she doesn't seem to need me to feel good. She smiles as I talk about Max's note and my response.

"Max loves you," she says dreamily. "She doesn't want to put you in harm's way."

"I'm still in it," I say, my hand idly reaching for my temple. "And I don't know where you get the idea she loves me."

She only smiles, which I find oddly irritating. Angry with myself for feeling that way, I come to my feet. "I should probably get going," I say.

She rises with me, following me to the door, where a doctor in a white coat waits in the hallway, looking up when we emerge from the room.

"Ah, Rain," he says, "I was just coming to retrieve you for your spatial training lesson."

"Thank you, Doctor," she says, still smiling sweetly. She turns back to me. "Everything will be all right, Hawk. I'm sure of it. Keep your head up...and clean that wound out."

"Yeah, yeah," I mutter as I walk away, then realize what she just said. How did she know I was injured? I spin, but she's chatting with the doctor as he leads her down the hallway, one hand on her elbow.

My hand goes to the wound again, where I feel some fresh blood. She must have smelled it. Rain told me that her other senses have sharpened since losing her sight. There's never a good time to be bleeding, but as it happens, right now isn't so bad.

I'm going to the hospital, and I'm going to find out what exactly is going on with this plague I'm being blamed for.

CHAPTER 13

The rain is still a downpour, and I keep my trench coat wrapped tightly, my wings hidden. The hospital isn't far from the Institute for the Blind, and I get there before I've come up with a plan. Squaring my shoulders, I walk through the sliding doors. Plans are overrated.

I stand, dripping, by the front desk until the woman working there lifts her head. "Hi," I say. "I'm a Council member and I need—"

"Stitches," she says grimly, coming to her feet. "You need stitches."

"What, this?" I say, my hand rising to my temple, where the bullet passed close by. "It's just grazed. I've had worse."

She looks me up and down, taking in my black boots, worn jeans, and ragged coat. "I believe you," she says, "but if you'd like the option of getting seriously injured in the future, you'd best let someone take care of that now."

I have to smile at that. I've always brushed off my own pain, and been downright proud of my scars. I'd never thought about taking care of myself now as ensuring I can get into more trouble later.

The woman leads me to a plain, small room and says someone will be with me shortly. I take off my coat and try to squeeze some of the water out of it over the sink. I shake my wings, spraying water everywhere. It hits the wall and slides down in little droplets, just like the rain outside.

"Oops," I say, surveying the damage.

There's a sign posted on the back of the door, printed in large, black letters.

Inform Staff Immediately If You Have the Following Symptoms:
  Fever
  Headache
  Rash

If You Display Any of the Previous Symptoms, Have You:
  Been in contact with a hybrid lately?
  Shared a public area with a hybrid?
  Had a hybrid in your personal space?

There's more, but I stop reading. I'd like to get in the personal space of whoever made this sign, and I'm not interested in hanging around and waiting for a doctor to poke and prod at me in a place where I'm clearly not wanted. I shrug my coat back on to cover my wings and crack the door. I don't spot anyone in the hall, so I slip outside and try to look like I know where I'm going.

But I totally don't. The hospital is a maze, and while there are signs posted, I don't know what half of them mean. I really wish one just said, HAWK, GO HERE. But I'm not that lucky, instead I'm stuck at a crossroads with options like HEMATOLOGY, INFECTIOUS DISEASE WARD, RADIOLOGY, and PRENATAL CARE. I know what at least two of those things are, and infectious diseases sound way more interesting than babies, any day.

I follow the arrows pointing to the Infectious Disease Ward, but there are two big red doors sealing the way forward. They're guarded by a serious-faced nurse behind a glass panel. She's wearing a mask that has smiley faces on it, but I highly doubt that's what her mouth is doing under there. She slides a glass panel to the side and beckons me forward. Caught, all I can do is obey.

"Name?" she asks, and I straighten my spine and decide to bluff this one out.

"I'm here on behalf of the Council," I say.

"Name?" she repeats, without blinking.

"Langford sent me," I try. I mean it's not *my* name, but it is *a* name.

"Name?"

I sigh and step back from the counter. "Never mind," I say. "I'll just come back another time."

"Stay where you are," the nurse says, her hand disappearing out of sight. I don't know if she's pushing a buzzer or going for a gun, and I don't plan on sticking around to find out. I bolt for the stairs, just as I hear her screaming for security. I slam into the door with my sore shoulder, and a grunt of pain escapes me. So much for future trouble—I've got enough on my hands right now.

I go down two floors, then dodge into a hallway. I'm sure there are cameras everywhere, so I've got to change my look. I duck into a patient room where an old man is asleep, a television squawking at him from the corner. His closet doesn't give me many options, but I leave my wet trench coat in a puddle, switching it out for a jacket and a baseball cap.

I crack open the door and eye the hallway, but all I can see is a doctor and a nurse, both leaning over someone's chart. They don't notice me, and they don't seem concerned. I slip into the hall, walking idly past patient rooms and planning my next move. I need to know what's behind those red doors in the Infectious Disease Unit. Patients with blistering rashes and bloody ears? Or hybrids like me and Calypso and Rain, being experimented on in the hopes of finding a cure?

My hands clench into fists. I won't allow that to happen again. I won't let someone like me be punished for something they aren't guilty of.

Behind me, the stairwell door crashes open, making the nurse squeal and the doctor jump, dropping his files. I don't wait to see who is coming for me—I break into a sprint and reach the elevator bank just in time. The doors slide closed, and for a split second I see the faces of two security guards, large and heavily sweating. I flip them the bird and push a bunch of different floor buttons at once.

I get off on the fifth floor, once more scanning for activity before wandering out into the hall. There's a large, circular nurse's station right near the elevators, but nobody's home. They might all be busy with patients, or following some sort of lockdown procedure. I have no way of knowing which, but I'll take my chances. I snag a vase of flowers off the counter and head down the hallway toward the patient rooms, trying to look innocent.

I peek into a couple of rooms where patients are distracted by what's on the TV, or simply sleeping. One older woman is staring out the window even though the view is only of a brick wall on the opposite side of the street. I raise the flowers to cover my face when I notice a camera in the wall, but I can hear the mechanical whirring of it following me as I pass.

Crap. I should have known I wouldn't be good at looking innocent.

I drop the flowers and the vase breaks, sending water and broken glass all over the floor. A girl comes to her door, pale blond hair falling to either side of her face.

"What is going—"

She doesn't get to finish. The door to the stairwell bursts open and the two security guards erupt from it. I spin to run, but my boots slide in the water and I go down, landing hard on one knee. A rough hand grabs the collar of my jacket and I'm hauled to my feet. I try to shake loose from their grip, but I'm no match for both of them. I struggle, kicking and fighting, almost wriggling out of the jacket.

The blond girl is yelling, telling the men to leave me alone.

She grabs ahold of one of the men, but he smacks her aside. She hits the wall and slides down it, dazed. Free from one of my attackers, I jerk out of one sleeve of the jacket, and the other tears. I bolt away, but don't get far. Two more security guards come out of the elevator, hands on their stun guns.

I eye their weapons, then their faces. They won't have any trouble using the guns. I watch them take in my wings, and one of them raises his a little higher.

"Can't a girl get medical attention without all this fuss?" I ask, but they're not going for it. All four of them have a good grip on me as I'm marched down to the entry-way, where the woman who told me I needed stitches stands with her arms crossed, her mouth thinning into a hard line when she spots my wings.

"Not worried about me now, huh?" I ask, right before I'm tossed into the street, literally. I actually roll down the steps and am rubbing my wrist when I stand back up. "I hope my insurance covered that!" I yell, but the guards don't even look back.

Some loose feathers blow down the street, knocked from my wings in the scuffle. I watch them go, the rain flattening them before they're sucked into a drain, headed for the sewer. I spit and am about to walk away when I spot motion in one of the windows. It's the blond girl, waving her arms to get my attention. We lock eyes and she points up, to the roof.

I nod and flex my wings. Maybe I'm going to find out what's behind those red doors, after all.

CHAPTER 14

I land on the hospital's roof just as the rain lets up. Puddles have gathered, and I take in my reflection. I don't look so great. My feathers are most definitely ruffled, and there's a bump forming above one eye where a guard clipped me a good one. At least it draws attention away from the little bit of blood running down the other side of my face. I swipe it away just as the door to the roof opens. The blond girl emerges, looking cautiously behind her before easing it shut again.

"Are you okay?" she asks, coming toward me.

"I'm fine," I nod, and take a step back as she gets too close.

"I'm not going to hurt you," she says. "And I'm not afraid of getting sick by coming near you."

"Why not?" I ask. "A lot of other people seem to be."

She shrugs and holds out one arm. There's a red plastic bracelet there. "I'm already going to die," she says.

"Why? What's wrong?" I ask, stepping forward.

"It's my lungs," she says, and for the first time I notice

how pale she is, and how heavily she's breathing just from climbing the stairs to the roof. "I grew up near the ope factories," she explains, and she doesn't have to say more. I know what the air was like near those places, and what it could do to the people who breathed it in.

"How long do you have?" I ask her.

"Two months, maybe," she says. "Unless someone checks out early and leaves me their lungs."

We both know the chances of that. In the City of the Dead, working organs are a hot commodity. I've seen bodies in the streets stripped like cars, nothing left behind but the chassis.

"What's your name?" I ask the girl.

"Melanie Hodges," she says, holding out her hand. We shake, and her fingers are cold and small in mine.

"Melanie, I'm Hawk. I'm on the Council," I say. "If you can help me out, I'll try to help you back." I'm careful not to promise anything, I know how dangerous hope can be. I spent ten years waiting for my parents to come back for me, after all.

"You're wanting to know more about the virus," she says, and laughs when she sees my surprise. "The security guards had their radios on pretty loud. They thought you were trying to break into the Infectious Disease Unit."

"I wasn't trying to break into anything," I say. "I just had some questions."

"Like what?"

"If there even is a virus at all, for starters," I say, and she nods vigorously.

"Yes, there definitely is. And it's killing people, all right," she says. "They've been carting the bodies out. They're trying to keep it quiet, but the nurses are scared, and they talk…especially when they think you're asleep."

She gives me a sly smile and I give one back. This girl might be at death's door, but she's eavesdropping, not dying. She has information—and I've got questions.

"Any idea how serious this is?" I ask, not wanting to use stronger words. But I shouldn't have been worried. She cuts right to the center of what I'm asking.

"How many dead?" she asks. "I can't give you a number. Too many to count. They're being carted out at night, when the patients are supposedly asleep."

"Carted out?" I repeat. That doesn't sound good.

"To the loading docks in the back, and the trucks." Melanie nods.

I whistle, low and long. "That's a lot of dead bodies."

"And those trucks don't go to the cemeteries," she adds. "I watch them from the window. They head for the Blazes."

I understand. Those bodies are never getting buried.

The Blazes are twin piles of garbage that have been burning outside the city for as long as I can remember. Trucks haul stuff outside of the city to incinerate, but most of the ash finds its way back in, either covering buildings or slipping inside our lungs as smoke. I cover my mouth and nose instinctively, not liking the idea of breathing in a bunch of dead people.

"They're burning the bodies? Why?"

"To stop the virus," she explains, walking me over to

67

the side of the roof near the west side of the city, where the Blazes burn. Two smoke spires rise in the distance, a view we've all become accustomed to. But now the smoke seems darker, the implications more sinister.

"Why blame the hybrids?" I ask, resting my hand on the barrier that reaches my waist. She leans against it, clearly tired, her eyes heavy with exhaustion.

"One of the first people to come down with it used to work in a lab," she explains. "She..." Her words stutter to a stop, and she looks at me apologetically.

"Performed experiments on hybrids," I finish for her. "It's not news to me."

"She died in agony," she says.

"Good."

"After that, a few more like her came in, all of them from that same lab. I heard some of the doctors talking outside my room, speculating that the illness had jumped from a hybrid to a human during the experiments."

"But they don't know that!" I say. "They did all kinds of crazy stuff in those labs. They could have been working on a biological weapon on the same floor, and it leaked to those people working with hybrids."

"You don't have to tell me," she says, holding her hands up in the air. "But that's the word that got out, and a lot of people believe it."

"That's for sure," I say, rubbing at the bump above my eye. "Have you seen any sick hybrids?"

I don't believe for one second that hybrids are the source of this virus—that just sounds like a nasty rumor. But if none of us are showing symptoms, that isn't going to help our case.

"Yes," she nods. "Not a lot, though," she adds, eyebrows coming together. "I think hybrids have been avoiding the hospital, maybe hoping to lay low and recover on their own. But I've definitely seen hybrid bodies being carted out, along with humans."

I'm almost relieved to hear that hybrids can get sick, that's how screwed up this situation is. We can't win—if we're not sick, we're the source. If we are sick, we're just as dead as the humans.

"Well…thanks, Melanie," I say. "I really appreciate you talking to me."

"You're welcome," she says, wrapping her arms around herself and rubbing her bare arms in the breeze. "Can I ask a favor?"

"Sure," I say, but my heart drops into my stomach. I can't promise her a top spot on the organ donor list. I should've kept my mouth shut.

"Do you think you could…maybe take me for a ride sometime?" Her eyes go to my wings, wide in wonderment.

"Uh…" I wasn't expecting that. She's my age. Even though she's no thicker than a stick, flying with a passenger can be tricky. I've tried short flights with Calypso in the past, but I don't want to take away what life this girl has left—even if it is only two months—because I drop her. Plus, it won't exactly help bring humans around to believing that hybrids don't mean them any harm if I start splattering teenage girls on the sidewalks.

"Can I give you a rain check on that?" I ask, rolling my shoulder. "I've had a couple bumps and bruises lately. Don't want to try hauling you around unless I'm sure it's safe."

"Of course," Melanie says, heading back to the door to go below, back to her room. "But Hawk..."

I'm on the concrete wall, ready to take off, but I turn back when she says my name.

"Don't wait too long," she says, holding up her red bracelet. I nod that I understand, then leap into the air.

I bank west, heading for the Blazes.

CHAPTER 15

I follow the trucks leaving the hospital, flying high through cloud cover so that I'm not spotted. I hate this new feeling that my wings are something to be ashamed of, that even being seen and recognized can pose a threat.

The trucks pause at the city walls—awkwardly built stone barriers meant to keep the wrong people out. Living in the city has a lot of downsides. Crime. Poverty. Belching smokestacks and the smells of a million people all gathered together, cooking in their own stew. But outside those walls is something worse—chaos and mayhem. I don't love the Council, but at least they try to keep something resembling peace in the streets.

Armed men hop onto the running boards of the hospital trucks at the city gates, making them look like big spiders, with guns for legs jutting out at all sides. I dip lower, knowing I'm safe for the moment. Any attack on the trucks— like the Marauders Pietro mentioned—will come from the ground, not the air. But I don't think they have anything to worry about. The bright-red crosses on the side mark them as hospital vehicles, and the smell alone lets everyone know what's inside—death.

A sudden gust of wind makes the smoke from the Blazes change direction, so I circle around, my eyes stinging. I land near the fires, hunkering down near a stripped-out vehicle someone left behind and attempted to burn. I lean against the metal, watching as the hospital trucks come to a stop nearby. The men jump down, tightening their masks as they pull open the double doors.

Melanie wasn't lying. The bodies are disgusting. I cover my mouth to keep from gagging as the men pull on rubber gloves and aprons. Men and women are hauled from the back of the truck, their hair hanging lank and stiff with dried sweat...and worse. Their eardrums have ruptured, blood and pus hang down from their scalps in dried chunks. The faces of the dead are forever stuck in a rictus of pain, their teeth biting into their lips, eyes squeezed tightly shut.

I've seen bodies before, and agony is nothing new to me. But the sheer number of corpses coming from the trucks makes my head spin as the men return, time and time again, arms full of the dead. The bodies—human and hybrid—are tossed onto the burning piles as if they were nothing more than garbage. Hair catches first, giving the dead bright, fiery haloes, making them oddly beautiful in the moment before their flesh begins to melt.

Clothes go fast, falling away to reveal the skin beneath. I

spot the rashes. Raised red blotches line their torsos, more than a few ribs showing underneath. These aren't only well-fed lab workers. A lot of these people look wild and dirty, like I was when I lived on the streets. That means the virus is spreading beyond the walls of the hospital.

And a hatred for hybrids is spreading with it.

CHAPTER 16

"We're going back to the forest," I tell Calypso, who sits up and wipes sleep from her eyes.

"Cool!" she says, the promise of an adventure waking her up completely.

"Is that a good idea?" Moke asks, his blue skin reflecting the last of the sunset that streams in through the windows of the Children's Home.

"Aren't all my ideas good?" I ask.

He smiles, but shakes his head *no* at the same time. Once again, I notice how tired he looks.

"Listen, Hawk," he says, "I know you need to get to the bottom of what's in the forest, but I don't see why Calypso has to be dragged along with you."

"I'm not being dragged!" Calypso says, crossing her arms. "I want to go."

"You want to go because you'll do anything Hawk asks," Moke says, a flash of irritation showing. "And she knows it."

"Hey," I say tightly, coming to my feet. "I wouldn't do anything to put her—or any one of us—in danger."

"Maybe not on purpose," he says. "But this is the City of the Dead, and you can't control everything that happens."

Control. Like I've ever had that, over anything. My life has been lived one day at a time, the only thing to look forward to, the chance—the slimmest possibility—that my parents were out there somewhere. Well, I found them. Then they left again, because they didn't think I was ready to handle the real world.

Nothing is more real than the City of the Dead, and I can handle anything it throws at me. Right now, the only person who believes that is Langford, and I've given her nothing to show for it. I need to find out what's hiding in the forest, and maybe locate Ridley's body, bring it back for a burial.

I shudder, remembering the bodies in the Blazes.

"Are you coming or what?" I snap at Calypso, who nods and scrambles out of her pile of blankets to find her coat.

"What is going on with you?" Moke asks, once the little girl is out of arm's reach.

I grind my teeth, hoping that I can find the words. "I have to *do* something, Moke," I finally say. "So many things are wrong, and I can't do anything about any of them."

I remember Melanie standing on the roof of the

hospital, her red bracelet in the air. I can't save her. I couldn't save Clete. And I can't give Rain her eyes back. I'm not a healer or a politician. I'm not good at speeches like my mom, who could probably find the right way to tell the whole city to calm the hell down and that the virus isn't our fault.

I'm a girl of action, and I need something to do. The ashes of the Blazes are still on my skin, and I can only hope there aren't tear tracks on my face as well. Calypso comes to my side, bright-eyed, her antennas wiggling. Moke looks from her to me, clearly uncomfortable.

"We're going to the forest," I tell him. "And we're not coming back out until we've got something to show for it."

I put my hands on Calypso's shoulders and we turn to leave, but not before I hear Moke's muttered words.

"If you come back at all."

CHAPTER 17

It's too warm for a coat, but I'm not comfortable showing off my wings. Not anymore. Calypso's antennas are
carefully tucked away, and I insist on holding her hand
as we walk through the city to the forest. She squirms
away from me the first time, dodges me the second, and
sullenly accepts defeat the third time I make a grab for
her fingers.

"What's the big deal?" she complains. "I've been out
by myself a million times. Why you gotta hold my hand
now?"

"Because somebody took a shot at me yesterday," I say
through clenched teeth.

"You've been shot at plenty," she snipes back. "What's
so different about this time?"

I glance around, but see nobody else on the sidewalk in
the dim evening light. I hunker down to her height, level-
ing my gaze at her. "This time, they shot at me because I
had wings. They shot at me because I'm different."

Her eyes narrow as she searches my face for the punch

line, the joke that isn't coming. "You weren't trying to take their stuff, or kick them in the balls or anything?"

"Nope," I say. "But I did kick him in the balls. *After* he shot at me."

"Cool," she says, and gives me a fist bump. We take off again, this time with her fingers enmeshed in mine. Her little legs keep up with my longer ones and we leave the residential area of the city, wandering closer to the dark, reaching shadows of the forest.

We find the spot where the footprint was earlier, but the rains have washed it away. That's okay, because what I'm really looking for is where the creature went in. If there's some sort of path that is used regularly, it would make my life a lot easier. But once again, my life is scoring a zero on the easy scale.

"We're going to have to hack through the brush," I tell her, letting go of her hand. I go a few feet into the woods, kicking down some of the taller grass. "Follow me," I say, and Calypso ducks under a low-hanging branch. We head into the deep woods, making very slow progress. I've got to crush, break, or bend something to gain every inch. We lose the light, fast. The canopy is so thick that I bet even high noon looks more like dusk in here.

"Stay close," I say. "If we get separated in here I won't be able to find you again." The little girl takes me very seriously, stepping on the backs of my heels. I can ignore it for a little while, but she also feels the need to apologize every time it happens. I'm about to tell her to can it when

I trip over a root. I go down hard, landing on my fist. All the air leaves my gut, and I'm about to take the next, painful breath, when Calypso comes crashing down on top of me, knocking my fist back into my belly button.

"Sorry," she says.

Short of breath, I wave off her apology. I rock back onto my heels and glance up at what I can see of the sky. The lights of the city have come on, but even those don't penetrate the gloom of the forest. It's not pitch black in here, but I doubt we'll be able to see each other much longer. Why didn't I bring a flashlight? Oh, because I was hell-bent on actually doing something, so I was impulsive and didn't come prepared.

At least I'm consistent.

"Look, instead of walking on my heels, why don't you just talk to me while I forge ahead?" I ask her. "That way I'll know you're behind me, but you won't be stepping all over me."

"Okay!" she says brightly, followed by, "Sorry."

"I'm fine," I reassure her. "Just…"

I don't really know what I am. Bored? Tired? Anxious? Fifteen? Probably all of those things are parts of the answer to what sent me out here, trying to prove myself. I don't bother finishing the sentence, just continue beating my way through the forest, teeth gritted every time I get whacked in the face by a branch.

"Well, we had some new take-ins at the Children's Home…," she begins, and soon my ears are filled with a steady stream of information. I grunt every now and then, partly to let her know I'm listening, partly because the forest is really, really wearing me out.

I climb over a huge tree that's been downed, hauling myself over the top, and then lean back over, arms outstretched to help her.

"...and I guess Langford told Moke—"

"What?!" I'm too surprised to hide it, and my words come out sharply. Calypso steps back, eyes wide.

"I'm not yelling at you," I say carefully. "I just don't understand why Langford is talking to Moke at all."

She only shrugs, her gaze downcast now. She's never said much about her life before the Children's Home, but I'm betting it involved a lot of getting yelled at.

"Hey, it's okay," I say, beckoning to her to come closer. She does, but slowly. I help her over the tree and decide to leave the conversation at that. It sounds like something I better talk to Moke about directly. Or maybe Langford. If she's got other hybrids doing favors for her on the side, I want to know about it.

"Hawk?"

Her voice is small and tentative, and I turn around, putting a hand on her shoulder. "We don't have to talk about it," I say, but she shrugs off my hand.

"No." She shakes her head. Her antennas are wiggling like crazy. "I smell something."

CHAPTER 18

"What is it?" I hiss, dropping my voice into a low whisper. "The same thing you smelled the other day?"

Calypso nods that it is, but her brows furrow in disappointment. "It's not a fresh scent," she explains. "But I think I can follow it. I'll have to lead, though."

I let her go in front of me. I didn't think our progress could get any slower, but apparently I was wrong. She stops every few feet to sniff the air, and she doesn't have half my strength for breaking through the brush. I'm about to tell her that we should switch places when she stops dead in her tracks, holding one hand up.

I go still and silent, listening.

But there's nothing, which in itself is kind of weird. I don't hear anything else moving out in the darkness. No bugs. No birds. No wildlife. The only things out here are us and whatever is leaving this smell behind.

"Hawk?" Her voice is low, barely even a whisper, but it's so quiet that it carries back to me, regardless. "I can't go any farther."

"Do you need me in front?" I ask, but she shakes her head.

"No, I mean like, there's a wall."

"A wall?" I repeat, coming to her side. She takes my hand and guides it through some branches until I feel it on my fingertips—cold, hard stone.

What is a wall doing in the middle of the woods?

"Get behind me," I tell her, grimly. She does, and we follow our way along the stones, finally coming around to some steps. She gasps, her astonishment making her forget to be quiet.

"It's a fairy tale!" she says. "A fairy-tale castle!"

"A what now?" I ask, confused.

"Oh, you know," she actually jumps up and down, clapping her hands. "Like in the stories with kings and queens and princesses and princes—"

"Yeah, no," I say, flatly. "I don't know."

And I don't. I didn't have anyone to read me bedtime stories. And if Max and Fang had done that and I was too young to remember, I doubt they read me anything close to fairy tales. Probably more like survival manuals on how to live off drinking your own sweat for a week.

"Can we go inside?" Calypso asks.

"No, sorry," I say. "It doesn't look safe."

It really doesn't. The stairs are crumbling, and the doors are hanging off the hinges. I can just see inside, and there is scattered glass everywhere. Her disappointment isn't long-lived. Behind me, I hear another gasp of surprise.

"Look! A lake! And a bridge!"

She's so excited she takes off, and I'm panting to keep up as she ducks under trees I have to climb over. "Calypso! Wait!" I shout, but she's lost in this new world, intent on exploring, no matter what the cost.

Sounds familiar.

I break out into a clearing to see her walking onto an old metal bridge that reaches across the still, placid surface of a lake. The bridge looks twice as bad as the castle and shakes even under her slight weight.

"Hawk!" She spins on her heel, delighted. "I found a—"

She doesn't get to finish. The bridge collapses.

CHAPTER 19

Calypso screams as she falls, a section of the bridge hitting the water right before she does. There's a splash, and the sound of breaking glass...which doesn't make any sense, but I don't have time to question what I heard. I take to the air and see a jagged hole in the face of the water, streams running down into it from all sides. I fold my wings in tight and dive, leaving behind the pale light from above as I plummet.

It's immediately dark, and I pull up, letting my eyes adjust. Water is falling from above, raining down on me as I continue to descend, toes reaching for the bottom. They find rock—slippery and slimy, but firm. Calypso is at my feet, bleeding from the forehead and gasping for air. But she's breathing, and she's conscious.

I grab her by the hand and pull her up. "You okay?"

"Yeah," she says, and looks toward the ceiling, shielding her eyes from the still-falling water to gaze at the hole above us. "What happened?"

I toe at some broken glass, kicking it off of the boulder we'd landed on, out into a lagoon. Pieces of the broken bridge aren't far, its spindled rusty arms poking up from the water.

"I don't know," I admit. "Looks like the lake had a glass bottom."

My eyes move from the hole twenty feet above our heads to the walls surrounding us. It's like a honeycomb, with stacked tunnels leading into and out of the main room where we'd landed.

Correction. Where we'd *crash*-landed.

"We gotta get out of here," I say, pulling Calypso close to me. My wings are soaking wet and stuck to my back. It's almost impossible to fly straight up, but if I can shake some of this water off and zigzag my way to the top of this cavern, it might be possible. She doesn't weigh much at all, and I think I can carry her.

We can probably get out. And we really, really need to. I can see well-worn paths snaking from the lower tunnels. Something lives here. And whatever it is, it's not alone. There are all kinds of footprints on the bank, the one I recognized from the forest, but others, too.

"Hold on," I say, and wrap one arm around her skinny chest.

"Uh…Hawk?" Her antennas squirm like crazy. "They're coming. I can smell them."

I don't bother responding, mostly because I can smell them, too. It's a dank smell, reminding me of the cold, wet nights I'd spent alone in rotting buildings before I found my orphans. I pull Calypso back against my chest and am about to expand my wings when something erupts from the tunnel across from us, followed by the sound of a gun being cocked.

"Don't move!"

CHAPTER 20

Calypso screams as I push her behind me and spin. There are more creatures coming from the tunnel behind us, all of them armed. The jutting rock we landed on is only so large, and one of my feet slips into the cold water.

"I said don't move!"

I spin again, always keeping Calypso close. I can't put myself between her and danger when we're surrounded, but I can keep a tight grip.

"I'll stop moving when you put your gun down!" I spit back. "All of you!"

The guy who yelled at me seems to consider that, his mouth going into a straight line. His lips are weirdly flat, almost nonexistent, and his face is scaled, fading in and out of regular human skin, then transposing again into thick scales on his arms and hands—one of which is pointing a gun at me.

"I said put it down!" I yell.

He looks at his cohorts, and the barest of nods passes between them. He doesn't put the gun down, but his arms do relax a little. Beside him, similar reptilian creatures do the same, following his unspoken orders.

"How did you get here?" he asks, his voice still gruff and suspicious.

"Front door," I say, pointing above, where water still spills in from the broken ceiling.

"Why did you come?"

I take a deep breath as the cold water drips between my shoulder blades. "We were looking for you."

It's not the right answer. The guns come back up, and the leader's face hardens as he takes a step closer.

"We're here because we don't want to be found."

"I know, I…" My voice fades away as I watch his skin ripple and change, the color now matching and reflecting the marbled wall behind him. "You're a chameleon," I say, and he stiffens. "No wonder I couldn't get a good look at you."

I remember the description I gave to Pietro—eyes and a tail. I couldn't get a good look at this thing in the forest because he was blending in with the greenery…and I'd been trying to penetrate the canopy in order to get revenge. My jaw clenches and my teeth grit together. This is who killed Ridley.

"You don't want to be found?" I ask, my voice low and gravelly. "Too bad, because I'm here. And I've got a damn good reason to be."

The chameleon shakes his head, the gun elevated again and trained on my head. "You're not one of us; that's all the reason I need to shoot you right now."

"Go ahead!" I yell, spreading my arms, welcoming the bullet. "I've got more lead in me than that bridge did, and I'm still standing. Take your shot. See what happens."

Calypso's arms tighten on my waist, crushing my stomach. A small gasp of terror escapes her, and I look down to see an iridescent hand reaching up from the water, creeping its way toward her ankle.

"No!" I shout, shoving the girl behind me. My wings spring out reflexively, preparing for flight and sending sprays of water across the cavern. A face looks up at me from underwater, eyes wide and blinking, my wings reflected back on either side of it.

"Down! Everybody put your weapons down!"

It's the chameleon's voice, and I turn to face him again, pulling Calypso up into my arms so that the creature at our feet can't grab her. I pump my wings, once, twice, and elevate out of its reach. But my wings are wet and heavy, and I can't keep us aloft for long.

But it looks like I don't have to. All along the perimeter of the cavern the reptilian creatures are putting their guns down, raising their arms to show me empty hands.

"It's okay," the chameleon says, edging closer to the bank, eyes focused on mine, his skin changing with the rock patterns. "We're not going to hurt you. You *are* one of us."

CHAPTER 21

"I ain't no fish person!" I yell, but there's not a lot of venom in my voice. My wings are heavy and we're losing height. They're waterlogged and I can't stay aloft for long. Calypso goes suddenly limp in my arms, her bloodied head resting against my shoulder.

"We're not all fish," the face in the water says, mouth and nose now above the lagoon. "Just me."

"Awesome," I say sarcastically. "I'll remember that for the quiz later."

The fish girl smiles and extends a slim, silvery hand. "Come, come," she says. "It's not deep here, look." She glides through the water like a mermaid and turns back smiling at me. "Follow," she says, her fingers beckoning.

I consider my options. Following the fish girl means joining the chameleon guy, and his entire reptilian army, on the bank. But... I look up at the ceiling, impossibly high above us, and my wings are so wet. Plus, Calypso's head weighs heavily on my shoulder, her warm blood sliding down my chest. I have no weapons, other than my hands, and those are full of an unconscious mutant.

All my alarm bells are going off, and everything inside of me wants to call these things my enemy, but what the chameleon said is right—I *am* one of them. So everything on the outside of me is telling me that I belong over there on that bank, with them.

"Okay," I say, taking a deep breath.

I begin easing my way off the rock, Calypso's warm, limp body growing heavy in my arms. Just as the fish girl promised, my feet find bottom quickly. The water is only up to my hips. I raise Calypso above the dark tides, just in case. Fish-girl might not be the only thing under the surface. I step onto the bank, and a hybrid, with scaled flesh and a turtle shell for a back, moves to take Calypso from me.

"No," I say, shaking my head. But my words are as weak as my arms, and he bobs his head slowly.

"It's okay," he says. "We mean her no harm. She's one of us."

His fingers are dark with yellow lines, matching his shell. They reach tentatively for Calypso's antennas, touching them gently.

"Insect?" he asks, and I nod.

"Her name is Calypso. I'm Hawk."

"Better keep Gila away, if she's hungry," someone says, and a small laugh ripples through the crowd. A girl with orange-and-brown-mottled skin pushes her way to the front.

"I would never eat this child," she says emphatically, then eyes me up and down. "Promise."

It seems like an odd promise to make, but I am at the bottom of a cavern covered by a glass ceiling surrounded by creatures that appear to be a mix of human and reptilian DNA. So I'm going to take the positives with the negatives.

"Thank you," I say, nodding to Gila.

"I can help," she says, holding out her arms. "I'm a healer."

"She's also poison, which is kind of ironic," the turtle guy says, and I pull Calypso closer to my chest, looking warily at Gila, who stamps her foot.

"Venomous! Geez, Tut! How many times do I have to tell you? If you bite it and you die, it's *poisonous*. If it bites you and you die, it's *venomous*."

"Whatever." Tut winks at Gila. But he winks very slowly, so it takes a second for me to realize he's flirting with her. She seems to miss it completely, having already turned away from him to take Calypso from me.

I reluctantly let the little girl slide from my arms. Her head rolls into Gila's chest, and she nestles there, her face very pale against the oddly patterned brown and orange of Gila's skin. "I'm taking her to the medical bay," Gila says to the chameleon, and I immediately step forward.

"Then I'm coming, too."

Gila glances at him. "You're the boss, Chammy."

He looks between me and Gila, his face changing colors with the slightest of movements. "All right," he decides, "but I wish you would trust us."

"Yeah, that's not going to just happen," I tell Chammy, shaking some of the water loose from my wings, accidentally spraying some of the reptilians. *Kind of* accidentally, anyway.

"Or...maybe it can," he says, his head tilted oddly sideways as he investigates my wings. "Tut, bring her out."

Tut nods, then turns to do as ordered, but it's taking too long. Chammy rolls his eyes. "Al? Maybe you instead?"

There's a sudden shuffling through the group and I see something with an alligator's body scurry out of view. It moves unnaturally fast, powerful legs pumping, human arms folded to the side. I am suddenly very glad that I got bird DNA instead of...that. But I don't have time to think about how much I love my wings, because suddenly there's another pair of them beating through the air, heading right for me.

"Ridley!"

CHAPTER 22

My hawk glides to my shoulder and settles there, her familiar weight bringing tears to my eyes. I swipe them quickly away.

"How?" I ask, turning to Chammy.

"One of my guards spotted you flying the perimeter, and took down your hawk as a warning. When he reported to me that he had seen a fellow hybrid, I immediately went in search of your bird. She had the wind knocked out of her—"

"And a broken wing," Gila adds. Chammy winces, like maybe he wasn't going to include that part in the story.

"Gila healed her," he says. "And I kept watching the skies for you. I knew you'd be back...somehow."

"And here you are," Gila says, nodding down at Calypso in her arms. "Breaking our house and bringing me more work."

"Yeah, I..." I glance up at the ceiling. "Sorry about that."

Chammy waves my apology away. "It's not the first time someone has found us."

"It's not?" I ask, eyebrows going up.

"Um...no," Chammy looks around at the reptilian band surrounding him, then turns back to me. "Would you like me to show you around?"

I look again at Calypso, but Gila reassures me. "I'll take her to the medical bay, see if any of these cuts need stitches. You can find us there, when you're done."

Her words are hard, and heavy. I can tell Gila doesn't like me, but her skin is what makes the decision for me. The orange-and-brown patterns are reassuring in a way that her attitude isn't. Gila would never hurt Calypso. And not just because she's a healer, but because they are both mutants. I nod my agreement, and Gila heads for the medical bay, the other mutants dispersing as Chammy leads me down a tunnel. The roof is wet and low. Water drips onto my back, and Ridley shifts uncomfortably on my shoulder, unhappy in such tight quarters.

"Welcome to our home," Chammy says over his shoulder. "It's not much to look at, but we can live in peace here."

"But not in the city?" I ask.

Chammy chuckles. "We're in the city, too. They just don't know that. It's kind of funny, really. We get in the same way they sent us out."

"What do you mean?"

"I'm assuming you know why you look the way you do?" Chammy answers my question with a question.

"Yeah," I say. "My mom and dad were experimented on. They're a mix of bird and human DNA. I'm guessing the same thing happened with your parents, except with reptile DNA."

"You'd be guessing right," Chammy says, brushing aside a curtain of hanging moss and motioning for me to step in front of him. I enter a cave with wooden boxes stacked along one wall.

"Our parents—mine, Gila's, Tut's—they all came from a lab, just like yours. When the experimenting stopped, the scientists didn't know what to do with them. My parents were supposed to be destroyed, but someone got lazy. Embryos in earlier stages of development were flushed down the toilet."

His voice, calm until now, rises with anger. "My parents ended up in the septic system of the city, floating in filth. They washed out down here and banded together to scratch out some form of existence, to try to make a life. A life that the humans would have denied them."

Chammy's skin mottles and flushes, reacting to his mood now rather than the environment. He's suddenly a bright red, his eyes an alarming blue that stand out strikingly in his face. "They managed...for a little while. The second generation was born, only to shepherd our parents out of existence. They were exposed so young to so many chemicals in all that waste. They were polluted from the inside out, and died because of it. Died horribly!"

His fist smacks into his palm, and I nod toward the wooden boxes. I'm no idiot. I've seen boxes like this before. Boxes stacked in the Pater gun stash. "So what's this, then?" I ask, trying to sound naïve.

Chammy walks over to a crate, hand resting lovingly on top. "For years we've been sneaking in the same way they sent our parents out—through the sewers. We've gathered enough guns and ammunition to stand a real chance."

"A real chance at what?" I ask, my stomach sinking. Chammy is clearly not okay in the head, and I've left Calypso behind, stupidly trusting this guy just because he's a hybrid, like me.

"A real chance at showing the humans that we aren't trash to be flushed away. We're alive. We're here. And we're going to make them pay."

He reaches into a box and pulls out a grenade.

"What do you say, Hawk? Are you with us, or against us?"

CHAPTER 23

I'm scared, but that doesn't mean I'm stupid.

Gazzy taught me a lot about explosives, and the thing about grenades is, they're really just a rock to throw at someone...until you pull the pin out. Chammy hasn't done that, so when he tosses the grenade at me, I catch it without blinking.

"With you, or against you?" I repeat. "Hmm...let me think. I'd say you've got two hundred hybrids down here, max. And I don't even know if I should count fish-girl, since I don't see her being super helpful in a firefight. Two hundred hybrids against a whole city? Yeah, I'm out."

I toss the grenade back at Chammy, who pulls it easily from the air. He begins tossing it from hand to hand.

"We're not against the whole city," he argues. "We just want to go after the scientists who tortured our parents." He tosses the grenade back, and I take it.

"Fair enough," I agree. "And that plan might have worked a week ago, but you've been living down here in the dark. You don't know what's going on above you. There's a pandemic in the city right now, and hybrids are being blamed for it. Somebody took a potshot at me the other day. You stick your heads aboveground, and everybody will be gunning for you."

I flip the grenade back to him, getting fancy and going under my leg with it. He catches it, smiling. But the smile doesn't quite reach his eyes.

"You're assuming I don't know what's going on aboveground. The sewers are connected to this entire city, and we can go wherever we want, whenever we want."

He tosses the grenade high, miming fear as it almost hits the ground, then scoops it up at the last second.

"We know about the virus," he says. "We've avoided it so far, by keeping our distance."

I shake my head. "That won't work in your favor. If people in the city see healthy hybrids it just makes them believe that we're the source."

"Ah," he nods, coming to the same conclusion I had earlier. "That's slick. If we're not ill, we're the carriers. If we are…"

"We die, like them," I finish.

"I understand the risks," he says. "I see everything you see. In fact," he goes on, "we even see you."

He pitches the grenade at my face, but I'm not in a teasing mood anymore. I snatch it out of the air and stare him down.

"You've been watching me?"

He shrugs. "You're hard to miss, with those wings. It might make citizens target you as a disease-carrier, but they've also bought you some pretty nice living conditions."

My jaw goes tense, teeth grinding. "You know where I live?" The grenade slips from my suddenly numb fingers and rolls across the cave floor to rest at his feet. He picks it up, his fingers toying with the pin.

"You're on the Council, supposedly representing the hybrid population. But what do you really do, Hawk? Other than whatever Langford and the others tell you?"

I bristle at that, alarmed that he knows so much. "I was trusted with finding you. I don't just sit and take notes and drink coffee and use big words."

His eyes darken and I realize my mistake. "They sent you here?"

"Not exactly," I hedge, wishing like hell I was the one with the grenade in my hands right now. "I came looking for you after I lost Ridley. I wanted revenge."

"Revenge," he repeats, a new spark dancing across his face. "Then I'd think you would understand. I'd think you would be on our side. The hybrid side. Against humans."

"It doesn't have to be that way," I tell him, shaking my head. On my shoulder, Ridley shifts, uneasy. "There are some good humans in the world."

"You just said someone took a potshot at you!"

"They did!" I argue back, my own volume rising. "But there's also people like Melanie. She's a girl at the hospital who helped me find out more about the virus. She's dying, and she put herself in between me and a security guard. She weighs half what I do, and she took a punch for me. There are good humans out there, Chammy. I'm sorry if you've never met any."

"I haven't," he says. "And I can't just take your word for it."

"Then I don't know what to say." I eye the grenade in his hands. "But I won't help you kill people that don't deserve it. And I won't be part of your revenge."

He considers that for a second, then tosses the grenade nonchalantly back into the wooden crate. "Then I can't promise you won't be caught in the crossfire."

A sigh of relief escapes me with the grenade out of sight. "I'll take my chances," I say. "Stray bullets aren't a new thing in my life."

"Fair enough," he says, and motions for me to exit the cave before him. I go, not exactly thrilled about having my back to him. But the tunnel is narrow and there's nothing I can do about it as we file forward. I'm alert, all my muscles tensed to react if he tries anything. On my shoulder, Ridley feels my nervousness and flutters restlessly.

We come out into the main room, where hybrids with suction pads for feet are climbing the walls, already repairing the ceiling. I flush at the damage. I might not be on friendly terms with this group but I know what it's like to have your home invaded and destroyed.

"Sorry about that," I say to him, as I see Calypso

emerging from another tunnel with Gila close behind her. There are some fresh stitches across her forehead, but other than that, she looks all right.

"That's okay," he says, resting a suddenly friendly hand on my shoulder. "You can help us fix it."

Calypso runs toward me, her little arms encircling my waist.

"What?" I glance up at Chammy, suddenly alarmed. "What do you mean?"

"Hawk," he says, his voice now low and charming. "Did you really think I was going to let you leave?"

CHAPTER 24

"*Let* me leave?" I repeat, anger slipping into my voice. "You can't tell me what to do."

Calypso's arms tighten around my waist, and I can't help but remember Moke's parting shot as we left the Children's Home—*if you come back at all.*

I *am* coming back. I've got an orphan to protect and a job to do. Langford trusted me with finding these hybrids, and I did it. Pride swells in my chest, and my wings puff out along with it. Chammy pulls his gun again, training it on me.

"Don't try anything, Hawk. It doesn't have to be this way. We're all on the same team."

"Your *team*?" I ask, putting some sass on it. "The team that wants to kill humans, and isn't too particular about who they are? Just kick back, right? Don't worry about who you hit? No daughter of Maximum Ride would ever agree to that."

"Hawk," Gila says, stepping forward. "You can't

possibly understand what it's been like for us down here. We watched our parents die—can you imagine that?"

"At least you had parents," I shoot back, edging away from Gila and Chammy. "I didn't, and neither does Calypso. All we have is each other, and she followed me out here because she trusted me. I won't betray that trust by letting her get hurt."

"*We* didn't hurt her," Gila says, her voice brittle with anger. "You're the one who let her wander onto a bridge and almost fall to her death. I gave her medical care. All you did was get her lost and injured."

"That's ridiculous," I hiss, but I know it's not. I'm reckless, and I don't think ahead. I came out here wanting to prove myself, but all I've done is put us directly in harm's way. Other hybrids fan out across the walls, hanging from their sticky, reptilian feet. I step backward again, getting my heel wet. I'm right at the edge of the bank. I can't back up any farther without risking fish-girl grabbing my ankles. There's a rustling at my feet and I look down to find the alligator hybrid has returned, with a smile as wide as my waist, all of it lined with teeth.

"It really is better for all of us if you stay," Gila says. I notice a flickering in her throat, a muscle spasming, and realize that she is filling her venom sacs, preparing to spray it at us. I tighten one arm around Calypso. Ridley feels the shift, and her talons grip my shoulder. She knows what's coming.

"You're right," I say, glancing at Gila and Chammy. "It might be better for all of us if I stay. But the thing is, I don't *want* to."

I spin in the air and extend my wings—dry now—and am suddenly horizontal with the ground. My chest is only inches from the water, and Calypso is dangling from my arms as I see the fish girl churning toward the surface, her face a mask of rage.

Ridley dives for Chammy's face at the same time, and he bellows. The gun fires, the bullet zipping past me and ricocheting off the cave wall. Everyone hits the ground as the bullet fires wildly, pinging off the stone surfaces. A jet of something warm sprays across my arm but I don't have time to register the pain. I'm straining my wings, pumping for the ceiling, aiming at the hole in the glass above us. Calypso is screaming, high and loud, directly into my ear, as all around us reptilians on the walls jump, trying to pull me out of midair.

A frog-like creature grabs my ankle, and we're jerked suddenly downward, Calypso sliding in my arms. I keep my grip on her, but barely. The frog thing flails wildly from the end of my leg as I kick at him with the other one. Below us, I see Chammy drawing a bead on me.

"Oh. No. You. Don't." I seethe, connecting my heel with the frog man's head with each word. He dangles, glassy-eyed, as I deliver one last kick. He falls, passing Ridley on the way up. More bullets fly past my ears, but they are shooting wildly, in a panic. I reach the fresh air and we ascend above the forest, Calypso clutching me with all her strength. I set us down at the edge of the forest. I'm winded, out of breath, everything spent, my arm on fire. Still, I've got bigger concerns than myself.

"You okay?" I ask Calypso, holding her at arm's length for an inspection.

She nods, then cradles back up against me. "I thought we were never getting out of there."

My hawk alights on my shoulder, and I nuzzle her. "We might not have, if it wasn't for Ridley."

"Are you going to tell the Council about them?" Calypso asks. "Are you going to tell Langford that they're planning an attack on the city?"

I look down at my arm, where Gila's venom has raised blisters. It hurts, but I've had worse. I shake off the pain, looking down at my orphan. The truth is, I don't know how I feel about informing on other hybrids. I'm supposed to be their voice on the Council, not the spy in their midst.

"Well," I tell Calypso. "I'm not too worried about an uprising."

Her eyebrows come together. "Why not?"

"Because they are terrible shots."

CHAPTER 25

We make our way through the city, two small shadows dodging larger ones in the night.

"What's going on?" Calypso asks me, holding tightly to my hand.

The truth is, I'm not entirely sure. We left the city just hours ago, and while it wasn't a beautiful pearl of a place, we've come back to something much different. I scuttle her past some graffiti that reads SEND HYBRIDS TO HELL, trying to distract her by asking about Gila.

"What was she like?" I ask, scrounging for conversational topics.

"Really nice," she says, words that stand in stark contrast to the burn across my skin from her venom.

"Huh," I say, peering around a corner before I walk out into the street. A man is carrying a woman in his arms, her legs and arms splayed on either side of him. She's out cold, and as they pass I can see twin streams of blood coming from her ears.

"Yeah, she was really nice," she repeats. "She even gave

me this." The little girl pulls a necklace out from under her top. The chain is grubby, but the pendant is a large and heavy turquoise teardrop.

"Gila said it was super special," the little girl goes on. "And that she was trusting me with it, that I should keep it close to me always."

I glance up and down the street again, ensuring we won't be seen when we move out of the alley and into the lights. I grab her hand and we run across the street to the opposite side, headed for an unlit doorway.

"Keep it close to you always, huh?" I say, cupping the teardrop in my hand. "It's probably a tracking device."

"A what?" Calypso snatches it back, eyeing me suspiciously. "Gila said it was for me. She said I could have it."

Crap. Gila isn't stupid. She gave a motherless orphan a nice piece of jewelry, and probably counted on it being the prettiest thing the girl ever saw. Of course, she isn't going to part with it. Inwardly, I fume. But I can't let her see that.

"Do you remember the warning signs we used to make fun of back at the Children's Home?" I ask her.

It's an old joke, and it brings a smile to her face despite our surroundings. At the Children's Home, we would laugh at some of the warning labels attached to things from before. Apparently, people had to be told not to throw their hair dryers into the bathtub with them, or that they shouldn't put their fingers inside a hot toaster.

"Remember what Moke said about those?" I ask her

now. "The fact that they have to warn everyone, means that somebody did it."

"Yeah, somebody super stupid," she says.

"Right," I nod, agreeing. "It makes me think about Gila promising not to eat you. Why would she have to promise not to do something so awful?"

"Because..." She gasps and her hand falls from mine. "Maybe she's done it before. Do you think she ate a kid?"

Actually, I seriously doubt it. But that mutant did burn my arm and try to charm my orphan out from under me. I'm not above accusing her of eating some children if that's what it takes to get that tracking device far away from her.

"Ugh," the little girl says, lifting the chain from around her neck. "You can have it."

"Thanks, kiddo," I say, dropping it into one of my pockets to investigate later.

Right now, I've got to get Calypso back to Moke, and that means going past the hospital. Unfortunately, it seems like that's where most of the foot traffic is headed, too. I pull her back into the unlit doorway as more people trek past, all of them in various stages of illness. Some are just sweating, others are barely on their feet. More than a few are bleeding from the ears.

"Can we fly?" she whispers.

I glance up at the sky. If I can get above the streetlights, I doubt anyone will spot us. Of course, flying will immediately mark me as a hybrid, and I won't be moving as fast as usual with her in my arms. On the other hand, I don't have a coat to cover my wings at the moment. Her antennas are out on full display.

I weigh the pros and cons, unsure of what to do, when another man passes, firing a gun into the air. "Murder the mutants!" he screams, shooting another volley in the air.

Crap. The farther away from him, the better. I grasp her under the arms and take three bounding leaps before unfurling my wings. They spread wide, and I give the guy a solid kick in the teeth before ascending. He goes down hard, the gun flying from his hand for anyone to pick up. I can only hope it's someone who won't point it at me.

From above, the city looks as desolate as ever, many streetlights burnt out or flickering. But what I can see is not good. The entire block around the hospital is filled with people on foot, and hospital beds have been set up in the intersection. The beds inside must be full, the disease spreading at an alarming rate.

Grimly, I head for the Children's Home.

Moke meets us in the stairwell and runs a blue thumb over Calypso's fresh stitches before giving me a hard glare.

"I know," I say. "I'm sorry. But she's okay. And by the looks of things she was better off with me in the forest than she would have been in the city."

Moke sighs. "I can't argue with that."

I glance around the empty halls. "Are you safe here?"

"We're all right," Moke says, pulling Calypso against his side. "I can protect her."

I try not to make a face. Moke is as skinny as one of my legs and probably couldn't knock over a cardboard box.

But I've already made him mad today, and I don't want to push it. I head down the stairwell, mind already on my next move.

"If it gets worse, I'll come for you," I yell over my shoulder.

Just barely, I catch Moke's response.

"If it gets worse, you'll be too late."

CHAPTER 26

I sleep hard and long, but pop awake to the sound of my alarm. I wear a long-sleeved shirt to cover the burns on my arm and sit quietly throughout the meeting. I have plenty to say, but the only person who needs to hear it is Langford.

The meeting is a circus. The illness cases have tripled overnight. The hospital is stretched to the max and the sick keep pouring in. A hybrid was found strung up on a lamppost, an electric cord digging into the scaled skin of its neck, with a sign reading DISEASED pinned to it. I feel heat rising through my body at the description. I have no idea if the hybrid was one who had managed to pass as human in the city until now, or if he was one of Chammy's people, plucked from the sewers.

If that's the case, he's not likely to wait long to roll into town with guns blazing.

The meeting adjourns and Langford comes to her feet. I meet her gaze and she gives me the slightest of nods. I follow her to her rooms, where she pulls the scarf from her neck and tosses it across the white sofa, falling onto it herself a second later.

"Please tell me you have good news," she says.

I don't know if she'll consider what I have to say a good thing or a bad thing. Honestly, I haven't decided how much to say in the first place. But the hopeful look on her face reminds me that I was trusted with a job, and I don't want to fail her.

"I found them," I tell her. "I found the hybrids living in the forest."

"Yes!" she cries, both fists in the air. "That's fantastic. Tell me all about them. How many are there? Do they seem well organized? Where are they living? What types of creatures do they seem to be?"

The last question is the one least likely to get me in trouble, so I choose to answer it first.

"Reptilian," I say, and her eyes light up. "There's one who appears to be part turtle; he's got a shell anyway. And a gila monster—she can spit venom. Quite a few of them must be some kind of frog because they could climb walls, and there was an alligator hybrid, too." I shiver, remembering the scuttling form and the mouth lined with teeth.

"Oh, and a fish girl," I say. "Kind of like a mermaid, but not in a pretty way. More like a gross way."

"Okay," she says, spinning her finger in the air, asking for more. I haven't mentioned Chammy yet, and I don't want to. Her knowing of his existence feels like a betrayal.

I couldn't give him what he wanted in the caves, but I can choose not to sell him out here in a high-end hotel suite, especially after he mocked me for living in one.

"There are maybe a hundred," I hedge, fudging the numbers a little and answering the questions that feel safe to me. "And I would definitely call them organized. They have medical facilities and everything."

Everything, as in a room full of guns, ammo, and grenades.

"What else?" she asks. "How did they come to be here in the first place?"

"Their parents were like mine, part of an experiment," I explain, happy to answer a question that won't get me into trouble. "Except they didn't get wings. They got things like venom sacs and sticky feet and shells on their backs and scales for skin."

I explain how the experiments were shut down and how embryos were flushed down toilets and sinks. My skin gets warm thinking about the tiny living creatures finding themselves alone, and in the dark, struggling together to survive. Was that what it was like for my mom and dad? And why haven't I ever asked them?

I shake my head, bringing myself back to the present. "Chammy said that first generation died out, and…"

And that their kids want to kill everyone in the city.

"…and I think that's really sad." I finish, lamely.

"Hmm…" She taps a finger against her knee. "Chammy? You didn't mention this person before."

Crap. "Yeah, he's uh…I guess he's a chameleon."

Her eyes narrow. "But you must have talked to this chameleon person, because you called him by name. You weren't simply watching and observing, were you, Hawk? You made contact."

She doesn't look like this in meetings. Usually she's controlled, always putting out fires that burn between others. Right now, she looks like she could start one, just with the lights in her eyes. She gets up, crosses to a desk, and grabs a sheet of paper and a pen.

"Here," she says, holding it out to me. "I want you to write down everything. Names. Places. Details. Descriptions. I need to know everything there is to know about these...things."

Her lip curls, and I see something else I hadn't seen before. Contempt.

"They're not things," I say, refusing to take the paper. "They're hybrids, just like me."

She waves my words away. "They're obviously not like you, Hawk," Langford says brightly. "You're smart enough to know what the right thing to do is."

Am I?

I look down at the paper and pen, feel the burn of Gila's venom against my shirtsleeve. I think about the hybrid hanging from the lamppost, his scaled neck stretched too far.

"No." I smack the paper from her hands. "They aren't hurting you. They aren't doing anything wrong. I won't tell you where they are."

I expect her to yell at me, to unleash the fire I see

115

dancing behind her eyes, this new side of her I hadn't seen coming out in full force. Instead, she calmly picks up the paper and pen and puts them back on the desk. When she turns to face me, her face is the cold, calm mask that oversees Council meetings.

"Clearly you aren't up to dealing with the situation," she says. "I'm removing you from the Council and sending for your mother. We'll let her represent the hybrid population."

My gut sinks. *What am I doing? Why am I defending a pack of hybrids who burned me, shot at me, and would've held me prisoner?* Still, my mouth remains closed, my hands in fists by my sides.

"I trusted you, Hawk. I believed in you," she says, shaking her head. "That's my fault. We need Maximum Ride back. Now."

CHAPTER 27

It's a cloudy evening, so I feel safe taking Ridley out for a flight. We sail through cloud cover as I sort through my options. Langford is not happy with me, and I doubt Max will be, either, once she gets back. She'll probably rip me a new one and give me a long talk about responsibility before sending me back to my room. Fine time to start parenting.

I bank to the left and look over my shoulder to see Ridley following my lead. There's a little jolt in my pulse at the joy of seeing her there again, where she belongs. I don't know if I'm doing the right thing, but Chammy gave Ridley back to me, and Gila healed her. Handing them over to Langford wouldn't have been the right way to show my thanks.

We pass over the hospital, where the throngs are thicker than ever before. I land on the roof, but Ridley wheels away. She's tired, and still recovering from her injury. I'll meet up with her back home. The roof door is locked, but there are enough pieces of castaway metal lying around that I can jimmy it, which takes less than a minute.

The last time I was here, I was the target of a manhunt—all the attention was on me. Now, I doubt I could get anybody's attention if I was on fire. I hear the chaos before I see it, shouts and cries echoing into the stairwell. I pull open the hall door to see harried doctors and panicked nurses moving from room to room. Some are wild-eyed and frantic, others have an eerily calm look, as if they know there's nothing they can do for their patients, but keep moving anyway.

I thread my way through the hall, dodging a crash cart being pushed by a woman who is yelling at everyone to get out of the way. She's wearing civilian clothes, and a trickle of blood snakes out of one ear.

A doctor grabs her. "What do you think you're doing? You can't just take that!"

"Nobody is helping him!" she screams at the doctor, struggling with him as he tries to pull the cart away from her, their scuffle drawing a crowd.

"You don't even know how to use it!" the doctor says, to which the woman pulls the shock pads from the cart and gives the doctor a blast that sends him against the wall.

"I figured it out," she shouts over her shoulder as she rushes down the hall. Some staff try to chase her, while other family members block the way. A few nurses are helping the stunned doctor to his feet as I turn my head, avoiding eye contact.

I push through more panicked people to make my way to Melanie's room, ducking inside just as a man erupts into the hallway, screaming that he needs someone in his daughter's room, *right now*. The door clicks shut behind me and I rest against it, my heart pounding.

"It's a madhouse out there," Melanie says. She looks up at me from the bed, her eyes weak and watery. There's a breathing tube in her nose, a cannula, and her voice is weaker than it was before.

"Hey," I say, cautiously approaching her bed. "You okay?"

She gives me a thumbs-up and manages a wan smile. "You're probably in more danger than I am. Coat hides your wings pretty good, though."

"Yeah," I nod. "I've been keeping them covered."

"Good." She closes her eyes, her breath coming out as a wheeze. "You're probably okay, though. My nurse says there's a nest of hybrids in the forest."

"A nest?" I repeat. I don't like the way it sounds, like Chammy and his people are rodents, or worse, an infestation.

"Yeah," she says with a nod. "The Council sent out a news alert this afternoon, saying that they had reason to believe that the virus originated from a group of hybrids there."

"That's not true!" I say.

"There aren't hybrids in the forest?" she asks in confusion.

"No." I shake my head. "There are, but they're not responsible for this sickness. They wouldn't—"

I bite off my words. I was about to say they wouldn't

hurt people like that, but I know that's not true. Chammy and his crew would love to take down the city, but they wouldn't let a virus do the work for them. They'd rather do it themselves, while holding smoking guns.

"Help me, Hawk."

I look up to find Melanie pulling her cannula out and trying to throw back her bedclothes. "Stop!" I cry, gently pushing her back down onto the bed. "You need to rest."

"No." She shakes her head, tears flowing down her cheeks. "You don't understand. You think this is bad? These are people who actually made it to the hospital—others are dropping dead in the streets. People are angry, Hawk, and the Council just gave them somewhere to direct their anger."

"The forest," I say, following her thoughts. "The Council can't do anything about the virus, but they can offer up somebody for the people to take it out on."

"Yeah." She nods, sinking back into her pillow. Her energy is spent, but her eyes are still bright. "How well do you think that's going to go?"

I think of crates of guns and ammunition, Chammy's itchy trigger finger, and grenades with the pins pulled out.

"That's going to go very, very badly," I tell her.

CHAPTER 28

I lift off from the hospital roof as the last of the sun's rays are dying in the east. I know where I'm going, but I don't know what I'm going to do when I get there. The path to the forest is easy to follow: a snake of light unwinds below me, leading the way.

"Those idiots actually have torches," I say, my words blowing away on the wind.

Some of the crowd outside the hospital have fallen in with the rioters leading the way to the woods. They can't get their loved ones inside or find them the medical attention they need, but they can punish the hybrids that got them sick in the first place. Or at least, the hybrids they've been *told* are to blame.

"Langford," I mutter, cursing myself for telling her all that I did. It's my fault that there are people marching on the woods right now. My fault that Chammy, Gila, and who knows how many others are going to die tonight. Because it won't just be hybrids, I know that for sure. The city dwellers might have fire, but they're about to face some serious *firepower*.

I touch down near the edge of a crowd that has formed along the perimeter of the forest. A man has climbed onto a box, a torch held aloft as his words ring out over the crowd.

"My wife died today," he says, and there's a sympathetic murmur. "My son died yesterday," he adds, and the sympathy grows in volume, as does his voice.

"They died in the street. Nobody helped them. Not even me...." He loses his momentum, stumbling over his emotions as they close his throat. "I couldn't help them," he goes on after gathering himself. "I couldn't *do* anything. But, by god, I'm going to do something now."

Across the crowd, heads nod in unison. Someone yells out in agreement, and the sympathy begins to turn into something else. Solidarity.

"I'm going in there," he says, gesturing with his torch to the forest. "I'm going to find whatever mutants are spreading this disease. I'm going to kill them."

There's a shout from the back: "Kill them!"

"I'm going to stomp out the monsters in our midst!"

"Monsters!" More than a few voices echo back at him, faces flushed with fever and with fire.

"I'm going in there," he says again. "And I'm not coming out until I'm painted in blood."

"Blood!" The crowd screams back in unison.

He turns and runs into the forest, his torch leaving a bright imprint on my eyes as he leads the charge. The first wave of attack hits the brush and is rebuffed, the under-growth far too thick for them to penetrate on foot. I cover a smile, knowing full well what it's like to struggle forever just to gain a few inches of progress in that bracken.

But these people have vengeance inside them and torches in their hands. The brush is aflame in a matter of moments, people stomping and breaking still-smoking branches as they penetrate the forest. The fire spreads, and the people follow behind, covering their noses and still screaming for revenge. I pull my coat tighter around me, aware that if anyone spots my wings I'm a dead girl.

I don't dare fly, can't risk being seen. And I don't know what I would do if I could. Alerting Chammy to the attack will bring a hail of bullets onto these people, most of whom wouldn't even be here if Langford hadn't issued that bulletin—which is my fault.

"Crap turds," I say under my breath. I'm in a battle and I don't know whose side I'm on. But I can't stand here and do nothing.

I rush forward into the forest, stamping out small fires as I go. The least I can do is keep this from spreading. There's smoke in my eyes and mouth when I hear the first *pop*. I stop, holding my position, ears alert. Was that a bullet? Or a burning pocket of sap inside a tree?

A torch sails past me in the dark, a woman's face brightly illuminated as she makes eye contact with me. "Where'd they go? Am I too late? Are they all dead?"

"What? No," I say. "Nobody's dead."

At least, I don't think so. In the distance another torch

blinks and the woman spots it, disappearing into the smoke within a matter of seconds. I follow her light as far as I can, when it suddenly winks out. There's a cry, followed by a gurgle, and then…nothing.

I hold still, remain silent, scan the horizon for another torch. I spot one, zigzagging crazily as it beats a retreat back to the clearing…and doesn't make it. It's snuffed out quickly, a small finger of smoke rising from where it landed. Nothing rises in its place.

There's a rustling nearby, and I throw off my coat, no longer worried about whose side I'm on. All I know is that this is a dangerous place to be, and I want to leave as quickly as possible.

I ascend just in time, the gator's teeth barely missing my ankle. Her smile flashes in the firelight, and I suppress a shudder as I rise, watching as torchlights are extinguished across the length of the forest. Soon there is nothing but darkness and smoke on the wind, the throats that yelled rhetoric only minutes before now torn open and bleeding onto the forest floor.

I spin in midair and head for the Children's Home as fast as I can.

CHAPTER 29

Moke is awake and on the roof, his gaze focused on the still-smoldering fires inside the forest. I land next to him, smoke wafting from my wings.

"You do that?" he asks, nodding toward the plume over the forest.

"No, actually," I say, catching my breath. "I tried to stop it."

He looks at me, the whites of his eyes standing out in his pale-blue skin. In the darkness, he almost glows. "What happened?"

I shake my head. "A lot of ugliness, but I'll explain later. Right now, I want to get you, Calypso, and Rain to my apartment. I don't think the city is safe for hybrids anymore."

I expect him to argue—something he's been doing with me a lot lately—but he only nods in agreement. "You get Rain," he says. "I'll bring Calypso and meet you there."

"You don't understand how bad the streets are," I say. "I don't think—"

"Hawk," he says patiently. "I can protect Calypso. Get Rain."

I'm not used to being told what to do. Usually I'm the one giving orders. But at the moment he sounds calm and efficient, two things I'm definitely not. My heart is beating a mile a minute, and the hems of my jeans are singed. Moke might be underestimating the danger, but I also know that he wouldn't risk taking Calypso if he couldn't ensure her safety.

"All right," I agree. "Meet you there."

I ascend again, passing over the Ope Center. The streets are full around the building, and I can see beds lined up in neat rows on the roof. I hope Pietro has things under control there, but I can't spare him a thought right now. He still has his family's resources to rely on, whereas I've got to focus on my family itself.

The Institute for the Blind seems much calmer, but I'm not leaving anything to chance. Rain might not be easily targeted as a hybrid, but right now I don't trust anyone I don't know from the Children's Home. Technically, visiting hours are over, but the nurse working the front desk must read the fear on my face.

"Rain is fine," she reassures me. "I just looked in on her an hour ago. Our building has good security, and the streets have been quiet here."

I nod my thanks, but there's no smile on my face as I go down the hall to Rain's room. She's at the window again, her hand pressed against the glass. A packed duffel bag is at her feet.

"I'm ready to go," she says.

"What?" My mouth flaps open. "How did you…?"

She turns her head, regarding me as if she can see me through her shut eyelids. "Shouldn't we go sooner rather than later?"

"Yes," I agree. She has some explaining to do, but she's right. Now is not the time. I sign her out so that the staff won't panic. My wings are easy to hide under a coat, and Rain can pass as human on the streets.

Calypso and Moke are waiting for us in my room, and they run to Rain for hugs as soon as we arrive. There's a ton of food sitting on the little table, and Calypso half apologizes for raiding my fridge.

"Sorry," she says, rubbing her stomach. "I was starving."

Suddenly, I realize that I am as well. Moke lights the gas fireplace and we move the food to the floor in front of it, sharing equally, our hands diving into the pile between us.

"It's like it used to be," Calypso says, crumbs falling from her mouth. "Back at the Children's Home."

Except Clete isn't here, I think, and see the same thought echoed in Moke's face. I don't know if he blames me for Clete's death, but it would make sense. It would explain his new attitude toward me. I swallow, and the bite of sandwich I was chewing feels like a rock in my throat.

"It's not like it used to be," I tell Calypso. "For a lot of reasons."

I explain to Moke and Rain about Chammy, Gila, and the other reptilians in the forest, their hatred for the city and its inhabitants, and how tonight's events won't improve relations on either side.

"The crocodile just took them down at the ankles," I say, shivering as I remember. "It wasn't pretty. I think Chammy was out there with a gun, too. People were falling all around me."

Moke considers this for a second, a frown on his blue lips. "And the reptilians will look at this as an unprovoked attack. You were right to bring us here. Who knows what could happen next."

"Nobody knows," I agree. "Which is why we need to prepare ourselves."

"How do we do that?" he asks.

"Tomorrow you're coming with me to meet with Pietro," I tell him. "We're going to arm ourselves."

CHAPTER 30

In the morning, Rain and Calypso are happy to stay behind. Whether she wants to admit it or not, Calypso is spooked by what happened last night. Rain is getting some food for the two of them, moving effortlessly around the kitchen while Calypso tells her all about meeting Chammy and Gila.

I send Ridley with a message for Pietro, asking him to meet us at the storage facility. She returns with an affirmative reply and nestles onto the back of the couch for a nap. She's still recovering, and I pat her head as Moke and I leave, thankful for her return into my life.

I don't agree with how Chammy does business, but I also can't argue with the reptilian response last night. They were attacked and invaded. They defended their home. It was a show of power, and the Council will have to determine how to respond. But I won't be at that meeting. I've got to worry about my own people first.

The storage facility is deserted when we get there.

"Where's Pietro?" Moke asks, pulling on the locked

office door. He cups his hands around his eyes and peers inside. Next to him, I do the same, but can't make anything out in the darkness.

"He said he'd be here," I say, pulling back from the door. "But I bet he's got his hands full at the Ope Center. It might be a little while."

He looks around cautiously. "Let's not wait long. I don't like being out in the open like this."

I can't say I blame him. I can cover my wings, but there's no way to disguise Moke's blue skin. I shade my eyes against the sun, scanning the ground for anything small and metallic.

"I might be able to pick the lock, get into a shed. Pietro wants us to be safe. He won't care if we take what we need now and let him know later."

"Works for me," Moke says, still glancing around.

I find a paper clip and get to work, fully concentrating on what I'm doing. Moke leans over me, watching. "You're in my light," I tell him, and he backs off.

Things have been weird between us ever since I became a Council member, but even before that. Since Clete died. Maybe it's a good thing Pietro isn't here. Maybe I can talk to Moke in private, find out what's eating him. Of course, it would help if I knew how to talk to people. Mostly I'm just good at arguing.

"Hey!" A male voice shouts. "What do you think you're doing?"

Moke jumps and so do I, the paperclip falling from my fingers. Four big, meaty guys are coming our way. They've got the look of Pater thugs. Guess it would've been better to have Pietro here, after all.

"It's okay," I say, lifting my hands in the air. "I'm a friend of Pietro's."

But the name doesn't stop them, and two of the guys jump Moke. A fist clips him on the temple, and he goes down face-first into the pavement.

"*That* is not okay," I say, my hands no longer open and empty. Now they're fists, and they are ready to fly. I land a strike square on the jaw of the guy in the lead, knocking him backward a few paces. But he's got a hundred pounds on me easily, and he doesn't go down. I lift into the air, dropping a jackknife kick into the second guy. It catches him in the ribs, and he lets out a rush of air and falls to the ground, clutching his side. I felt a few ribs give way underneath my foot, and he is going to have a beautiful bruise to show for it as well.

"Moke!" I yell, as the two guys he's struggling with haul him to his feet. He's dazed, his eyes rolled back into his head. But when I yell his name he comes back to consciousness, focused on me.

And he is furious.

Suddenly there's a ferocious *crack* that splits the air. The men holding Moke are blown away from him, their bodies hitting the storage units hard enough to dent the metal sides. Both of them slide to the ground, lifeless, smoke coming from their ears and the blue light of electricity dancing around their teeth for a moment before sizzling out.

Stunned, I stare at my friend, whose hands are blazing with the same blue light.

"What the hell?" I ask, but Moke can't answer. Whatever he did, it zapped him completely. He falls to the ground, unconscious.

"Moke!" I yell again, right before a bag is put over my head. I kick and scream in the dark, lashing out all around me. But I can't seem to connect with anything. My arms are pulled behind my back and tied together, pinioning my wings. I'm pulled to my feet roughly, elbows bending painfully.

"Pietro will kill you for this," I threaten.

"We don't work for him no more," someone says in my ear. And then I'm lifted and tossed, landing hard next to Moke, whose body is completely relaxed. He's out cold. I hear a car trunk slam over my head and the rumble of an engine. My body rocks against Moke's as the car pulls out of the storage facility, heading who knows where.

We've been kidnapped.

CHAPTER 31

"Moke? Moke? You okay?"

I can't see anything in the dark, but I can feel his legs against mine, his shoulder blades digging against my wings. I press back against him, hoping for a response.

"Moke!"

"I'm okay," he says, but he doesn't sound like that's true at all. His voice is weak and small, wrung out like the laundry we used to do back at the Children's Home.

"What the hell was that?" I ask him, raising my voice, as if to transfer some of my strength to him. "What did you do to those guys?"

"Electricity," he says, slurring the word slightly.

"What? How?"

"I . . ." He fades out, and I brace my legs against the side of the trunk, pushing back against him violently.

"I swear to god, Moke, if you pass out on me—"

"You'll what?" he asks, followed by a small chuckle. "Hit me over the head and throw me into a car trunk?"

"No," I shoot back. "I'll pee on us both. I can. I can and I will."

As threats go, it's the only one I can really follow through on right now. And even though it's not terribly compelling, it does make him laugh. And if he's laughing, he's conscious. I wait for him to stop, and when his shoulder blades are still, I try again.

"Seriously, man. What's up?"

He sighs, and I feel him relax against me.

"Remember how we always said we didn't know what my DNA was mixed with?"

In the dark, I nod. "Yeah. I'm part bird, Calypso is an insect, but you and Rain—"

"We just didn't know," he finishes for me. "Remember when Calypso said maybe I was part blue crayon?"

It's my turn to laugh, but it hurts my shoulders, and my wrists chafe where they're tied.

"Silver," he says, so quietly I'm not sure I heard him right, until he repeats it. "I've got colloidal silver in my bloodstream. It makes my skin look blue, but it also means I can conduct and store electricity."

"Dude," I breathe. "That is awesome. You're like that god guy who can throw lightning bolts."

"Well...not quite yet," he admits. "It takes time for me to build up a charge, and once I throw it, I'm exhausted. Langford has been teaching me how to control my abilities, but—"

"Wait—Langford?!"

Too late, I remember Calypso's words in the forest. Words I never had the chance to follow up on. She'd said that Langford was talking to Moke, and my surprise at that admission had sent the girl into silence, fearing that she'd said the wrong thing. Calypso had clearly led a life where saying the wrong thing meant getting into trouble, but I should know better. I should know that not asking the right questions is what gets you into trouble.

But right now I've been kidnapped and thrown into a car trunk with just the person I want to talk to. No better time than the present.

"What does Langford want with you?" I ask.

He is quiet for a second, but I know this silence. He hasn't passed out and he isn't refusing to talk. He's weighing his words.

"Langford told me I was special," he says. "She said I was made for a purpose and that we would figure out together what that was. She taught me how to feel electricity in the air, in the ground, all around us. She told me how to hold it, store it, and how to release it when I wanted to, against whoever I wanted to."

"She told me the same things," I admit, my heart sinking. "I was special and smart and capable and amazing."

"Amazing, really?" Moke asks, and I give him a small kick.

"Okay, so maybe I made that one up," I say. "But yeah, she pulled that same trick on me."

Heat has begun to burn in my cheeks, but in my

stomach, too. If I get back to the City of the Dead I will not be missing the next morning meeting, and damnit, it'll be one hell of a wake-up call for Langford.

"She made me feel special, made me want to do more. Do what she asked," he says. "I never had a mom, so..."

His words die off, but I'm nodding in agreement.

"She does a good job of stepping in," I say.

"But you've got a mom," he objects.

"Yeah, and my real mom is going to kick my fake mom's ass if she has anything to do with why we've been kidnapped."

I feel his head moving next to mine. He's shaking it *no*. "She doesn't," he says. "I'm sure of it."

"How do you know?"

"The reason why she was training me on how to use my powers was because she wanted a personal bodyguard. She doesn't think the Council is effective. She told me that a dictatorship is much more efficient than a democracy."

"So is she going to overthrow them?"

"I don't know," he says. "I just know that she taught me how to feel electric currents because she wanted someone to protect her. Someone who was loyal only to her."

"But how did she know all of this?" I ask. "How did she know about electric currents and that you had silver in your DNA?"

"You don't know?" he asks, and I shake my head. "She was one of the original scientists who made hybrids in the City of the Dead."

"Wait, wait, wait," I say, "hold up. If that's true then

she would have already suspected that Chammy and the reptilians were what was in the forest. She wouldn't have needed me to go in there at all."

"That's right," he agrees, then asks as if he already knows the answer, "So why did she send you?"

"Because," I realize as the building heat inside me roars into a full-on flame, "I wasn't supposed to come back at all."

CHAPTER 32

"That bi—"

I don't have time to finish. The car comes to a sudden halt, and Moke and I are both quiet, listening. Doors open, then shut again, and footsteps move toward the trunk.

"I'll do the talking," I say.

"When do you stop?" he asks.

The trunk flies open, sunlight making me wince and close my eyes. I'm roughly hauled out by my armpits, and nobody moves to help me when my cramped legs don't hold me. I go down, toppling face forward into dirt. I spit a mouthful out.

"When Pietro finds out you treated us like this—"

A boot comes down next to my nose, hard enough for me to reconsider talking. My eyes follow the length of leg up to the familiar face of one of the guys who jumped us at the storage facility.

"I told you," he says. "We don't work for him no more."

"Anymore," I correct him. "And I don't believe that

for one second. You've got Pater goon written all over you."

He yanks me to my feet so that he can stare me down. "I'm muscle," he says. "And muscle works for whoever is paying. Oh, sorry…*whomever* is paying."

Oh, dang. I was wrong. This guy isn't a run-of-the-mill enforcer, and I have definitely put my foot in it. But that's okay. I've got two feet.

"So who's paying?" I ask.

"I am," a voice says, and I turn to find a man walking into the clearing. He's shorter than me, and neatly dressed, his suit in stark contrast to the meadows that stretch out to all sides of us. He approaches us with a smile, his eyes sliding over both me and Moke.

"I'm Dr. Tanning," he says, and offers me a hand to shake. I give him a very dirty glare and one side of his mouth rises sardonically. He damn well knows that my hands are tied, and probably gave the orders in the first place.

"My apologies," he says, giving me a mock bow. "Devin, if you would?"

The big guy, Devin, moves behind me. There's the sound of a blade being drawn, and suddenly my hands are free. A bright, sharp pain follows and I know that Devin just gave me something to remember him by. Sure enough, when I bring my hands around to the front, a bright ribbon of blood is running from the base of my thumb. I pretend not to notice, blithely shaking hands with Tanning, who wipes his hands clean on his pants.

"Why the suit?" Moke asks.

"Dress for the job you want," Tanning says, nodding to Devin to cut Moke's bonds, as well.

"So, you want to be a funeral director?" I ask, and he turns back to me, still smiling.

"Of course not," Tanning says. "I want to be exactly what I already am. A scientist. A visionary. The man in charge."

"Of?" I ask, turning a half-circle. "This gravel road? All that grass?"

Suddenly my arm is jerked upward and back, my wrist touching the back of my neck. I cry out at the pain, sharp and hot.

"No, little girl," Tanning whispers in my ear. "I'm the leader of the Marauders."

My mouth goes dry, any smart-ass response I had evaporating on my lips. The Marauders. These are the guys Pietro warned me about, the ones who have been making inroads into the city since the Six were no longer around to patrol the walls.

But what do they want with me and Moke?

"I'm a guy who gets what he wants," Tanning goes on, his voice a harsh whisper in my ear. "First, I wanted to become a scientist. Then, I wanted to draw men to me, men who could do things I can't."

"Like a pull-up?" I ask.

I expect a crack to the back of my knee, or maybe a hand around my throat. But neither happens. Instead, there's a chuckle in my ear.

"Exactly," Tanning agrees, twisting my arm a little bit. "I'm the brain, they're the muscles. I've always known where my strength lies, and it's most definitely not in my body."

He lets go of my arm, and I bring it around to my front, massaging it. But that's a mistake, because I realize—too late—that what he's really interested in...is my wings.

"I'm a scientist," he says again, and I feel the sharp point of a scalpel probing the spot between my shoulder blades where my wings sprout.

"And I'd like for you to be a part of my next experiment."

CHAPTER 33

"Are you asking me, or are you telling me?"

Tanning's scalpel is still at my back, his fingers poking their way through my feathers. Meanwhile, a string of vehicles has appeared on the horizon, bright flashes with a plume of smoke rising behind them. I make eye contact with Moke, who can only shrug in response. He doesn't have a charge built up yet, and we're going to be greatly outnumbered once those vehicles get here. I might be able to twist out of Tanning's grip and take to the skies, but I'd be leaving Moke behind.

And that won't happen.

"I'd like to think I won't have to *tell you* to do anything, once I've finished explaining myself," Tanning continues, stepping back from me. I turn to face him, ignoring the trickle of blood running down my back and the squeal of tires as six vans pull up, surrounding us.

"Okay, then," I say. "Explain yourself."

Tanning nods, addressing both me and Moke.

"You see, in the city you're both looked at as mutants, monsters, as the source of the scourge that is dropping people like flies. But that's not how we think," he says. "Many of us are engineers, scientists, and doctors."

The sliding door opens on one of the vans, and a handful of men get out. They're all older. A few have glasses, and one is sucking on a ventilator.

"These are the Marauders?" I ask. My disbelief must show on my face, because Tanning chuckles again.

"I know we're not much to look at now, but in our former lives we were on the cutting edge, leaders in our fields. And like all men ahead of their time, there were those who opposed us. Who felt that our vision was too far reaching, too..." He pauses, taking a breath. "Too extreme."

"Why?" I ask, but it's hard to get even that one word out, past the weight in my stomach. The weight of dread.

"We're not like the people in the city," Tanning goes on. "We don't think you're less than human. In fact, quite the opposite. We think—*I* think—that hybrids are the next step in evolution. You might have been concocted in a lab, but you're here now. You're here, and uniquely situated to continue the human race."

"But...we're not human," I counter.

"You are, though...at least partially. The parts of you—of all hybrids—that aren't human are exactly what makes you adaptable to this new world."

"What new world?" I ask.

"Where we've found ourselves," Tanning says, hands

in the air. "The old world. The one we battered and broke, polluted and poisoned. We ruined it, and that's what our children will inherit. But sadly, I don't have children. Not human ones, anyway. So, I've made my own."

He turns to Devin. "Bring them out."

Devin goes to the back of a van and pulls the double doors open, reaching up to help down...something.

"What...?" Moke's single word is lost on the breeze, and for once in my life, I have nothing to say.

It's human, or at least...it has the legs of a human. The torso has been scraped and stretched, and I can see where scales have tried to grow. But they didn't get far. Combating the scales is the spotted hair of a leopard and, beyond that, a patch of porcupine quills. A dog's flapped ears sprout from either side of the head, and it cocks them toward us as Moke makes a gagging sound, trying to keep his lunch down.

The thing walks past us, and a chain drags behind it. A chain connected to another creature. This one has horse legs, but one is dragging badly from an abscess on the knee joint. Its fingers end in bear claws, and bat wings sprout from its back, out of proportion and grotesquely small.

The worst part is that Tanning has left the humans' faces untouched, so I can see who they used to be. And I can see the suffering in their eyes.

The one with the horse legs stumbles, pulling down the entire chain of creatures, the last one falling with a shriek from the back of the van, unable to catch itself with its arms, which are stubby and short, like a pig's. The group rolls on the ground, a horrible mix of animal and human sounds rising up from them.

"Stop it!" I shout at Tanning. "Make it stop!"

He smiles, pulls a revolver, and calmly executes the horse creature. The shot rings out sharply, and the other animals immediately cower. Tanning spins back to me, tucks the gun into his shoulder holster.

"You know how it goes," he says, shrugging. "A horse breaks a leg, you've got to put it down."

"That wasn't a horse." I seethe. "That was a human, a hybrid. You said yourself—one of your own children!"

"Yes, yes," he agrees dismissively. "But a defective one. For all our expertise, we haven't had much luck. Grafting wings, surgically implanting teeth, attaching tentacles... that all takes time, spotless surgical environments, and willing test subjects."

A feathered hand reaches up from the pack around his feet, touching his knee as if asking for forgiveness.

"Back in the old world, we had the first two things," Tanning admits. "Although we may have loosely interpreted the word *willing* when it came to our subjects. For that we were ejected from the medical community, and from the world at large. Tossed out beyond the walls of the city, we've had to make do.

"And these are the sad results," he says. "It's become clear that surgical means of creating hybrids are not feasible. So we've decided to go another route. One that's, let's say, a little more...natural."

"Natural," I repeat, eyes still on the crawling monstrosities, their hands held up, supplicating their master. "Natural is probably better."

"I'm so glad you agree," he says, smiling. "We're instituting a breeding program. And you two showed up right on time."

CHAPTER 34

"We didn't exactly show up," I tell Tanning, rubbing my wrists together. "We were sort of kidnapped. And by 'sort of' I mean, that's totally what happened."

"Yes." He nods, agreeing. "And you'll remember that I said we loosely interpret the word *willing* for all of our test subjects, including you."

"So that's the deal?" I ask, my temper flaring. "You just kidnap whoever you want and use our bodies to make more hybrids?"

"There is a bright side, of course," Tanning says. "It's our own genetic lines we're looking to improve. We wouldn't want anything to happen to children carrying our genes."

I look at the group of men who had exited the van. "Yeah, that's not really a bright side, in my opinion. I can't say that I know what my type is, but I definitely think anybody over fifty is out of the running."

"The benefit to you is not in choosing your mate," Tanning says patiently. "The benefit is in carrying a Marauder's child, and all the perks that entails. You'll have the best of everything. Lodging, food, protection, and medical care. You'll never have to raise a finger to ensure your own survival, or that of your children."

"Right, just be a good little incubator," I say. I'm running my mouth, hoping that Moke will have a decent charge built up soon. I may not have an escape plan ready, but I'd really like to see Moke fry Tanning and figure it out from there.

"What about him?" I ask, nodding toward Moke. "He can't be a hybrid baby vending machine. What do you want with him?"

"Oh, we're interested in the males, too," Tanning says, approaching him. "We'd love to continue our lab experiments with some fresh hybrid DNA at our disposal." He raises a hand to touch Moke's shoulder, one finger tracing the pale-blue skin. "What exactly are you, anyway?"

"Careful, boss!" Devin says, but it's a second too late. Moke squeezes his eyes shut and the hair on my arms rises as electricity gathers in the air, all of it funneling toward Moke. There's a sizzling sound, and Tanning cries out as a spark jumps from Moke's skin to his hand. He backpedals, sucking on his finger like a little kid that just got smacked.

Devin moves toward Moke, fist raised, but Tanning intervenes, grabbing him by the elbow. "No, wait!"

Exhausted, Moke sags to his knees, eyes watching Tanning warily as the doctor approaches him. "Are you finished?" Tanning asks. Moke can only nod, any pretense of being a danger long past.

"You're a conductor?" Tanning says, but it's more of

a statement than a question as he circles Moke, reaching down to pull my friend to his feet. "Cut his bonds," Tanning tells Devin, who circles around behind Moke, clearly afraid to make contact with his blue skin.

"I said cut his bonds," Tanning barks, irritably shaking the hand that was shocked. Devin pulls a knife and I can't help but make a small *zzzt* noise when he leans in to release Moke. Devin jumps, and the other muscle men try to hide their smiles.

"Bring the girl," Tanning instructs, and I'm flanked by guards who direct me toward one of the vans. I gingerly step over the line of mutants, ignoring when one of them barks at me, soft puppy ears flapping beside beseeching dog eyes, the human mouth working as it tries to speak.

"What will happen to them?" I ask, as one of the men pulls the sliding door shut behind us.

"They're a drain on resources," Tanning explains, settling into the middle seat, Moke by his side. "They require feeding and medical care that we can't funnel into wasted projects."

"Projects!" I spin in my seat to watch as we drive away. The *pop, pop, pop* of bullets can be heard from inside the van, but the spray of dust from our tires hides the pitiless scene. "You made them!" I yell at Tanning. "And that's how you treat them?"

"I thought it best you be made aware of the end game for our less successful results," Tanning says, eyes blank as our van makes a turn and begins climbing. It falls silent inside the van and I shoot a worried glance at Moke, but he's almost completely out, his head sagging to the side as we turn again, the switchback taking us to the top of a ridge.

It comes to a stop in a shaded area, trees twining their limbs above us as the sun begins to set. It would be beautiful if I weren't terrified about what monstrosity Dr. Tanning has to show us next. We climb out, Moke kept on his feet only with the assistance of the men on either side of him. Tanning motions for me to follow and moves toward a clearing. Tanning holds aside a low-hanging limb for me, and we break out of the trees onto a rocky point, the red rays of the sun barely peeking out over the horizon.

There's a hum in the air, something I can barely hear but am highly aware of, a vibration moving through my body, jarring my teeth and making me shake my head.

"What is that?" I ask Tanning, still following as he moves toward a bulky object at the edge of the rim. It's covered by a tarp, and his face lights up in admiration as he pulls it away, revealing his grand surprise.

"I know we're not impressive to look at," Tanning says, eyes still on his grand creation. "But the things Marauders can make...well, *those* are quite incredible."

I can't argue. Even though I don't know what I'm looking at, it feels ominous. Coils wrap around a mountain of metal, gears clicking and whirring, everything churning and gyrating along with a low pulse I can't ignore. I plug my ears and step closer. Wires spill from all directions, small clamps pinching onto the electrodes of a bank of batteries.

"So this is why you've been raiding the city. You've got to power this thing," I say, peering closer. The innards of the machine have glass tubes, some filled with different colored liquids. As I watch, the large, awkward head—eerily shaped like a rocket—spins to settle onto the horizon, the crosshairs set directly on the City of the Dead. My city.

"What does it do?" I ask, turning to Tanning. I'll tear it apart with my bare hands if I have to. Rain and Calypso are in this thing's sights, and so are Pietro and Melanie.

"Not much," Tanning says with a shrug. "With enough power and in the right conditions, it can raise the temperature about ten degrees."

"Oh," I say, relief washing through me. There's not a bomb or a weapon of mass destruction in the hands of these madmen.

"Which is exactly the right temperature for the virus to flourish," Tanning finishes, smiling at me.

My gut bottoms out. "What do you mean, 'flourish'?" I ask, advancing on him, my hands in fists. "It's already chaos down there! People are fighting for hospital beds, and Langford has them all convinced that the hybrids are the source of the sickness."

"Oh, Langford!" Tanning claps his hands together in mock glee. "How is she? Still kind of a bitch?"

"You know her?" I ask.

"Of course I do," he says. "We all worked together back in the old days, before there were so many protocols and rules. I have to say, she wasn't a big fan of ethics back then. I doubt much has changed, hmm?"

"Says the man with a thermometer aimed at a city tearing itself apart," I mutter.

"It's more of a radiator, dear," Tanning says smoothly.

"It can't get any worse down there," I snap back. "Langford's got everyone convinced the sickness jumped from hybrids to humans, and that we're to blame. There's already riots and blood in the streets down there. All you'll do is make everyone a little sweatier."

"Oh, it can get worse," Tanning says, his voice dropping low. "I engineered that virus, and trust me when I tell you that what you're seeing is tame compared to the mutations heat will bring on."

I think of the feathered hand reaching up from the pile of ruined hybrids at his feet, Tanning walking past them like they were nothing.

"What?" I ask, almost not wanting to know. "What will it do?"

"If I raise the temperature in the city, those already infected will become delusional, convinced that the very people who are trying to help them actually mean them harm."

"That's horrible," I say. Calypso had a fever once when she was very little. I was worried we were going to lose her, and I sat up with her all night. She'd raged and babbled, kicking off her blankets and screaming at me, certain I was a monster trying to hurt her, not a friend with a cooling cloth trying to help.

"You created the virus." I repeat Tanning's words, realizing their significance. "You weren't just coming into the city for batteries, were you? You were infecting the populace."

"Slowly but surely." Tanning nods. "It should be reaching peak infection rates right about now."

Moke stumbles into the clearing, the men tasked with holding him up barely able to do their jobs as he moves toward Tanning. "If you touched her, I swear—"

"Relax." Tanning waves away Moke's threat. "This has been more of an informational meeting."

Moke turns to me, confused.

"They created the virus," I explain. "And it'll kick up a notch, turning every infected person in the city into a homicidal maniac, if they raise the temperature, which they can do with this machine."

"You said yourself that the humans and hybrids are at each other's throats. They don't want you there. But we want you. We want you very much," Tanning says, fingers drumming against the weapon. "We want all of you."

"So that's the deal?" I say, a ball of dread in my chest. "You tell Langford you'll take the hybrids off her hands in exchange for not making the virus even worse? Not making everyone turn on each other?"

"Even better." Tanning smiles. "I have the vaccine, and I'll happily distribute it right into the atmosphere. No one else will get sick, and the ill will recover. Everyone goes home happy."

"Except for the hybrids," I say. "As usual."

Tanning shakes his head. "You haven't been listening. I said you'll be treated well. Better than you ever have, I'm sure. There is one nonnegotiable item, though."

"What?" I ask, suspicion rising.

"We absolutely must have Maximum Ride."

CHAPTER 35

"What do you want with my—"

Moke shoots me a glance, just in time, and I clamp my mouth shut. There's a chance Tanning doesn't know Max is my mom. I mean, hell, I didn't even know until a few months ago. And once he figures out that I'm the child of one of the most famous hybrids ever—and the prize catch for his experiments—I'll be his number one bargaining chip.

"Why her?" I ask. "Why Maximum Ride?"

"She's the best example of our work from long ago," Tanning says, eyes alight. "I've not had the honor of meeting her, but can you imagine what wonderful children a creature like that might produce?"

Moke snorts, and it's my turn to shoot him a glare.

"Think about it," Tanning says, his gaze lost somewhere on the horizon. "Her advanced DNA, my gifted mind... our children would be amazing specimens."

I try not to puke a little bit in my mouth. Tanning wants Max for himself. That's both gross and ridiculous. Plus,

Fang would tear his lungs out of his back and give him a quick flying lesson by dropping him from a thousand feet after the fact. But I've got to keep my head clear. Like Tanning said, so far this has just been an informational meeting—and right now, I know something he doesn't. Namely, that I'm Maximum Ride's daughter.

"So you want us to go back to the city and deliver your message to Langford. We'll let her know that you can cure everyone in exchange for her hybrid population, which she doesn't want anyway. Sure." I shrug. "I mean, no skin off my back."

But Tanning is shaking his head like I'm a child that hasn't played this game before and doesn't know all the rules.

"I can't let you both go," he says. "That would be a major tactical error on my part, wouldn't it? Two hybrids in my power, and I release them for...what? To build goodwill? I'm holding all the chips, dear."

"I won't leave her here with you," Moke says. "There's been more filth coming out of your mouth than I've seen in a lifetime on the streets, and you're insane if you think I'm going anywhere without Hawk."

Tanning cocks his head at my friend, reminding me of the puppy-like creature on the ground in the meadow, the *pop, pop, pop* of the execution squad as we drove away. "You assume I want to keep the girl, but that's a miscalculation. You're of much more worth to me than she is."

My fists clench at my sides, blood still running down my thumb from where Devin pricked me with his knife.

"You're the one who's miscalculated, if you think I'm going anywhere without Moke."

"Friendship!" Tanning claps his hands together. "How adorable! However, those bonds are cut as easily as the ones that were on your wrists. With your pretty blue friend here, I won't need to risk sending my men into the city any longer to salvage batteries. He can power my machine for as long as I need."

Tanning glances at Moke, sharp eyes assessing. "Maybe even with a few tweaks we can take care of this troubling recharging issue."

"Never," Moke says, straightening up as he stares down Tanning. "I won't do it."

"You will," Tanning argues. "Or I raise the temperature now and take out everyone in the city below us." He licks a finger and holds it up in the air. "If the wind is right, we might even be able to hear the screams."

"You sick—"

I don't get to finish, my mouth snapping shut in fear as Tanning approaches me. "No, no, no," he says. "That's exactly the point. I'm not sick, not at all. But I can make everyone else that way, if you don't do what I want."

There it is. Everything depends on me...again. I've looked out for my band of orphans for so long that worrying about them is second nature. But a whole city? And I don't even like half of those people! Yet somehow I've become responsible for their well-being. I hang my head. I might be stubborn as hell, but I know when to run and when to fight. And right now, I've got nothing to my benefit except my wings.

"I'll be back, Moke," I tell him, pumping my wings to rise a few feet into the air. Tanning watches, unable to hide his fascination as I take off.

"Hawk...don't...," Moke says, his blue lips twisting into grief. He might still be arguing, but he knows as well as I do that we lost this round.

"I'll be back," I say again, catching a draft and wheeling for the city. "I won't leave you, and I won't lose you like I did Clete."

CHAPTER 36

I can't go right to Langford, not after what I've learned.

If she really is planning a coup against the rest of the Council, I can't stand the thought of letting her think I'm still her little pet. I might flat-out be stupid sometimes, but I'd still have a hard time pretending to be *that* dumb. I need to clear my head, so I aim for my apartment balcony, the cool fog of the evening beginning to settle. The glass doors slide open as I land, Max and Fang coming out to greet me. I'm surprised, and stumble a little on the landing, bringing a blush to my cheeks.

"That was fast," I say. "Langford sent for you?"

"Yes," Max nods, ruffling Ridley's chest feathers, while my falcon nuzzles her fingers. What a traitor.

"Langford said that the situation here in the city between the populace and the hybrids was out of control," Fang explains, leaning against the balcony railing and airing his wings. "She said you weren't up to the task of keeping any kind of peace between them."

"Well, I can tell you a few not-so-nice things about her,

too," I say, walking into my apartment and kicking off my shoes. "Where should I start?"

"How about with where you've been and why you're bleeding?" Max says, grabbing my wrist.

"That's a longer story," I tell her. "You should both sit down. And where the hell are Calypso and Rain?"

"I moved them over to our apartment, so that the three of us could talk," Max says easily.

"You've got your own rooms here?" I ask, embarrassed that I didn't know. Of course, Max and Fang have a room. They've probably got a suite just as nice as Langford's, because they're everyone's favorite hybrid couple.

They settle on the couch, and Ridley comes to my shoulder, nudging my ear as I stroke her neck. "There's a colony of hybrids in the forest," I begin. "Calypso and I discovered them after Langford put me in charge of figuring out what lived there. They aren't exactly the nicest hybrids I've ever met, and a few of them are hard to look at."

"What kind of hybrids are they?" Max asks.

"Reptiles," I tell her. "Chammy is a chameleon, Gila is a lizard, and Tut is a turtle. But there's also a fish girl, and a crocodile." I shudder, remembering the crocodile and the screams from the forest, as it took humans out at the ankles.

Max turns to Fang, her eyebrows furrowed. "Almost makes you wonder if those old rumors about alligators in the sewer system were actually true."

"Probably," I say. "Langford and her team dumped them down drains."

"Wait," Max says. "Her team?"

I nod. "She was one of the scientists working here in the City of the Dead to create hybrids. When the plug was pulled on their lab, they did away with the specimens in the easiest way possible. Now their children want revenge for what happened to their families."

"Revenge," Fang repeats, his eyes darkening. "How many of them are there?"

"Maybe two hundred, total," I say. "They have weapons and aren't afraid to use them. Now Langford has told everyone that the hybrids are the cause of the virus, so people are ready to kill any hybrid they see."

"Smart," Max says, with admiration. "Her own creations want to come for her, but she's got the bodies of citizens to put in between them. Tell someone who their enemy is, and they will fight to their last breath."

"She's the real enemy!" I say, voice rising. "She manipulated me—and Moke, too! I wasn't supposed to come back from that expedition into the forest. She already knew what was there; she just didn't have a use for me anymore once I made it clear I don't just follow orders blindly. But Moke—we found out he can conduct electricity—Langford has plans to make him her personal bodyguard, once she makes a move to disband the Council and rule this city on her own."

"Hard to rule a city in chaos all by yourself," Max says.

"It gets worse," I tell her. "The Marauders are the real source of the virus, and they manufactured it to take a violent turn once the weather reaches a certain temperature.

Everyone who is sick will become a cold-blooded killer if it gets hot enough in the city, and the Marauders built a weapon that can raise the temperature, and now they're using Moke to power it. They've also got the vaccine, and will make a deal with Langford: they'll release it into the atmosphere in exchange for all the hybrids of the city. Or, they make it hot enough to cause a bloodbath that brings the population of the City of the Dead to zero."

"What do the Marauders want with hybrids?" Fang asks. "And how do you know all of this?"

"That's where my bleeding comes in," I say, lifting my hand. "Moke and I got kidnapped, and the leader of the Marauders—a Dr. Tanning—sent me back with the message for Langford. They want the hybrids for..." My voice breaks off, the blush in my cheeks rising further.

"Uh...breeding purposes."

"*Ewww,*" Fang says, nudging Max. "Breeding."

"Yeah, reproduction. Gross," she says, smiling back.

"I'm serious!" I yell at them. "And so is Tanning! He wants you, particularly Max, and he wants you for himself!"

"Okay, that's definitely not funny," Fang says, blood rising to his cheeks as well. "Obviously I have to kill him now."

"All yours," I say. "But first we've got to figure out what to do about Langford, and this virus."

"And the reptilians," Max adds, her eyes turning to me. "You should never have taken Calypso into the forest with you. You had no idea what was waiting for you there, and you put her in danger."

"Seriously!" I screech, coming to my feet. "I just tell you about a plot that's going to end the city and that a mad doctor wants you to make babies with him, and all you want to do is point out my bad decision-making?"

"I'm your mom." Max shrugs. "This is a parenting moment."

"You're too much," I say, walking away from them into the kitchen, where I rinse my bloodied hand in the sink, rubbing my sore wrists. "I get kidnapped and all you've got is criticism."

"Yes, you did get kidnapped," Fang says, following me over and leaning against the counter. "And it was bad decision-making that led you there. Your mother is right; you could learn some lessons on how to survive."

"Survive!!" I spin, water flying off my hands. "I survived for ten years when you guys abandoned me!"

"On the streets," Max corrects, joining us. "You survived on the streets. You have no idea how to take care of yourself—or others—in the wilderness. And if you want to take action now, it sounds like it's time for you to learn. Street smarts won't help you in the forest, or out in the wilderness with the Marauders."

Max and Fang lock eyes, both of them smiling.

"What?" I ask suspiciously. "What are you thinking?"

"I think class is back in session," Max says.

CHAPTER 37

"This is your worst idea ever!" I yell at Max, as she flies in front of me. "Everything is falling apart and you want to go on a field trip."

"Not everything is falling apart," Fang says. He's on my right, gliding easily, pumping his massive wings once for every three times I exercise mine. "We're together, after all."

"Oh, boy, family camping trip!" I snap, glaring down at the endless trees below us. We'd left the city behind more than an hour ago, after I gave a quick update to Calypso and Rain, who flinched when I explained about leaving Moke behind.

"I had to," I explained, but it didn't feel good to follow up with the information that I was leaving again, and Calypso refused to hug me good-bye.

"This better be worth it," I grumble, as Max begins to circle for a landing, aiming for a break in the trees below. Fang and I follow her down, and I give her a critical look once we're all on the ground.

"I know you're pissed," she says, "but the truth is that

I need fresh air and some time to think this over. This is a complicated house of cards, and if we play our hand wrong, people will die. Maybe a lot of people."

"Okay," I say, grudgingly. It's nice to know that she doesn't have a quick and simple answer to this problem. She looks tired, and for the first time I have to consider the fact that maybe she isn't perfect. "So what are we going to do?"

"Make shelter," Fang says. "It's the first thing you need to know about being in the wilderness. You get wet, and you'll be miserable for as long as you're out here."

"Um…which isn't long, right?" I ask, following him into the trees. Max stays behind, resting on a rock, her chin in her hands. Fang points to a tree with a fork in its trunk about five feet up.

"You want to find something like this," he says, kicking dead leaves around until he uncovers a fallen tree about twice the size of my arm. "Help me out with this."

I bend down and pick up the other end, maneuvering as he fits it into the notch of the forked tree. He nods, like we've accomplished something. "Now, look around and find branches to cover the sides."

"Okay," I say dubiously, "but we're not like, actually sleeping out here, are we?"

"Doubt it." He shrugs. "That's not the point, though."

"What is?" I ask, tossing my hair from my eyes as I gather branches in my arms. "I don't even know what we're doing right now. Max said she needs time to think, fine. But she can do that in the city—which is where I belong. Why do I need to learn how to build a shelter in the woods? It's not like I'm ever going to have a sleepover in the forest with Chammy and his pals."

Fang shakes his head and begins leaning the branches he's gathered against the propped tree, lining either side to produce makeshift walls. "You're not thinking big enough," he says. "Your mother and I have talked a lot about all the ways we've failed you. You know leaving you behind was an accident—and believe me, Max has beaten herself up over it plenty. We should have been teaching you everything we know for your entire life."

"Right," I say, following his lead and propping my sticks along the other side. "Instead I'm getting a crash course in deep woods survival when all my enemies are back in the city."

"Will you always be there, Hawk?" Fang asks, grabbing an armful of leaves from the forest floor. He spreads them along the outside of the branches lining the fallen tree, creating a canopy. "You've got wings on your back and a brain in your head. You can go anywhere, do anything. And we want you to know how to survive, wherever life takes you."

I watch as he continues to cover the stick frame that we've erected, his words spinning through my mind. "I guess I never really thought about my life outside of the city," I say, mouth dry at the thought.

"That's what I'm telling you, kid," he says, stepping back to admire what we've built. "You're not thinking big enough. When your mother and I were in Antarctica—"

"Antarctica!" I screech. "What? How?"

He shakes his head and smiles. "See what I mean? You

never know what's going to happen, or where you'll end up. Your mother and I want to be sure you're prepared for everything. Now"—he claps his hands together—"get in!"

Still shocked, I do as I'm told, creeping in under the opening at the base of the forked tree. He crawls in after me, and it's a tight fit. We lay side by side, shoulders touching, only small amounts of sunlight coming through the leaf covering.

"If it's winter, use snow to cover the sides," Fang says. "It's a fantastic insulator. Bet you didn't know that snow could actually keep you warm, did you?"

"No," I say, honestly surprised. "I guess I could probably learn a lot from you guys."

I stare straight ahead, way too embarrassed by this admission to turn my head and look at Fang...my dad. Maybe it was easier to tell him than Max. She's always fast with criticism, eager to point out when I've made a mistake. Sometimes it makes me feel like she's embarrassed that I'm her daughter. But now I realize that maybe her sharp tone and quick temper don't come from the fact that she's disappointed in me—she's mad at herself. Upset about all the lost time and chances to teach me everything she knows.

"Maybe this wasn't such a bad idea after all," I say. But my throat closes up and I'm not quite ready to say more. I can't say what's on my mind, even though I want to let Fang know that I'm impressed—no, that I'm proud.

I'm really, really proud of my mom and dad.

"Your feet are sticking out, Fang," I hear Max say, and

he grunts when she kicks his heel. "Come on out, you two," she says. "We need to talk things over."

I crawl out, followed by Fang.

"First things first," she says. "We need to make sure Moke is safe."

"Yes," I sigh, relieved. She must understand that my orphans are like her flock is to her—family.

"But I don't think he's in any danger right now," she goes on. "Tanning needs him to power his weather machine. That thing is his ace in the hole. If he can't raise the temperature, he poses no real threat."

"He has the cure," I argue, but she's shaking her head.

"Langford has her own team of scientists, and I guarantee you they are all working around the clock on creating a solution themselves. Tanning's power is in the machine, not the vaccine."

I look at Fang, and he nods. It makes sense.

"Okay, so what about Chammy and the reptilians?" I ask.

"It's tricky," she says. "They're determined to destroy Langford, and I'm half tempted to let them. She's a dictator waiting to happen. But they aren't just angry with her. They've been attacked by the regular citizens, and it doesn't sound like they'll be willing to just accept an apology."

"Probably not," I say. "But I know something Chammy doesn't. Langford was one of the scientists working on the hybrid program. She created his people, then flushed them down the toilet."

"True," Fang says. "Will he believe you if you tell him?"

"And can we trust him to not kill you on sight?" Max adds.

I think of the crocodile in the forest, and Chammy tossing a grenade from hand to hand. "I don't trust him, not entirely," I say. "But in the end, he's a hybrid. And I won't trade him—any of them—in order to save the city."

"Good," Max nods, like she was hoping I'd say that. "Which means we're going to have to either overthrow Langford, or convince her not to divide the population, hybrids versus humans."

I think of the morning meetings, all eyes turned to Langford. "I don't know if the Council will be on board with—"

I'm interrupted by a high-pitched screech, and the sound of wings overhead. I look up to see Ridley descending, a rolled-up parchment in her mouth. She settles onto my shoulder, and I unroll the message with shaking fingers.

Calypso's handwriting is large and awkward, the writing of a child who never got a real education. But I can still read it, and my stomach bottoms out.

Marauders attacked the city. Come home.

The last inch of paper unrolls under my hand to reveal one more word.

Please.

CHAPTER 38

I keep my I-told-you-so to myself as we wing back to the city. By the look on Max's face when she read the note, she wasn't expecting Tanning to move so quickly. She'd made a mistake, but instead of being angry with her for leading us astray, I feel bad for her. I know exactly what it's like to make the wrong decision and have others pay for it.

But that doesn't relieve her—or me—of our responsibility. I knew the threat that Tanning and his machine posed. If it really can turn the sick into bloodthirsty murderers, the whole city is going to be at war with itself...and those stuck in the hospitals will be under the first wave of attack.

"I've got to go check on someone," I say, peeling off from Max and Fang, who are headed toward the spire of the hotel and our apartments there.

Max shoots me a worried look, but it's my turn to make the decisions. "Ten minutes," I shout over my shoulder as I veer toward the hospital. The roof door is unlocked, and the halls are oddly quiet as I make my way to Melanie's room. I knock briefly, then push the door open and slip inside. She's in her bed, eyes open, her lips blue-tinged, skin gray. Oh, no, am I already too late?

"Hawk," she says, the tubes in her nose bouncing as she speaks. "I didn't think I'd see you again."

"I'm here," I tell her, and sit next to her on the bed. It sinks with my weight, and her hand finds mine. Her fingers are cold and clammy.

"Listen," I say, leaning forward so she can hear my whisper. "The sickness that's moving through the city isn't from hybrids. The Marauders created it."

Her eyes go wide. "I heard they're in the city," she says. "One of the nurses was saying that they muscled their way right into the middle of the square, and that they've got some sort of weapon, but nobody knows what it's for. Things have quieted down around here, mostly because I don't think people know who to fight. The Marauders? The hybrids? Or each other?"

"Sorry to tell you, but things are about to heat up again—literally."

I explain what the weapon is, and what it can do. She blinks rapidly and her eyes go even wider, the machine tracking her heart rate beeping fast. "That's horrible! The sick will turn on whoever is closest to them, the very people giving them care."

"That's right." I nod. "Which makes a hospital the worst place you can be. I was going to offer to take you out of here, but..."

I look at her bedside. She's hooked up to more machines now, some of them to help her breathe. Some to track her heart rate, some I don't even know what for. I just know that unhooking her from them is probably a bad idea.

She shakes her head. "I can't leave, Hawk. These machines are keeping me alive. But thank you for coming for me. Thank you for...for caring." Her lip trembles and it seems like she's about to cry. I squeeze her hand.

"Spread the word," I tell her. "Let people know to keep cool, and I mean that. Ice packs, cold water soaks, whatever. If the sick can keep their body temperature down, we all have a better shot at surviving this."

"I'll try." She nods.

"Best not to say why, though," I say. "The last thing we need is a panic...well, more of a panic. Maximum Ride is here, and she'll know what to do about the Marauders and their machine."

The sound of my mom's name makes Melanie light up. "Maximum Ride!" she says, real hope gleaming in her eyes. "If she's back, everything is going to be fine."

Not that long ago I might have agreed with Melanie. But now I've seen worry lines on Max, and her mouth go thin at the mention of the virus. My mom is scared. And when Maximum Ride is scared, that means everyone else should probably be crapping their pants.

But Max and Fang have taught me more than they think; they've taught me how to instill courage, even when there's little hope. I pat Melanie's hand.

"We can win this," I tell her.

But as I fly into the night sky, I can't help but remember the gray cast of her skin and the blue tinge of her lips.

Even if we do win this, she might not be around to celebrate.

CHAPTER 39

When I walk into the Council room, I think it might already be too late for all of us. Voices are raised, fingers are pointing, and most of them are directed at Max and Fang.

"That's the most ridiculous thing I've ever heard!" Langford snaps as I enter the room. "The Council does not bargain with terrorists."

"You don't seem to have a problem with instilling terror, though," Max says slyly, and Langford's eyes narrow.

"What did I miss?" I ask, strolling to my chair. "No fur—or feathers—flying yet?"

"I'm trying to convince them that a show of brute force against the Marauders is not in our best interest," Max says, her eyes not moving from Langford.

"They've come into our city with a weapon of mass destruction," Langford says. "Tanning says he'll raise the temperature one degree every hour until we hand over our hybrid population...which normally I'd be more than happy to do. But I won't set the precedent of bargaining with anyone who poses a threat. This city will be overrun with opportunists."

"She wants Pietro to hand over the Pater weapons stash," Fang tells me. "Langford wants to arm the populace and sic them on the Marauders."

I remember the panicked woman in the hospital who had shocked a doctor with a crash cart. She certainly shouldn't be handed a gun, and neither should anyone else without the proper training and emotional stability to handle it. Plus, these same people had attacked the forest with fires and pitchforks, only to be set back by Chammy and the reptilians, carrying their dead and wounded. Giving them guns will only escalate that situation.

"And did Tanning also tell you that the Marauders are the ones responsible for the virus?" I ask, and Langford looks away.

"I don't see how that's relevant at this point," she says stiffly, but other Council members are muttering among themselves.

"It's relevant because you need to make a citywide bulletin right now, making it clear that the mutants aren't the source!" I say, voice rising.

"That ship has already sailed," Langford says blithely, waving her hand. "As soon as the citizens attacked the mutants the seed was planted. The reptilians will want revenge. Revealing that they had no part in the outbreak won't save them now."

"How convenient," I sneer, and one of the Council—

Holden—gives me an odd look. I might actually be heard for once in these meetings.

"Regardless," Max says, "handing out weapons should not be considered an option. Hawk, tell the Council what you witnessed at Tanning's camp."

I explain about the parade of monstrosities, the Marauders' plan to create a kind of super-human of their own progeny, mixing hybrid and human together. When I mentioned the breeding program, Holden is visibly shocked.

"That's horrible!" he says.

"They want our hybrids—they want me, my husband, my daughter," Max says. "I have a problem with that. I won't go willingly, and no other hybrid should be asked to make that sacrifice for the sake of a city that has mal-treated them for generations."

Langford rolls her eyes, but other Council members appear to be listening.

"But there's a way to get out of this without more bloodshed. The Marauders are unethical, surely, but a life outside of civilization has contributed to that. They're here, now, in our city. They want our hybrids, but what they're really asking for is to continue their experimenta-tion. Why not allow them access to our scientific facili-ties and laboratories? Why not give them the ability to continue their project—in an agreed-upon and humane manner—instead of handing over our hybrids, or risking the city being turned into a war zone?"

"No!" Langford shouts, her hand slapping the table and making a few people jump. "I will not treaty with Tanning! He's a monster, a viper, a—" She breaks off, suddenly aware that her tone is rising, and her face is flushed. She's losing control.

"Sounds like you're putting personal issues in front of what's best for the greater good," Max says coldly, eyeing her. "Not very democratic of you."

Another uneasy ripple moves through the conference room, and Langford straightens her shoulders, aware that she's losing the confidence of the Council.

"Very well," she says, her tone controlled again. "Can I ask that we consider both options? We'll send a message to Tanning with the offer of our scientific facilities for his use, in exchange for the cure to the virus. Meanwhile, I'd like to send Hawk to see if she can persuade her friend Pietro to share the location of the other weapons caches throughout the city. Make no mistake—if Tanning rejects our offer, we *will* use force against the invaders."

Max looks at Fang, and something passes between them. She nods to him, then Langford, finally turning her eyes to me.

"Go, Hawk," she says. "And hurry."

CHAPTER 40

The Hope for Opes Center looks like it's short on hope...
and opes.

Much like the hospital, the streets around it are filled
with those sick with the virus, and their loved ones are
demanding treatment. Beds overflow onto the street, and
Pietro looks harried when I find him in a crowded hall.

"Hawk!" he says, face lighting up briefly, right before
an orderly stops him with a question. He nods and signs
off on something, then returns his attention to me.

"Sorry, things are crazy here. The virus is out of control, and news that the Marauders are in the city has made
people more wary. I've been moving through the lines
outside, asking people for their patience and understand-
ing, but that's not something people are handing out right
now."

"No," I agree, shaking my head. "But Langford would
like to hand out guns."

"What?" he asks, brow furrowing. "That's insane! Half

these people have never had any training with a weapon, and I wouldn't trust anyone with a gun right now. Everyone is out for themselves, Hawk. It's getting ugly."

A doctor pushes past us, barely bothering to say *excuse me*. "Can we go somewhere?" I ask. Judging by Pietro's reaction to what I said about Langford, this isn't going to be an easy conversation.

"Sure." He nods. "The roof is just about the only place we can be alone."

We head to the end of the hall. He climbs the stairs ahead of me, and I can't help but notice that while he wouldn't trust anyone with a gun right now, that apparently doesn't apply to him. The grip of a pistol sticks up above the waistline of his pants.

We break out onto the roof and into slightly cooler air. But not by much. There's still lingering smoke from the fires in the forest, and if I'm not mistaken, it's warmer than it was when I first got here. Has Tanning already started the weather machine? He clearly doesn't trust anyone; he didn't give me enough time to return with an answer to his message for Langford. I wouldn't put it past him to start cranking the temperature as long as he's ignored.

"What's going on?" he asks. "You look pissed."

"I am," I admit. "You want to make the rules about who should and shouldn't get a weapon in a world gone crazy, but you're packing."

He reaches behind his back, fingers brushing the gun. "This is keeping the peace," he says. "My staff has been attacked more than once already, and this thing isn't showing any sign of slowing down."

"And it won't," I tell him. "The Marauders designed the virus, and it will turn the infected into homicidal maniacs if it gets much warmer. To make things worse, they can *make* it warmer with a machine they built."

"So that's what it is," Pietro says, scratching his chin. "I sent some of my men to the square to report back, but all they could tell me was that there was some sort of weapon there, and that they had a blue hostage. I assume that's Moke?"

"Yeah," I say, dropping my gaze. "They're using him to power it, and they'll make it hotter here if they don't get all the hybrids in the city to use for a screwed-up breeding program."

"Breeding program?" he echoes, his nose scrunching up. "That's awful! Please tell me that you already drop-kicked all of them?"

"I tried," I say. "But they nabbed Moke, and I can't do much alone. Max and Fang are trying to convince Langford to offer a more humane method of experimentation here in the city, but Langford wants to attack—and now."

"Oh," he says, a small smile forming. "So that's why you're here."

"Of course that's why I'm here," I say, irritated by the smile.

"I guess it would've been too much for me to think maybe you were worried about me," he says. "Or just checking in to make sure I'm okay."

"Seriously?" I say, my wings bristling outward as my temper rises. "You really want to play pity-party right now? I need—"

"My guns, yeah, I figured that out on my own, Hawk," he says, his own face flushing red with anger. "Who are you asking for? Langford or Max? Whose messenger girl are you right now?"

"Are you serious?" I seethe at him. "I'm not a messenger girl, I'm—"

What am I? A member of the Council? Maximum Ride's daughter? Or am I just Hawk, Pietro's friend, who needs a favor?

"That's *exactly* what you are!" he snipes back. "You're just running around at everyone else's beck and call. And here you are, standing in front of me, not because you care about me, or anything ridiculous like that. But because someone sent you here."

"Listen," I say, crossing my arms. "We can argue about the benefits of friendship in high-stress situations another time. Right now, I need to know where the other weapons caches are."

But he's already shaking his head. "I won't tell you," he says. "And not because I'm mad at you, either. It's because it's the wrong thing to do. I saw a woman tear a chunk of scalp off a guy earlier today because a nurse brought his kid ice chips before—"

"Ice chips," I say, interrupting. "Be pissed at me all you want, but make sure you're keeping your infected cool. Ice, cold water, whatever."

"I can do that," he says. "But I'm not telling you where the rest of the Pater guns are stored. And I already moved the stash you knew about."

"Nice," I spit. "You want to talk about friendship but your first reaction to me not showing up to our meeting was to clear out the stash?"

He shakes his head, anger all but evaporated. "It wasn't the first, no," he says quietly. "There was a lot of blood in that alley, Hawk, and two dead men. When I couldn't find you, I almost lost my mind."

"Came back to you pretty quick though," I say. "Must have, with you calling the shots and making big decisions without thinking twice."

"It's not a hard choice," he says. "Give weapons to an already unruly mob, or hope common sense prevails." He raises both hands in the air, as if weighing them on a scale.

"Then we're done talking," I say in a huff, walking past him toward the edge of the roof.

"Wait, Hawk—"

He reaches out to grab me, but I've always been the quicker of the two of us. I grab his wrist and spin him, pressing his back against me. I slip the gun from his waistband and run for the edge of the roof. His fingers slide off the edge of my boots, but I'm hovering in the air already, beyond his reach and holding his gun.

"Hypocrite!" I yell, before wheeling away to fly back to Langford and the Council.

"Hawk!" he yells, his voice bleeding away into the night. "Wait!"

But I don't have time to wait, and I don't feel like talking. I sail through smoky air, sparing a glance downward at the city's center, where Tanning and the Marauders are gathered around the weapon. Among them, I spot a bright flash of blue.

"Hold on, Moke," I say. "I'm coming."

CHAPTER 41

I'm angry, worried, and a little beyond stinky.

I can't remember the last time I showered, and it takes me back to the Children's Home, how all of my orphans eked out a life. I would steal food, pick pockets, and trade some of my better finds for medicine. We weren't always clean, and we weren't always safe, but we were always together. Now, I've got a swanky apartment with hot running water and a kitchen full of food. But I don't have all my orphans, and I definitely don't feel safe.

I approach my door cautiously, fingers resting on Pietro's pistol. Max was worried when I left, the line between her brows deepening as she told me to hurry to meet Pietro. She might have misjudged Tanning, but she'd never met the man. Langford she's dealt with, and she was picking up what the other woman was throwing down. Langford has little patience left, and she'll deal with Tanning—and the hybrids—in her own way, not waiting for the Council to vote.

I can't let that happen. It won't go well for hybrids,

particularly Maximum Ride, who Tanning clearly has his eye on. Weird. For ten years I was hoping my mom would come back for me, and now I find myself wanting to protect her, instead of asking for protection. It feels funny, but good, too. Like maybe I can do something useful, not just be a messenger girl, like Pietro said.

I lean against my door, ear pressed against it, but I don't hear anything inside. The orphans should be in there, maybe Max and Fang, too. The quiet makes me uneasy, and I'm about to try my parents' room instead, when a soft voice calls out from inside.

"It's all right, Hawk. You can come in."

It's Rain's voice, and I open the door, walking in without a second thought. She's standing near the window, the last of the sun's rays soaking into her skin. Her face is upturned, light falling on her round cheeks, pale lips… and her sewn-shut eyelids.

"How did you know that was me at the door?" I ask, but she only smiles and presses her palms against the glass.

"Calypso is sleeping," she says. "She's worn out. There's a lot more excitement here than at the Institute for the Blind."

"She's good, though?" That little girl has seen more than her fair share of violence and death, and I was holding her hand through most of it. I feel bad I wasn't here for whatever today brought her.

"She's fine," Rain says calmly, as Ridley flutters to my shoulder, nudging my earlobe in welcome.

I scribble out a quick message and roll it into a scroll.

I need to let Max and Fang know that I wasn't able to get access to the Pater weapons, and I don't want to share that information in front of the entire Council. Max might be able to figure out a way to spin this so that it doesn't send Langford on the warpath, but she'll need time to think that through. If Ridley can get a message to her, it might give her a head start on a plan.

I release Ridley on the balcony. If the Council is in session they'll have the double doors to the conference room closed, and she won't have access. The evening is getting warm (I try not to think too hard about why that might be), and if the Council has the windows open, Ridley might be able to reach Max. If not, at least seeing her through the window will let Max and Fang know I'm back and have a message for her.

Messenger girl.

"Stop," I seethe. I'll have to work on a better retort for the next time I see Pietro. For now, I need to put him—and his nasty words—out of my mind. Rain comes out and joins me on the balcony, her hand cool on my shoulder.

I keep an eye out for Ridley. The Council conference room is on the other side of the building, but she should be back before long, whether she delivers the message or not. As if following my thoughts, my hawk comes fluttering around the corner, scroll still in her claws.

"Ugh," I say, as Ridley lands on my shoulder, concern suddenly spiking. "Where is Max? Is she okay?"

The words are for my hawk, but it's Rain who answers.

"She's still in the Council room," she says, her voice

calm and soothing. Surprised, I turn to look at her. Rain's face is screwed up in concentration, her lips pressed tightly together.

"Rain?" I ask. "How can you possibly know that? And how did you know it was me at the door earlier?"

"Hawk," she says patiently. "Just because I don't have eyes doesn't mean I can't see."

CHAPTER 42

I stare at Rain as the tension floods out of her face, her lips return to normal, and her cheek muscles relax.

"You're going to have to explain what you mean about not having eyes but still being able to see," I say. "Don't think I haven't noticed you knowing things that you shouldn't."

"I can see," she says, calm again as she takes my hand and leads me back inside, Ridley riding on my shoulder. "Sit down," she gestures at the overstuffed chair, not missing a beat. I flop down, tired, worried, and confused. She sits across from me, her head eerily following my movements as I shift in my seat.

"When the scientists took my eyes, they weren't just doing it as a form of torture," she explains, her voice cool and even. "It had a purpose."

"Yeah, the purpose of being a bunch of assholes," I say.

"No," she shakes her head. "It was part of an experiment involving remote viewing. Do you know what that is?"

"No," I tell her. "But it sounds asshole-y."

"When they first took me—all of us—they performed a series of tests. One of those tests was meant to measure our psychic abilities. Some of us have a greater natural capacity. We're more open to different aspects of the world around us, and aware of things beyond the normal five senses.

"I scored high on those tests, and I became a pet project for one of the experiments. They wanted to know if they could strengthen those latent abilities, and use me as a remote viewer. That means that I could see something far away, using my psychic abilities...but not my actual eyes."

"Wait, wait, wait," I say. "How do you mean? That doesn't sound possible."

She tilts her head and thinks for a moment, then turns her blind gaze to Ridley, who is shifting on my shoulder.

"Think about Ridley," she says. "I want you to imagine if, every time you sent her out, she wasn't just carrying a scroll to deliver. What if you could actually see what she sees? She could fly anywhere—to the square to spy on Tanning, to the Opes center to check in on Pietro—"

"Yeah, apparently I don't do that enough already," I say, smirking. "I guess I'm not a good friend," I add, putting that last part in air quotes.

She ignores my interruption, continuing on. "Remote viewing is like that. When my eyes were taken, it strengthened my inner eye, my mind's eye. I can see things that are very far away, in places that my body isn't."

"Huh," I consider that for a second, amazed. "So it's like you've got an inner Ridley that you can just send out, and...use her eyes? See what she sees?"

"Yes," she says, smiling. "I like that. My inner Ridley."

"Wow," I say. "That could be incredibly useful."

"That's exactly what the scientists thought," she says. "I could be their ultimate spy, go anywhere in the world, be in any room, and know exactly what everyone was saying."

"Nice," I say.

"But it didn't work out that way," she continues. "My vision has limits. I can only see a place, or be somewhere, if someone I am connected to emotionally is there as well. I can send out my inner Ridley to be with a person that I know, or sometimes even a place I'm familiar with. But I can't go just anywhere. If I haven't been there before, or don't know a person well enough, it doesn't work."

"But it's still super cool," I say, my mind already spinning. All the times I've worried about Calypso or wondered if Moke was all right could've been easily settled by just asking Rain to do a quick check-in. Which reminds me...

"So where is Maximum Ride right now?" I ask.

She focuses, the line between her brows furrowing again as she sends out her mind's eye. Suddenly she snaps to attention and grabs my wrist.

"Get to the Council room," she cries, grinding the small bones in my arm. "Go now!"

CHAPTER 43

I crash through the door into the hallway, sprinting for the stairs. There was panic in Rain's voice. Maximum Ride is in trouble, and it's bad enough to have Rain sending me in as the rescue. I sprint up the stairs, calf muscles burning as I break out into the main hallway, the double doors at the end securely blocking the entrance to the meeting room. But I'm going in, and I'll turn myself into a missile to do it.

I hover for a second at the end of the hallway, pump my wings hard, and zip down the hall. Windows pass in a blur, doorknobs are just shiny spots in my vision as I lower my shoulder and hit the big doors right in the center. They blow open, the lock cracking, as I roll to my feet, wings tucked protectively around my body. Everyone is yelling and screaming, and it's not just because I crashed their party.

Max has Langford in a headlock.

"Holy crap, Mom!" I dive in, but it's hard to get to the two of them. The other Council members are crawling across the table and pushing chairs out of the way, trying to protect their leader. Fang has the high ground, floating above them and kicking at faces as they try to intercede.

"Max!" I yell, watching as Langford's lips go purple, her skin turning a grayish hue that means her oxygen has been cut off way too long.

Mom glances up, loosening her hold. Langford slides to the ground, eyes rolling back into her skull. I smile, relieved, but Max only stares at me for a second in shock.

"No!" she suddenly yells at something behind me. "Not my daughter!"

But I don't have time to spin, and Fang can't get to me. There's a dull thud, pressure on the back of my skull, and then blackness seeps into my vision, crawling in from the edges and filling everything as I sink to the floor, my wings useless, my legs limp.

I'm losing consciousness as everything fades, and think of Rain as all my senses slide away. I can't see anything, noises are scratchy and high, the smell of blood—my own, I assume—barely registers. But I can still feel, and someone is picking me up and carrying me away. I don't know who hit me, or where they're taking me.

But I swear when I wake up, I'm going to find out, and I promise myself, I will make them pay for this.

CHAPTER 44

I wake up with one hell of a headache.

That, and a burning desire to kill something. Unfortunately, the only thing in front of me is a brick wall, which makes killing something...difficult. I struggle into a sitting position, my vision popping with black spots, and look around.

I'm in some sort of holding cell, and judging by the décor, I'm somewhere underneath the Council building. Everything is blank and gray, and badly lit. Whoever put these cells down here did not want the occupants to feel welcome. And yes, that's plural—occupants—because I turn to find Calypso is down here with me.

"Calypso!" I cry, falling to my knees beside the little girl. She's lying on the floor, as unconscious as I was. But she's breathing. I can see her chest moving up and down under her thin shirt. Those bastards must've grabbed her while she was still sleeping. Some courage, sneaking up on a little kid and knocking them out while they're napping with only a psychic blind girl to protect her.

Wait, where's Rain?

"Rain!" I yell, but my voice only echoes back at me, bouncing off the concrete walls. She's not here. I can only assume that Langford—if it's her pulling the strings— must have sent some goons to my apartment, telling them to nab Calypso. I didn't exactly share that I had a blind stowaway sharing my pad. It's possible Rain had just enough warning to hide, and maybe, escape and go for help after they took Calypso.

At least, I can hope. That's all I can do. Right now I'm limited to sitting here and sweating. Like, a lot. Crap. The Marauders must still be cranking the temperature up. I don't know how long we have before it turns into a murder-fest outside, but if it's soon, maybe I'm lucky to be down here in this cell, and Calypso, too.

Her eyelids flicker and I lean down over her still body once more. "Calypso?" I ask, but there's nothing. At least, not from her. What I do hear is a steady *click, click, click.* Someone is coming. Someone in high heels.

Langford turns the corner, and I erupt into a rage. I fly against my bars, yelling all the bad words I know— and that's a lot. I grew up on the streets of the City of the Dead, and the first thing you learn is how to insult some- one. I'm good at it, and the words fly thick and heavy, but it's really all I can do. I press against the bars and let Langford know what she can do with the chair she sits on during Council meetings. It does involve her ass, but it's certainly not sitting on it.

I run out of steam and sag against the bars, winded.

"You done?" she asks, her voice thick and scratchy. There's a dark line around her neck where Max had her in a chokehold, and I can't help but smile at the sight of it.

"Done with words, yes," I tell her. Then I spit on her. She doesn't even blink, just calmly wipes it away with the back of her hand, which I notice also glistens with sweat. If it's hot down here in this basement, I wonder what it's like on the higher floors.

"Tanning has made his move," she says. "I'm sure you've noticed."

"I'm kind of living inside a rotisserie oven right now, so yeah," I shoot back.

She nods, still completely unemotional. "How's your head?"

"Hurts," I admit. "That happens when you get hit from behind by a coward with a...?" I let my words trail off, raising my eyebrow and letting her finish my sentence.

"A nightstick," she says, with a shrug. "For what it's worth, I told them not to break your skull."

"For what? Old times' sake?" I ask.

"No." She shakes her head. "We're going to need all the able hybrid bodies we can get in order to satisfy our deal with the Marauders."

Despite the heat, I go cold. "You didn't."

"I *had* to!" Langford shouts, suddenly hitting her limits. "Tanning isn't messing around. It's getting hotter by the hour out there, and the virus is responding. People haven't turned on one another yet," she adds, seeing my dismay. "But the heat appears to help it spread, as well.

We've got sick people wandering on the street, people dying on the sidewalks, and your little friend won't give us what we need to fight Tanning and his men."

Little friend. I'll have to remember that and use it against Pietro later, in return for his *messenger girl* jab. That is, if both of us get out of this.

"He wouldn't give you his cache?" I ask. "Good. He's right. You can't arm panicked people. It's asking for trouble."

"Maybe, but that left me with no choice," she says. "The hybrid population of the city will be handed over. That includes you, your cohort of friends, and that damned lying blue bastard."

"Oh...," I say, a sneer slipping into my voice. "Your little pet didn't play by the rules, did he? You're not in charge, Langford! You're not in charge of Moke, and you're not in charge of this city, either. The Council is! Moke didn't want to help you become a tyrant, and I won't do your bidding anymore, either."

"You don't have to," she says, skipping her fingers along the bars of my cell. "My bidding is in the past. It's my *will* you bend to now. And you're my captive. I only regret not gagging you."

"Oh, trust me. I'm gagging," I say.

"I really am sorry it had to end this way, Hawk," she goes on. "You were mildly interesting. But in the end, this is the best answer for everyone. The hybrids leave, Tanning gets what he wants, and my city returns to health and peace."

"It's not the best answer for the hybrids," I snarl. "It's what's best for *you*."

"Then I'll take it," she says, turning away. "Good-bye, Hawk."

My helplessness hits me. My wings are useless, the bars around me as good as a birdcage, and my words got me nowhere. Well, the bad words, anyway. Maybe I should try something else, something with less swearing.

"We have rights!" I shout at her back. "Hybrids are also human, and we have rights. If you do this, if you sell us off for your own sake, how will you be remembered? Do you think it will play well in news clips a hundred years from now that you bartered with a madman and sold off your own citizens? You'll be remembered as a tyrant and an overlord who barely held on to power only by trampling those she thought were beneath her."

That gets her. She stops under a bare lightbulb, her shoulder blades rising and falling as she takes deep breaths to calm herself. I lean against the bars, hoping she comes back. It's the only card I can play.

She spins, her cheeks now red with anger as she stalks back to my cell.

"How will I be remembered?" she asks, walking right up to me. "How will history tell my story?" She reaches into her pocket and pulls out a folded paper. "What about you, Hawk? What will people say about *you*?"

"What is that?" I ask, eyeing the paper warily.

"The most powerful thing in the world," she says, sneering. "Politics."

"Your politics couldn't keep my mother's hands from around your neck, so I'd rethink that statement if I were you," I say.

"Remember all those boring meetings?" she asks, rolling her eyes. "All the times you could barely be bothered to get out of bed and participate in the running of the city, the representation of your own people?"

I'm still, my eyes following the paper as she unfolds it.

"This is from one of those meetings, something I asked you to sign. You were bored, not paying attention, half-asleep and trusting. You signed without even reading it."

A chill runs up my spine. What have I done?

"May I read it to you?" she asks, with mock politeness. She dives in, not waiting for my answer.

" 'I, Hawk, daughter of Maximum Ride, representative to the City Council for the hybrid population of the City of the Dead, do hereby forfeit all rights of hybrids during times of civil unrest. Should such a time come, hybrids shall willingly give up their lives and bodies for the continued advancement of the human race, up to and including the use of hybrids to be sold, traded, or used for breeding purposes. Signed, Hawk.' "

She turns the paper around, but I don't need to look. I know it's my signature.

"You tricked me," I seethe.

"You signed it, that's on you," she says. "I may be a tyrant, but you'll be remembered for much worse. You'll be a traitor."

CHAPTER 45

"You utter bitch!" I scream. I don't need anything more polished to describe how I feel. I'm scrambling against the bars, reaching as far as I can, flailing for the paper. Langford holds it just outside my reach, taunting me.

"You lying, manipulating—"

"Yes, yes," she says, bored now, as she folds the paper and puts it back inside her pocket. "I'm a terrible person. We all know that. But at least I'm a *person*," she says. "Not a hybrid."

"Hybrids are people, too!" I yell, beating my hands against the bars. "We feel and we love and we hurt and we bleed. I spent ten years of my life in the streets with hybrids, barely making it. And we held on, all of us. Held on and stayed true to each other, and never, ever sold anyone out!

"You don't know," I fall back from the bars, my righteous anger spent. All that's left is sadness, and the deepest feeling of failure. "You won't ever know," I go on. "I bet you've never had it tough, had to worry about what you'll eat the next day, or how you'll protect someone you love. Sure, you can stand there and talk about being a person, but I don't see it, Langford. Whatever was human inside of you is gone. You're a machine."

"A machine?" she asks, and now it's her turn to come up to the bars, staring me down with eyes so bright and intense I back away, and am almost glad my cell door is locked. It might keep me in, but it also keeps her out.

"A *machine*?" she repeats. "You don't know anything. Oh, boo-hoo, I spent ten years on the streets, finding food and shelter. Those are basics, little girl. I only wish my life had been that simple. Keep your belly full and a roof over your head? That sounds wonderful to me!"

"Easy to say when—"

But I don't get to finish. She's burning with rage. "Do you want to know where I was during those ten years? What I was doing? Making decisions that affected the entire human race, that's what. Deciding what was best for the whole planet! And you...you want to talk about caring for a pack of snot-nosed brats when I was responsible for a *species*! Do you hear me?"

Her words ring out in the empty hallway, bounding off cement walls and iron bars, her voice as cold as our surroundings.

"I've had to do things in the name of science that make handing you and that little girl behind you over to the Marauders easy by comparison."

There's a rustling behind me and a hand on my arm. Calypso is awake, leaning against me for support as she

199

comes around. She's confused, her eyes dazed. But they meet mine and I see comfort bloom there, which only makes me feel worse. Poor kid. She thinks that just because I'm here, everything is going to be okay. My heart drops into my stomach, and I pull her close against me.

"What could be worse than handing over innocent children to madmen?" I ask Langford, looking up, tears in my eyes.

Cold and steely, she answers me.

"Abandoning my own."

CHAPTER 46

"What?" I ask, stunned. *"Your children?"*

But Langford is clamming up now, backing away from the bars. Her eyes go to Calypso and for one second, I think she might even be ashamed of herself, but she brushes her hair out of her eyes, squares her shoulders, and faces me.

"Yes," she says crisply. "My children. I abandoned them in the pursuit of science, and in the hopes for a political career. As you can see, it worked out."

I want to fire back, *Probably not for them.* But for once, I reconsider shooting off at the mouth. I was telling the truth earlier when I said that she comes across as more of a robot than a human. But her eyes had glistened over when she mentioned her children. It might be the only angle I've got right now, and I'm going to play it.

"You have children?" I ask again, hoping to pry that door open. But she is straightening her spine, and I know once she's back in full Council meeting mode I'll have lost any chance I have at appealing to what emotion she has left.

"I thought my parents abandoned me," I tell her. "For years I showed up at the same spot, every day, hoping they would come back for me. That was the deal. That was what they told me to do, and I never gave up hope. I got mad—definitely. All the time, in fact. But I kept showing up, because the memories I had of my mom and dad... they were good memories. I knew they were good parents, and even on my bad nights, I thought about the few things I could remember.

"I almost gave up—many times," I continue, "and there were plenty of days when I hated them, when I thought they'd left me behind because I was too much work, too much of a weight, just... too much."

There's more than sweat running down my cheeks now. What started out as a strategic move to keep Langford talking has turned into a confessional. Even Calypso is looking up at me, eyes wide, as I share things she's never known.

"I never gave up on them," I say. "Even though all the facts were telling me I should. And it turns out they always wanted me, they never stopped trying to get back to me, and now that we've found each other..."

I raise my hand to wipe away a tear. It's real enough, and so is the rising temperature in my cell. I lift my heavy hair off my shoulders, feel a trickle of sweat sneak down my neck, slip onto my spine, and roll down to where my wings attach—and where Pietro's gun is stashed. Whoever patted me down wasn't used to dealing with hybrids; they'd forgotten to check my wings for weapons.

"Now that we've found each other," I repeat, still holding Langford's gaze as she listens, rapt, "I'm sure as hell not letting you separate us!" I snatch the gun from its hiding place and blow the lock off my cell. Calypso screams and falls to the ground, covering her ears at the shot and ducking as metal flies. Langford yells and jumps away from the cell, but I'm faster than her, pinning her up against the wall before she can make a run for it. Gunpowder tickles my nose as she squirms under my grip, her face pressed against the wall.

"Calypso!" I yell, and she's at my side in a second. "Find her keys," I say, motioning toward Langford. The little girl goes through Langford's pockets, coming up with a digitized ID badge.

"That should work," I say, eyeing the cells. "Swipe it against that pad on the wall."

She does, and the door on the empty cell slides open. The door of the cell I was in makes a high, malfunctioning whine as it tries to operate even after I blasted it.

"Hawk! Please, listen to me—" Langford begins, but I grab her by the neck and toss her into the working cell, cutting off her words. Calypso swipes the badge again, and the door swings shut, locking Langford in.

"It's not the corner office," I say. "But you'll find the heat works very well."

"Hawk!" she yells again. "What are you going to do? Really? Think about this, please. Just *think*!"

"I have been, for a long time," I tell her.

"Yeah, me, too!" Calypso hops in. "And I think you suck!"

"You're making a mistake!" Langford pleads, clutching the bars of her cell. "Without hybrids to trade, the Marauders will let the virus run wild. Everyone will die. What kind of world are you escaping to? What kind of future are you creating for that little girl?"

She motions to Calypso, who hides her face against my side, suddenly scared.

"It's better than what you would give to her," I say. "A life of captivity. Used for breeding purposes."

"But a life!" Langford argues. "And can you even stop that from happening? The Marauders have weapons, and they want what they want. If they decide to come after you on their own, your fate is the same."

I hesitate, knowing she might be right.

"Or"—her face suddenly twists, turning ugly—"were you just going to leave? I can see it now, you and your happy, reunited family just flying away into the sunset. Meanwhile, the humans of the city die, and you leave the wingless hybrids to their fate at the hands of the Marauders."

"I would never leave behind hybrids!" I shout back, my grip on Calypso tightening.

"But you don't deny you'd let thousands of humans die to save your own skin?" Langford asks, swiping sweat from her face.

"I...I don't know," I tell her honestly. "Humans have never been kind to me, after all."

"And they won't be any kinder now," Langford says, her mouth twisting into an ugly approximation of a smile. "As soon as you step outside this building, you and your little friend with antennas will be pulled into pieces. The people of this city will tear you apart with their bare hands."

I swallow, suddenly unsure, as Calypso starts to shiver with fear. Langford's smile widens as she presses her face against the bars.

"Tell me, Hawk—where are you going to go?"

CHAPTER 47

You know things have taken a turn for the worse when the scariest place in the city now seems like the safest. I'd left Langford cursing my name—and my choices—in her lonely cell, and grabbed an extra jacket and cap from the security closet as we let ourselves out of the cellblock.

Calypso looks at me now from where we stand at the edge of the forest, wide-eyed under the brim of her cap. It's much too big for her. I carried Calypso in my arms, intent on looking like just another stricken citizen, not what we really were—hybrids who would likely be killed on the spot for no crime greater than simply existing.

It'd been a harrowing walk, and I was glad I'd encouraged the kid to pretend to be unconscious. Sick people roamed the streets, the well leading the ill, everyone looking for comfort and no one able to find it. I avoided the streets near the hospital, and the flickering flames that leaped out of one alleyway made me glad I did. I stowed Calypso away in a dark corner, slipped off my jacket—grateful to be free of it in this heat—and took to the sky to get an idea of where the fire was and how to avoid it.

Turns out the hospital staff had set it, lighting up barricades at each city block to keep the unruly mob away. Whether they meant to or not, this actually helped the Marauders, who now sit contentedly in the square, the manned hospital barricades protecting them as well as the hospital staff. It wasn't the smartest thing the hospital could have done, but I can't exactly question their choices. They're full up of the sick and can't even help the ones who have beds, anyway. Not with this heat rising and hope fading. I grimly find Calypso again and hold her hand tightly in mine as we made our way to the forest.

"Did you see Rain?" I ask her, and the girl only shakes her head. I press forward, needing the right answer. "When the men came and got you, before you woke up in the cell—was Rain with you?"

"No," Calypso speaks this time. "She must have hid inside the apartment. They didn't know she was there—"

"—so they weren't looking for her," I finish. "They don't know she's a hybrid, either, or what she can do. Right now, Rain is our best weapon."

I rub my temples, anxious for an answer to come to the surface. I don't know what to do. Not knowing where my parents are or what's happened to them is not a new feeling to me, but before, I hadn't cared. Before, I hadn't loved them. Now, I realize, I do. And honestly, it kind of sucks.

"Shit," I say, glancing around. Calypso gives my hand a warning smack.

"Language!" she says, with a little-girl glare.

"Sorry, kiddo," I say, swiping her cap off her head to give her hair a ruffle. "Listen," I bend down closer to her, so that we're eye to eye.

"You're not the only person I'm responsible for," I tell her. "I've got to make sure Rain is okay. We can't just leave her—"

But she is already panicking, clutching my hand. "Don't leave me here!"

"I'm not...I mean, I won't! I'll be back, I swear. You know you can trust me."

She gingerly lets go of my hand, visibly gulping as she nods. "Yes, I trust you."

"Okay," I say. "I can travel a lot faster on my own, and I'm only making one stop. You will be fine here. It's getting dark, fast. With those fires going, the smoke will block the sun even faster. No humans are going to be coming close to the forest, anyway. Not after what happened with the reptilians."

At the word *reptilians,* she can barely hide a shudder.

"They won't hurt you," I say. "They won't hurt another hybrid."

At least, I don't *think* they will. In the current climate, I'll trust Calypso to Chammy, Tut, Gila, and the rest of them, before I'd hand her over to humans for safekeeping.

"It'll be all right," I say, shedding my jacket and pumping my wings as I rise in the air. She grows smaller, but I can still see the fear on her face as I lift above the smoke, find a good draft, and head for the one place I can find someone I trust.

I touch down on top of the Hope for Opes center to find Pietro on the roof. He's sitting on the edge of the building, his feet hanging over the drop into nothing. Alarmed, I perch next to him.

"Hey, man," I say. "It's not all that bad. The world is ending and everything is on fire, but you've still got your good looks. Except, you are definitely sweating like a pig. So that doesn't help."

Amazingly, I coax a smile out of him. He shakes his head, still looking down at the drop—hundreds of feet—under his shoes.

"I'm not thinking about jumping, if that's what you're worried about," he says, casually.

"Oh, good," I say. "Because I kind of like you."

He looks at me, raising an eyebrow. "Even though I called you *messenger girl*?"

I shrug. "I've called you way worse."

"When?" he asks.

"Well, it's mostly just in my head," I confess, and he laughs.

"I'm glad to see you," he admits. "I felt bad after..."

"After not handing over all your guns?" I finish.

"Yeah, that," he says. "Although you did sneak off with my side piece."

"Needed it," I say, pulling it from the back of my pants to show him I still have the pistol. "Came in handy. I had to blow my way out of jail."

"Sounds about right," he nods, still smiling. But his humor fades when he glances back at me. "I'm still not giving you guns, Hawk."

"Like I'd think you'd change your mind," I shoot back. "You've always been pig-headed. No, I need something else."

"Shoot," he says.

"Langford nabbed me and Calypso, had us locked up under the Council building. I don't know where my parents are, but I'm afraid she might have them somewhere, too. She's ready to trade all the city's hybrids over to the Marauders in exchange for turning off their machine, and providing her with the vaccine against the virus. The only ace I have up my sleeve right now is Rain."

"Rain?" he asks. "How can she help?"

"She can do remote viewing," I tell him. "And I don't have time to explain what that means. Right now, all you need to know is that she's hiding in my apartment, and I can't go back there. I need you to go get her, and keep her safe."

"I can do that," he says automatically, without question.

I exhale, relieved. It's not like I thought he would tell me no. But the last time we talked I stole his gun, so I'm sure I'm not exactly high on his list of favorite people right now.

"Thanks," I say, standing and perching precariously on the ledge, ready to dive, ready to go back to Calypso, ready to keep fighting.

"Hawk," he says, and I pause, looking down at him. "I'll take care of Rain, but who is going to take care of you?"

"I'm going to take care of myself, as usual," I say.

Then I dive, and I'm gone.

CHAPTER 48

The smell of smoke from the city permeates even this far into the forest. Calypso's antennas are practically useless with the scent of burning clogging the air.

"It's okay," I tell her, one reassuring hand on her shoulder. "We can find them again, I'm sure of it."

"But this is what I'm good at," she says, lower lip poking out. "This is how I help out, and now I'm just...just—"

"Don't say useless," I cut her off. "We never would have found the reptilians in the first place if it wasn't for you."

"Yeah," she agrees with a sniffle. "Me falling through the roof of their house."

Which gives me an idea. I don't normally like to fly with a passenger. I'm just now getting really good at finding vents and pockets in the air, riding them like a bird with my wings outstretched. Having a passenger means having to reassess everything—elevation, distance, weight, amount of energy needed. But Calypso is small, I've practiced short trips with her, and we'll be flying over the forest, where no one from the city will spot us.

"Want to take to the skies with me?" I ask her with a grin. She holds her hands up like the little kid she still is, begging to be lifted into the air. And with me as her stand-in parent, that means literally in the air.

I find a spot where the earlier fires from the people attacking the reptilians had stripped the trees bare, leaving space for me to rise above the canopy. I clutch her tight against my chest, and even though I know she trusts me, the girl quakes with fear. I pump my wings, gliding left and right, searching for a break in the trees where the lake should be. The lake…and the giant hole in the glass ceiling where the bridge had collapsed and fallen into the reptilians' subterranean chambers. In the moonlight, it's easy to spot. The hybrids must have dammed off some of the water from the breach; I can see water glistening and a gaping black hole where we crash-landed through their roof.

"Ready?" I ask. My voice is a little thready, and I take a deep breath, hoping that I sound stronger by the time I need to speak to the other hybrids. My words will matter then more than ever, and I need to be convincing.

"Ready," she says, with no hesitation.

"Here we go."

I dive, the wind pushing our hair back from our faces, my feathers rippling and rustling as we descend. We pass the waterline, the cold dankness of the earth underneath enveloping us, lit only by a spot of fire below. I aim for it and pull up just in time to land feet-first on the little island where we'd come to rest before. Calypso slips from my grip, antennas on high alert.

But I don't need her extra-powerful sense of smell to know our enemies are near. They're right beside us, on the other side of the water, huddled around a small fire. Chammy makes eye contact with me and leaps to his feet.

"How dare you!" he shrieks, moving to the water's edge. The fish-girl rises, drawn by his voice. She follows his gaze to us and hisses, then disappears beneath the black water once more. I pull Calypso closer to me, hoping she's far enough away from the edge that nothing can grab her ankles.

"Listen," I say, raising both my arms to show that I don't have a weapon. Well, not in my hands, anyway. It's stuck in the back of my pants.

"Listen to *you*?" Gila asks, hissing as she comes to join Chammy. "Why should we? You betrayed us! We've lived here peacefully for two generations and suddenly humans are crashing into our forest and burning our trees—right after you refused to join us, and left."

"It looks bad," I admit, hands still in the air. "But you didn't exactly lie down and burn, did you? I saw more than a few humans disappear into those flames. Trees can grow back. Those people won't—and you killed them."

"I'll kill more if I have to," Gila snaps, her eyes flashing. "Any human who sets foot here. And any hybrid who calls them a friend."

"They're not my friends," I snap, but Chammy shakes his head.

"Gila has a point, you know," he says, eyeing me cautiously. "Last time you were here, you blasted your way in and damaged quite a few of my people on your way out."

I shiver, remembering the crazed ascent, reptilian hybrids leaping at me from the walls as I clutched Calypso to my chest, hoping to break into free air.

"But I'm here now," I counter, straightening my shoulders. "I came back, even after all that. Aren't you just a little bit curious why I would take that risk?"

"Taking risks is what you do," Gila snarls, and I can't exactly argue with that. She's not wrong. But her wrath has stirred up the others, and more reptilians crowd the beach across from us, cold black eyes staring us down.

"Listen," I try again. "I know that you don't trust me." One of the reptilians snorts, but I ignore it and keep going.

"But I'm not asking you to trust me," I say, steadying my voice. "I'm just asking you to hear me out."

Gila shakes her head. "I'm done listening, and I'm done talking." She gives a nod, and suddenly a pale, white cord whips out of the water, wrapping itself around Calypso's leg. She shrieks, but the tentacle is wrapped tight, suckers doing their job as she's dragged toward the edge of our island. I dive and manage to grab her hand just before she slips into the water. Her horrified eyes lock with mine as I pump my wings, ascending just in time, as another tentacle reaches for my legs.

This was a mistake. My words aren't working, and now whatever is in the water—some type of octopus is my guess—has a tentacle wrapped around Calypso's leg. She kicks at it with her free foot, but her shoes only slide off the slippery surface. I'm being pulled back toward the water, refusing to let go of the little girl.

"Screw. This," I say, and pull out my gun.

Firing blindly into the air, I hear glass shattering far above us, and the whooshing sound of jagged edges slipping past me. There's a sharp pain in my left wing and feathers fly, but I get off easy. A huge shard of glass severs the tentacle holding Calypso, blood flies, and I lift off rapidly now that she's no longer being held.

"Octavian!" Tut yells, crawling to the edge of the water and calling to the thing whose arm now lays, severed and flopping, on the bloody island.

"Don't move!" I yell, aiming at the turtle hybrid. His head turns toward me, slowly, and he blinks, slowly, confused and hurt. I feel bad, pointing a gun at this reptilian—but seeing Tut on the wrong end of a pistol seems to affect Chammy. His face has gone white at the sight of the blood, and his mouth is a sharp line when he looks back up at me.

I pull the gun away from Tut, pointing at the ceiling now. "I can do this all night," I say. "Keep sending your people at me, and I'll keep shredding them. Or do you want to talk?"

There's a long, heavy silence. Then a sharp gasp comes from Gila as a white, contorted body rises to the surface of the water. It's a reptilian, bled out and nearly dead. She dives into the water without waiting for Chammy's permission, and hauls Octavian to dry land, ripping off her scarf to tie a tourniquet around the stump of one of his tentacles.

"All right," Chammy says, still eyeing the bloodied end of Octavian's arm. "We can talk. But if you hurt any more of my people—"

"I won't, if you won't," I say darkly, eyeing the bruises rising on Calypso's skin in the shape of sucker wounds.

"Deal," Chammy says. "No one touches her!" He raises his voice and his cold, hard gaze sweeps the cavern, each reptilian in turn. "Hawk or the girl. Can I get the same reassurance from you?" he asks, as I touch down on rock, only a few feet away from him.

"Yes," I tell him. "But I won't give you my gun. You'll have to take me at my word."

Gila hisses, but Chammy holds my gaze.

"Done," he says. "Now, tell me, Hawk. What made you come back? What's so important that you'd return to a place where you almost died?"

CHAPTER 49

I snort. "I've almost died in the city a thousand times, but I keep hanging around."

"That's different," Chammy counters. "The city is your home. And the forest is ours. You came back knowing you wouldn't be welcome. So why are you here?"

I glance around at the other reptilians who crowd us. I was hoping for a private conversation, but I think I've already cashed in any favors Chammy is willing to grant. I'm here, I'm alive, and so is Calypso. That's about all I can hope for.... Well, not *all*. There's a big ask coming.

"Have you ever heard the saying, the enemy of my enemy is my friend?" I ask Chammy, who only shakes his head.

"I don't know it, but I agree with it."

"We share an enemy," I say. "Langford—the woman who runs the City Council—convinced the citizens that hybrids were the cause of the virus sweeping the population. She encouraged them to target you, and practically lit the torches for them."

There's some muttering among the reptilians, along with some low hisses.

"And what'd she do to you?" Tut asks, joining Chammy. Gila is crouched next to Octavian, who is propped against the cave wall. She's managed to stop the bleeding and his color is coming back. I'm secretly relieved; if he'd died, I doubt I could spin that in my favor.

"She kidnapped me," I tell Tut. "And she plans to capture all of the hybrids and trade them to the Marauders in exchange for a vaccine."

"The Marauders, huh?" Chammy repeats, arms crossed. "I've heard of them." He smiles when I start in surprise. "Surely you didn't think we live out here in complete isolation? We've got eyes in the city. Mostly in the abandoned subways and the sewer, but you can see—and hear—a lot from underneath people's feet. But what do the Marauders want with hybrids?"

"A breeding program," I say, earning audible gasps from those around us. "The Marauders are led by a guy called Dr. Tanning, and he doesn't hate hybrids. Instead he thinks we're the next step in evolution, and he wants to make sure his own bloodline is riding the wave of the future."

"Ewww," Gila says, wrinkling her nose.

"You're all healthy," I continue. "You'll be prize catches for Tanning, and his needs—hybrids that haven't been in contact with the virus."

"Definitely a common enemy, then," Chammy agrees. "In both Langford and Tanning." He thinks for a moment, arms still crossed. "What do you propose?"

Encouraged, I plow forward. "My friends are hybrids, and one of them is being used by Tanning to power his machine."

"A blue guy?" a reptilian with a snake's head asks, tongue slipping in and out through his teeth. "I saw him, Cham." He turns to his leader. "A blue guy with a bunch of older humans. They've got something going on in the square."

"It's controlling the weather," I inform them. "Tanning created the virus, and heat can make it worse." I don't add that pretty soon the hordes of untrustworthy humans will likely all be infected and gunning for hybrids. This is hard enough to sell as it is.

"So you want me to take my people aboveground to face an entire city of humans who have been primed to kill us on sight?" Chammy asks. "What for? Why should we agree? I've got nothing but hate for the humans. The Marauders can take them all out, as far as I'm concerned. Let him handle that problem, then we can sweep in after the carnage and wipe out the Marauders on our own, take the vaccine, and rule the day."

Heads are nodding, and unfortunately, I see the wisdom in his plan. Why not just let all the humans die? The reptilians certainly have no reason to love them, or even spare a tear for their fate. But I think of Pietro and Melanie, the little kids who used to wave to me in the streets on my morning flights.

"Not all humans are bad," I say, and there's a grumbling response that tells me exactly what they think of that. "They're not!" I insist.

"Even if one or two of them are decent people, I'm not bringing my reptilians into your war, Hawk," Chammy says.

"Then you'll be rounded up with the rest," I tell him, crossing my own arms. "The Marauders want all the hybrids, not just the ones aboveground."

"They can't catch what they can't find," Gila says, easily.

"And they're old men," the snake guy agrees. "They aren't going to crash through brush and search for days. They'll take the easy pickings—you city dwellers—and go."

"They won't," I say, shaking my head. "You haven't met Tanning, you didn't see the look in his eyes. He'll burn this forest down to find you, and send goons in—not just sick people with pitchforks and torches."

"You're right," Chammy says. "I haven't met Tanning. I haven't met Langford, either. And that's not my friend shackled to a machine in the square. So tell me, Hawk— what's in it for me?"

I pull Calypso closer to me, thinking hard. I've got an ace up my sleeve and I'll use it if I have to. Damnit! If only Chammy would've let me talk to him in private. With his whole crew circled around popping in with their opinions, I can't win any arguments. I'm about to take a step backward, cut my losses, and fly for the sky, when there's a crashing noise, and a reptilian comes barreling out of a side tunnel. He collapses onto the ground, his fingers splayed like a frog's, with tiny, sticky bulbs at the tips.

"Chammy," he wheezes, out of breath, long tongue lolling. "I came as fast as I could." He spots me, bulgy eyes going wide with disbelief. "How did you get here so fast?"

"What?" I ask, sputtering.

"You...you just blew out a window in the Council building," he says, confusion evident on his splotchy face. "I saw you! There was an explosion and glass went everywhere, and you and another one blasted out of the window like bats out of hell."

I start laughing; I can't help it.

"That wasn't me," I say, when heads turn. "That was my mom. Probably my dad, too. Sounds like Langford must have been keeping them under guard far away from me, in the upper rooms."

Relief washes over me. Langford doesn't have Max or Fang. They got away. But right on the heels of that relief is a cold, familiar fear. It's like I'm ten again, still stuck in the city, wondering where my parents are.

"Does this change anything?" Chammy asks. "Now that you know your parents are safe, do you still want to pit yourself against the world? Or is it time to give up?"

I square my shoulders and pull up my chin. Max might be safe, and Fang, too. But Melanie is still in a hospital bed, and Pietro is fighting for the lives of strangers in a battle he can't win. Moke is chained to a machine, and Rain is out there somewhere, silently watching.

"No," I shake my head. "I've still got people I care about up there, and I won't trade any one of them."

Chammy smiles sadly. "I guess that's where we're different, Hawk. I don't have people I care about up there. It's just us, and we're not marching into your war just because you've got some friends in trouble. This isn't our battle."

I take a deep breath, ready to throw down my ace. I clutch Calypso to me tightly. If this doesn't work, we'll have to get out of here, fast.

"There might not be anyone up there you care about," I tell Chammy. "But there is definitely someone you need to meet."

His eyebrows furrow. "Who?"

"Your human mother."

CHAPTER 50

Chammy's face collapses into confusion, quickly followed by anger.

"How dare you?" he shouts at me, blood rising into his face as his colors swerve in and out, moving with the flecking of the cave wall behind me as he comes toward me. "You think you can just come and go as you please? Say whatever you want? No matter how hurtful, or untrue?"

"Oh, it's true," I say, and I've never been more sure of it than I am right now. "So, you want to talk in private, or what?"

He shares a look with Gila, who only shrugs. "I've never cared," she says, backing away. "If I could be all reptile, I would."

"Me, too," Tut says, and a few heads nod in agreement.

"What about you?" I ask Chammy, whose eyes are slits now, his thoughts flashing across them nervously. "Five minutes," he says, giving me a glare. "And you better talk fast."

The crowd parts and I follow him down a tunnel, clutching Calypso's hand. I might have won a few moments alone with the reptilian leader, but that doesn't mean she's any safer here than she was when Octavian's tentacle was around her leg.

"All right," he says, turning to face me. "Shoot—and I don't mean that weapon." Here, without his posse around him, he gives me a smile.

"Okay." I take a deep breath, hoping this was a good idea. I can't take to the skies this deep under the earth. I'm trusting him. And—I realize—he's trusting me.

"Here's the deal. All along I've thought Langford was just the head of the Council, a politician like the rest of them."

"She's certainly played the game like one," he agrees. "Pitting people against one another while she grabs for more power."

"Right, but there's more to it. I found out from Dr. Tanning that Langford was one of the scientists involved in the hybrid projects here in the city, years ago. He told me she used her own DNA on her subjects, and when the project was stopped she was told to get rid of her samples. Not knowing what else to do, her team simply..."

I let my words fade out. He knows well enough what happened to his ancestors.

"They flushed them down the toilet," he says harshly, red blooms of anger blossoming on his cheeks again. "My parents. Gila's and Tut's and Octavian's and everyone else's, too."

"That's right," I agree. "They flourished down here,

made a life of their own, had kids, and created a community of hybrids. But their mother—your grandmother, I guess—had no idea any of her subjects had survived."

"I bet we were a hell of a surprise," he says, his teeth flashing white in the dim room as a smile forms.

"I couldn't figure out why she was so interested when I told her I'd seen something near the forest, and when I described what I saw...well." I remember the flash in Langford's eyes—a look I would become familiar with over time. At first, I'd mistaken it for affection, maybe even a little bit of pride in me. Now, I know better. Now, I see myself for what I was—her pawn. But I saw something else in that moment, too.

"I didn't realize it until she had us in that cell," I admit, pulling Calypso closer to me at the memory. "I wish I would've seen it sooner. I might have put everything together if I had."

"Seen what?" he asks.

"Her eyes," I tell him. "They're your eyes. And Gila's, too. I'd never seen Langford lose control. She's always cool, calm, and collected. When she had me in that cell, she lost it. Flipped her lid when I told her she'd never had to make hard choices. She told me..."

I lose my conviction, not sure if sharing the rest will help bring him over to my side, or drive him further away. Calypso presses back against me, her little body warming mine.

"What?" he pushes. "What did she say?"

"She said I didn't know what it was like to abandon

your children," I say, dropping my eyes. "You should've seen her, Chammy. She lost her temper, made me glad I was behind bars where she couldn't get to me."

He chuckles quietly. "So she lost her shit and got aggressive—"

"And she looked like you, in the eyes," I say. "Sorry, I know that's not the nicest thing I could say right now."

He only shrugs. "Doesn't have to be nice in order to be true. In fact, the worse something sounds, the more likely I am to believe it."

"Yeah," I say, scuffing my toe on the floor, my words catching in my throat. "Yeah, me, too. I'm sorry, Chammy."

"Well," he says, tossing some hair from his eyes with a quick shake. "It's not like I thought anyone was out there looking for me."

"Sometimes it's better if you don't," I say. "That way you don't hang around, waiting."

"Oh, I've been waiting," he contradicts me, his eyes taking on a glimmer. "I've been waiting for revenge."

"I can give it to you," I say. "You and all the rest of your people. Langford didn't have to flush her experiments. You might all be her children, but believe me, she has no love for you."

I remember how she always shrank from my touch, kept a careful distance, and always seemed to have the right words. The ones to be polite, but not the ones that really mattered. Langford had praised me up and down, but she'd never mastered the tone of affection. Maybe she couldn't.

"She's a cold, hard woman," I say. "I think she sent me into the forest just to get me out of the way. And if I killed you—or you killed me—it's still one less hybrid."

"But now she wants us," he says, thinking. "Needs us, even. To trade us to the Marauders. Still just pawns in her game."

"I've got a plan," I say. "What do you say? Tired of being a pawn? Ready to be a player?"

I put a hand out, and he eyes it, hesitating a second before reaching out. But I pull back at the last second, forcing him to meet my eyes.

"I need you to let me take the reins on this," I say. "You'll get your revenge, but only at the right time. My plan *will* work, but only if it's executed perfectly, to the very last detail. I can't have you, or Gila, or any one of your people losing their heads at a bad time. One slip, and this all goes to hell—and we all go to the Marauders."

His hand stays out. "I'm with you," he says.

We shake on it, and I should feel relieved—I just conscripted an army to fight in my war. But I know he's not interested in fighting for the rights of all hybrids, or achieving equality and peace within the city. All he wants is revenge, and the look in his eyes—so like Langford's—weighs heavy on my mind. She couldn't be trusted, and I learned that lesson way too late.

Am I making the same mistake again?

CHAPTER 51

When we emerge from the cave the other reptilians are watching us cautiously. Gila's eyes go to Chammy's, and he gives her a nod.

"It's okay," he says, and his people gather around him. "Hawk can give us something we've been looking for our whole lives. Revenge on the person who tossed our parents aside, threw them in the sewers like trash."

Gazes turn to me, disbelief in them.

"It's true," I tell them, and go on to explain about Dr. Langford.

"So she's our...what? Mother? Grandmother?" Tut asks, his head turning ever so slowly back and forth between Chammy and Gila in his confusion.

"I'd say more like our creator," Chammy says. "But we've got nothing to thank her for. Langford condemned us to a life of darkness and hiding, deemed us unhuman and unworthy of her company. I've wanted to avenge our parents ever since I could walk, and I'm not letting this opportunity get away from me."

All around us, heads go up and down in agreement. Even Octavian—back on his feet now, and white as a sheet—seems to be in. The fish-girl is perched on the edge of the lagoon, hissing and smiling. Calypso takes one look and a shudder passes through her tiny body.

"Good." Chammy nods solemnly. "Hawk has a plan."

"Uh…"

When I said I had a plan, I meant it more in the sense of that I *would* have one, hopefully sooner rather than later. But time is running out, and I don't think I can bluff myself out of this one. I fake a cough.

"Sorry," I say. "It's really dank down here."

"I'm sure it is, for someone who is used to freedom in the sky," Gila snarls at me. I may have handed her an enemy, but that girl is never going to like me. I don't bother correcting her about the skies, either. With the fires burning up above, the free air isn't much better than what they've got down here.

"Could we go somewhere a little warmer?" I ask, curling my arms around Calypso, whose shudder from spotting the fish-girl has morphed into a full-body shiver.

"Of course," Chammy says. "Gila, Tut, come with us. Everyone else, stand by."

The five of us head down a familiar path, and my hand tightens on Calypso's when I realize that we're heading for the room where Chammy has weapons stockpiled. Is he going to double-cross me? I'm surprised when we enter the weapons cave to find a small fire burning. I turn to Chammy, eyes wide.

"It's okay," he reassures me, indicating a small fissure in the ceiling where the smoke funnels out. "We have to walk a fine line between risking being blown up or having all our weapons rust and the gunpowder grow wet and useless."

"Fun life," I say. I'm not totally jazzed about the flames being so close to live rounds, or that Calypso is standing so close to them.

"Hey, you wanted somewhere warmer," Gila shoots back.

"Yeah, but less explosive would've been nice," I say.

Chammy holds his hands up, calling for silence. "Let's hear your plan, Hawk."

Luckily, the hike back to the weapons cache gave me time to think. I've come up with something, and I actually think it might be pretty good.

"Langford wants hybrids to trade," I begin. "But I've got a trade of my own in mind. I'll offer the reptilians up in exchange for my parents."

"Um, your parents are free," Gila says, crossing her arms. "Looks like all that fresh air might not be good for your head after all."

"But Langford doesn't know that *I know* Max and Fang are free," I counter. "I'll tell her I'm bringing her the entire forest population of hybrids—all the reptilians—in exchange for my family, friends, and their freedom."

Tanning wanted Max specifically for his breeding experiments, and he'd never take this offer from Langford in exchange for the vaccine without Maximum Ride as part of the goods. But I didn't tell Langford that, and I'm sure as hell not letting Chammy know, either. I've got a lot riding on this house of cards, and if it falls, I'm totally screwed.

"So you hand us over to Langford, who gives us to Tanning. She gets the vaccine and the humans live happily ever after, while you fly into the sunset?" Gila asks. "Why would we ever agree to that?"

"Because Hawk isn't selling us out to anybody," Chammy says, eyes going to mine. "She wouldn't do that to another hybrid."

"No, I wouldn't," I say, then turn back to Gila. "Langford knows you've got big numbers here. You should've seen her face when I told her how many. Even Tanning won't expect that many hybrids to populate his experiments. If I promise I can deliver you—all of you—they might just bite."

"And?" Chammy asks, rolling his hand to encourage me to keep going.

"Oh, yeah." I plow forward. "And of course, none of you will actually be involved in any experiments. Langford has never played straight with me. Now it's my turn."

"How..."

We all look at Tut, waiting for him to mentally put together his sentence before speaking. "How would you do that, though? There are way more of us—"

"Yeah." Gila jumps on this. "How could you bring two hundred of us to Langford, all by yourself?"

"You're sick," I explain, and her eyebrows fly up.

"Langford wants to convince everyone that the hybrids were the source of the virus to begin with. Having all of you crawl into the city looking like hell will only reinforce the lies she's told to the population. It all works in her favor."

"I'm not crawling," Gila says, crossing her arms.

"Fine, shuffle, whatever," I say. "Just look sick, march into the square, and let me take care of the rest."

"And the rest is?" Chammy asks.

"You'll be armed," I say, nodding to the crates of weapons all around us. "You'll have weapons under your clothing. We'll call a meeting for all interested parties—Langford, Tanning, and us—at the Square. At my signal, you'll show your weapons and use them, if necessary."

"And if I clip a few humans in the melee, oh, well," Gila says.

"I'd really rather you didn't," I say. "Think about it—we'll still have to live here after this is settled. Do you really want more strife between humans and hybrids? Or is there a better way?"

"We've got too much riding on the present to think about the future, Hawk," Chammy says. "You're asking a lot of us."

"I know," I tell him. "But I can't let you just open fire on a bunch of humans. They've been misled, and a lot of them are sick."

Chammy and Gila walk into a corner for a private conversation. Their harsh whispers echo around the cave, but I can't make anything out. Tut gives me a slow, unsure smile. From the corner, Calypso whimpers in her sleep.

"All right," Chammy says when he and Gila rejoin the group. "We won't fire first, but that's all I can promise. If humans attack us, we *will* defend ourselves."

"Of course," I say. "I wouldn't expect anything else. Do we have a deal, then?"

Chammy sighs, gaze going back to Gila, who nods almost imperceptibly. "Deal," Chammy says. "And I swear, this better work, Hawk. Or else—"

But he doesn't get to finish his threat. A scream echoes down the hall, followed by raised voices.

"Get back!" I recognize that voice. "Get back, or I'll shoot!"

It's Pietro.

CHAPTER 52

We spill out into the lagoon area to find all the reptilians on high alert, guns and hard gazes aimed at Pietro, who stands on the center island, a rope dangling from the roof above. Next to him stands Rain.

"Pietro!" I scream. "What the hell!"

A shriek erupts from above, a reptilian alerting those below as a shadow dives down the opening. Everyone ducks, but I stand still, waiting for Ridley to light on my shoulder. She nuzzles my ear, and despite the chill in the air—and the weapons still pointed at my friends—I feel the first glimmers of real hope.

"Everyone calm down," I yell, holding my arms out. "These are my friends. Rain is a fellow hybrid."

"Hello," Rain says calmly, her blank gaze sweeping the group.

"She doesn't look like a hybrid," Gila says suspiciously. "Where's her fur, or feathers?"

"Rain's not like that," I explain. "She's blind, but she can see things from far away, without having to be there."

"Cool trick," Gila concedes. "And the skinny one?"

"Hey!" Pietro bristles, but his gun arm is lowering.

"The skinny one is Pietro," I say, trying to keep the smile from my voice. Calypso, tucked under my arm, can't quite suppress her own giggle.

"A human," the reptilian with a frog head snarls, his tongue flicking in and out of his mouth rapidly. Chammy looks at me, expecting an explanation.

"Yes," I say, with a sharp exhale. "He's human."

There are gasps from all around the cavern, but no bullets fly.

"He's okay," I tell everyone, locking eyes with Pietro. "He's my friend."

Chammy gives a nod, and all around us guns lower. I motion to Pietro, who leads Rain from the island over to the beach. The fish-girl flicks her tail playfully at Rain, who giggles and splashes back, landing a perfect wave right into the girl's eyes.

"Blind, but not blind," I remind everyone.

Chammy meets Pietro at the bank. "Before we get too friendly, care to explain how you found us?"

"It was Rain," Pietro explains. "She can see where people she cares about are at, and she knew I'd been here before. When she saw Hawk and Calypso in an underground place with other hybrids, it didn't take long for her to figure it out. We couldn't exactly make Ridley stay behind. She's a hard-headed bird."

"Just like her owner," Chammy says to me.

I ignore that, turning to Pietro. "But why risk bringing her here? Surely Rain was safer in the city?"

"Not really." He shakes his head. "It's getting hotter up there, and I mean that in about a hundred different ways. Things are bad. Some people are beginning to turn, and it's..." He glances around, not wanting to say too much. "Well, it's ugly. And there's more."

"What?" I ask.

"My doctors at the Hope for Opes centers have been working on a vaccine ever since the pandemic began. We're close. And if we can achieve that, then produce it in quantity, we won't have to deal with the Marauders at all."

"How long will that take?" I ask. "Even if they get it done, how long to produce enough for everyone in the city?"

"At the rate Tanning is raising the temperature, too long," Pietro admits.

"So it doesn't matter," Chammy interrupts. "If you can't make the vaccine quickly enough, it won't do us any good. The hotter it gets, the more violent and enraged the infected people will become."

"Yep," I agree. "Sorry, Pietro. I know you'd like to see this all come off without any violence, but I just don't think it's possible. We don't have time to wait."

His head hangs, the turbulent, murderous past of his father still weighing heavy on his shoulders. "I know," he admits. "But I had to try."

In the silence that follows, Rain's voice rises, calm and cool. "Max is with her people."

"What? The Flock?" I perk up immediately, moving Ridley onto my other shoulder as she begins to pace.

"Max...and Fang..." Rain's voice is dreamy, her eyebrows coming close together as she accesses her power. "They're safe, escaped. They are together, and gathering with..." Her brow furrows as she struggles to clarify what she's seeing, "...more." She finally finishes, shaking her head, as if to clear it.

"I'm sorry, Hawk," she says, turning to me. "My connection with you is strong, but I do not know Max well. I only felt that moment because of the joy she was feeling, at being with her own people. But I cannot see where they are, or what they are doing."

"Probably making bombs, if Gazzy's got anything to do with it," I mutter.

"Bombs?" Chammy asks, immediately interested. "That would be amazing. If we can coordinate our arrival in the square with an attack from the air—"

"It doesn't work that way," I tell him. "Rain can't talk to them, and they don't even know that she's watching them. All we can do is trust what Rain is relaying, and it looks like we won't be getting all that much information out of her, since her connection to Max is weak."

Somewhat disappointed, Chammy backs away.

"It's still a good thing," I say. "Great, even. You don't understand. The Flock—my parents, Gazzy, Angel, Iggy, Nudge—with them in the skies, we've got artillery in the air."

"With no idea when it will arrive," he shoots back.

"And we're the soldiers on the ground—where the casualties happen."

"We can count on the Flock to go wherever the fight is," I say. "No matter when they get here, it can only be a good thing."

"Allies with no communication and no ETA?" Gila steps in. "Artillery in the sky falling from people we don't know? What if reptilians get caught in the crossfire?"

"You won't." I shake my head. "They'll know you for fellow hybrids, and they'd never harm you. Unless you give them reason," I add, when I see her eyes narrow.

Chammy nods, like he's come to a decision.

"All right," he holds a hand out to Pietro, who takes it. Rain reaches out, touching his shoulder. "I can't say I like it, but I guess we're all together now," he says. "The enemy of my enemy is my friend, huh?"

"Yep," I say. "Good thing we've both got plenty of enemies."

CHAPTER 53

Excited as I am about this plan, my heart is heavy when I send Ridley out with the message for Langford. I'd written the note with a shaking hand, anger almost making it unreadable. It says I'll trade the reptilians for my friends, signing off on handing over my fellow hybrids for a life of experimentation. It's a lie—I know that, and so does Chammy—but it's still my words, with my name put to it. Langford already has one piece of paper she wants to use to establish me as a traitor to my kind. And here I am, handing her another one.

"This better work," I say to Ridley, as she nudges her beak against my nose. "Or else I'm going to go down as the most hated hybrid in history."

But like Chammy said, we've got too much riding on the present to worry about the future. Ridley is gone in a flutter of wings just as dawn is starting to light the sky, the scent of smoke heavier in the air than before. Despite the heat—and it is definitely hotter than it was when I got here last night—a chill runs down my spine. So much could go wrong. I close my eyes against the fear, willing myself to be brave.

I slip back down the tunnel entrance that Tut led me through, meeting up with him inside. He gives me a quick glance, then touches his cheek right below his eye. Taking the hint, I swipe at my face. I hadn't even known I was crying. I'm so glad it's Tut with me and not Chammy. Or even worse, Gila.

He's quiet as we move slowly down the tunnel, taking turns that I'm pretty sure we didn't take on the way to the surface. A young reptilian—a chameleon—leads the way. Chammy introduced me to him as Stick, so called not because he's as thin as one, but because he's bioluminescent. He glows in the dark.

"Like a glow stick," Chammy said, a little note of jealousy in his voice making it sound like Chammy wished he'd received that particular chameleon gene.

Stick is quiet, doing his job as our light source but not contributing to conversation. Tut moves along beside me, reaching out to tap Stick on the shoulder whenever he wants him to turn.

"Your fearless leader doesn't trust me entirely, does he?" I ask when we pass a rock formation I know I didn't see on the way up. "You're taking me through a maze so I can't find my way back to the surface on my own, aren't you?"

Tut sighs, a long, slow exhalation while he puts together what he wants to say. "We haven't lived this long by making friends," he finally says. "And Chammy isn't fearless.

Did you see his face when you mentioned his human mother?"

"Yeah," I say. "It definitely threw him."

"Mmm-hmm," Tut agrees, as a warm, orange glow lights the end of the tunnel. "Gila and Chammy, both of them would be happy to give up on their human side altogether, become completely reptile. It's not easy for them to be reminded that they are part human, like it or not."

"What about you?" I ask. We're nearing the light, and I can hear murmured voices from the central cave. I slow even further, wanting to learn more about Tut and how he feels. Stick reaches the exit and looks back at us. Tut waves for him to go on, and the kid disappears into the light, a flutter of voices welcoming him home. There's a long silence, and for a moment I think Tut isn't going to answer me.

"I think..." He scratches his head, his claws leaving red marks behind on his close-cut scalp. "I think...very slowly."

His eyes twinkle at me and I realize Tut just made a joke. I laugh, which brings a few curious faces to the lit end of the tunnel.

"But I'm glad I can think," Tut finishes. "I like the part of me that is human."

"I do, too," I say, putting my hand on his shoulder. "I like the reptilian bits, too. I like all of you. If you took either part out, you wouldn't be Tut anymore. Just like I wouldn't be Hawk."

"Chammy doesn't want me going up top," he says

suddenly, and I know the words must have been held back for quite some time in order for them to come out so quickly. He's held them there, ready to fire. "I'm too slow. He says I can't fight. That I'll just be in the way."

"Oh, Tut," I say, squeezing his shoulder. "I don't think that's true at all."

He shrugs. Chammy might not be entirely wrong. But I know what it feels like to be left behind, and my heart hurts for Tut.

"I just didn't want you to think that I don't agree with your plan," he goes on. "I think it's a great idea. And I think it's going to work."

"So you're just supposed to stay here, keep the home fires burning?" I ask.

"Something like that. Me and the other turtle hybrids."

I don't like it any more than he does, but Chammy has already gone out on a limb for me—more than once. I can't argue against him again, and I can't tell his own soldiers to defy his orders.

"Listen," I blunder forward, not wanting to contradict Chammy, but not wanting to let Tut down, either. "Don't believe for one second that you're useless. You might not be the fastest, and maybe that's what Chammy is looking for right now. But there'll be another time, another place, where you'll have what he needs. I'm sure he'll call on you then, and I know you'll do whatever is asked of you. We all have different strengths."

"Right," Tut says. "I just need to figure out mine."

We approach the cave entrance, and he hops out ahead

of me, reaching down to give me a hand over the loose rocks that rest in front of the crumbling cave mouth. I don't need his help, but I'm not about to refuse it, either. He already feels like he's not doing anything useful.

"I guess I'll see you when I get back," I say, then add, jokingly, "*if* I get back."

"You'll make it," Tut says. "You're the strongest, hardest person I've ever met."

"Not quite as hard as you," I say, tapping my knuckles against his shell.

He blushes, and Pietro's eyes meet mine as we approach the campfire, still burning low for light, even though it's getting warmer even here, underground.

"You took your time," Pietro says, his voice oddly harsh as he cuts his eyes at Tut.

"Tut and Stick brought me back a different way," I explain. "Guess I don't have my all-access pass yet."

"I think he'd like all-access," Pietro says, still glowering at Tut. I smack his shoulder a little harder than necessary. He's rubbing it gingerly when there's a call from above, a high-pitched shriek as Ridley circles to us.

"That was fast," Chammy says, hovering over me as Ridley alights on my shoulder. Her heart is beating so quickly I can feel her pulse against my neck, as she nestles closer to me for comfort. Looking closer, I can see why. Langford hasn't sent her back with a scroll—she sent a phone.

With trembling hands, I unloop it from Ridley's leg. Everyone gathers around me, with Chammy, Gila, and Pietro leaning in close.

Suddenly, it vibrates in my hand, the high, shrill ring echoing around the cave. I gasp and jump, jostling against Chammy, who tries to grab the phone from my hands. I snatch it back, willing my heart to settle and my words to be strong when I answer.

"Hello?" I say.

"Hawk," Langford replies, her voice a ball of iron, my name a bullet in her mouth. "Did you really think I would fall for this?"

CHAPTER 54

"Fall for what?" I ask, trying to inject innocence into my tone. "I'm offering you a truce that benefits both sides. You don't fall for truces," I tell her. "You accept them."

Gila leans in closer to my left, Chammy on my right, trying to pick up Langford's end of the conversation. I break away from them, wandering to the water's edge.

"You're right," Langford says. "Treaties are accepted when they come from trusted people. And I don't trust you."

"Last time I saw you I was locked up in a cell with a child, and both of us were just coming back to consciousness after you had us knocked out. I don't exactly trust you, either," I say.

"Hmmm..." She pretends to mull this over. "So how do two people who don't trust each other come to an agreement?"

"You have my parents," I say, my knuckles tightening on the phone. It's a gamble, but it might work. Langford doesn't know that the reptilians have eyes in the city, or that Rain caught a glimpse of Max and Fang free in the outside world, gathering the Flock. If she thinks she still has that ace in her hand—that I *believe* she has them—I just might be able to get away with this.

"I won't risk them," I hiss into the phone. "These reptilians are a repulsive, dirty, stupid species. They're nothing like my kind. We fly in the clean air, they crawl in the dark. Trade them for my parents' freedom and a fresh start somewhere else? Hell, yeah, I will," I say.

Hackles are rising all around me, deep breaths and tight exhales mix with a grumbling that rises. Calypso pulls in close to Rain, making herself smaller. Pietro comes to my side, holding up his hands, pleading for them to let me finish this charade, this necessary lie in order to convince Langford that I'm on the up-and-up, willing to sign off on the reptilians in order to save my own skin. Chammy gives everyone a sharp look, and they remain in a holding pattern—but I didn't win any friends with that little speech.

On the other end, Langford deliberates. I hear the ping of the coffee maker in the Council room and imagine the scene. The rest of the Council will be in their seats, hands dutifully folded as they wait for their orders. Some—Holden and maybe a few others—might be trading glances, weighing the options as the power shifts from Langford to Tanning in the square below.

I bet they're all sweating, and not just because of the Marauders' weather machine. I close my eyes, thinking of Moke and the endless stream of energy he's feeding it. Can

I get him out of this alive? And even if I do, will he ever be the same?

"All right," Langford comes to a decision with a huff. "I guess there aren't any other options, are there?"

In the background, I hear a gust of breeze and the rustle of a tarp. I have to cover my smile. Max and Fang must have busted out of the Council room, raining glass and feathers in their wake. That blast of air has to remind Langford of her failure, just like the rising noise from the Square does. I can hear it over our connection: a gathering of people, none of them happy, all of them ill.

"No," I tell her. "We don't have any choices at this point. Neither of us do."

"Bring me the reptilians, Hawk," she says, the steel back in her voice. "But know this—I will be watching you. *You,* specifically. And I won't be the only one."

I imagine snipers positioned on the high-rises, my flashing wings in their sights. She's letting me know that if I go against my word, I'm a dead girl. But telling lies to survive is nothing new to me, and neither is staring down a bullet.

"See you soon," I whisper to Langford and hang up, turning to the hybrids, who eye me suspiciously. "She went for it," I say. "Langford agrees to the terms."

There's a round of jubilant yells, and everyone starts practicing their sick walks as Pietro models for them what most of the citizens above look like, dragging their legs and hanging their heads. We won't have to work too hard to make them sweat and have flushed cheeks; I can still feel the heat from the air above trapped in Ridley's wings as she fans them out, a warm breeze on my face. I duck my head beneath her feathers to hide my own flush.

"Please, please, let this work," I mutter to her, or whoever is listening.

Because if it doesn't, I'm not the only one in the crosshairs.

If it doesn't work, this whole army of hybrids is as good as dead.

CHAPTER 55

Calypso, Stick, and some of the younger reptilians are given the job of doling out weapons. After grabbing a few hours of sleep, I slide past the line of hybrids waiting to get their guns. They're all wearing bulky clothing to make it easier to hide the fact that they are armed.

I get to the munitions cave, where Calypso is handing out grenades, smiling and joking with the other child hybrids. I'm glad she's found people here, a group of hybrids her own age. So weird that they can bond over something like handing out military-grade weapons right before a possible apocalypse.

Suddenly there's a cool hand on my shoulder and Rain's voice in my ear. "I can't see Max anymore," she says.

"What was the last thing you saw?" I ask. "Are they on their way?"

Her ability is impressive, but like Chammy, I'm frustrated by the limitations. If she can't see clearly where exactly the Flock is, it's going to be almost impossible to coordinate our attacks. I don't want to be caught on the square facing down Tanning and Langford with two hundred hybrids pretending to be sick while we wait for reinforcements from the sky. It'll be hard enough to keep humans from hassling the hybrids as it is, and I doubt Gila can keep her itchy trigger finger under control for long.

But she only shakes her head, squeezing her eyebrows together, like squinting can help. "What I can manage to see is cloud cover," she says. "That's all. Or maybe it's haze."

"Is it cloud cover, or is it haze?" I push. "Because haze means smoke and that means they're close."

Rain's mouth goes into a flat line of frustration. "It's called remote viewing, not remote smelling, Hawk," she says. "All I can tell you is what I see. They could be right above the city, or a hundred miles away. I just don't know."

"Okay," I sigh. "Sorry. It's just..."

"Everyone's on edge," she says. "I understand."

My eyes wander over the line of reptilians. They've been practicing looking like they're sick, but they're obviously healthy. They're mostly young, and their skin looks good, their eyes bright. I can only hope that they stay that way. Exposing them to the virus—and possible infection—is a risk. But the sickness won't have its way with them if they're torn limb from limb by an angry mob of humans.

"I'm glad we're doing this at night," I confide. "I don't think Langford is going to buy that all these hybrids are sick, not looking as good as they do. And if even one human suspects something, it could turn into a riot, fast."

"I'll keep you updated," she reassures me. "As soon as I see something that tells me where the Flock is, I'll let you know. But I can't guarantee anything."

I nod in agreement and we head back to the main cave, Rain's step as sure as mine as we come out into the light. Chammy spots me and approaches us, handing me a radio.

"Walkie-talkie," he says, motioning for Pietro to join us. "I only have three," he says, giving the last one to Pietro. "Hawk, you'll be the closest to Langford and Tanning. Will you be able to hide that you're carrying this?"

"I have my ways," I tell him, slipping it into the spot above where my wings attach. "Langford's guards didn't frisk me there when they took me to the cell," I explain.

"Okay," Chammy goes on. "I'll be with the rest of my people, waiting for the signal. Pietro, I want you and Rain somewhere high, somewhere you can see everything in the square below you. And Rain, as soon as you have any indication that the Flock is coming, tell Pietro. He can notify me and Hawk over the radios."

Rain nods but doesn't say anything. She's already frustrated enough over the limitations of her gift. I don't blame her for not wanting to share with a stranger that she might not *ever* be able to tell us the whereabouts of the Flock.

"The hospital would be the best place for Pietro and Rain," I say. "It's right on the square. You'll be able to see us, the Marauders, and Moke. He can't get hurt during all this. He just *can't*."

"You know we'll do our best," Chammy reassures me.

"But I can't guarantee anyone's safety. My own people know this. Yours need to, as well."

"Yeah," I say, sadly agreeing. "But you should see how tired Moke is after he unleashes a bolt. After powering that machine for so long, he's got to be completely drained. I don't know what Tanning is giving him to keep him going this long, but"—I fan my hand in front of my face—"it's obviously working."

Pietro clears his throat. "I'm sure Chammy and the rest will do everything they can for Moke," he says. "But once the fighting breaks out, it's going to be everyone for themselves. And I don't just mean the Marauders and Langford's people, either. People are scared, and the citizens will jump into a fight just because they want someone to blame. It'll be chaos."

"Right," Chammy agrees. "Which is why a high point is important for you. As long as one person can have some idea of what's going on, we stand a chance. Stay in contact." He points at Pietro. "And I'll make Moke my priority," he says to me.

"Thanks," I say, but something else has occurred to me. "Chaos," I repeat what Pietro had said, turning to him. "I need you to do me a favor. There's a girl in the hospital named Melanie."

I give him her room number and tell him what she looks like. "She helped me out, more than once. If there's rioting in the streets, it could spread inside. Try to get her on the roof; at least there's some sense of safety there."

"I'll do my best," Pietro says grimly. "But you need to be realistic, Hawk. We're all going into this with our eyes open."

"I'm not," Rain says lightly, raising a smile from Chammy.

"But," Pietro finishes, "make no mistake. People are going to die."

CHAPTER 56

We file out through the tunnels, two hundred reptilians shuffling and moaning, already pretending to be sick. It's an eerie sound as it echoes around the rock walls, and the hairs on the back of my neck stand up. Once we're all gathered in a clearing, Chammy climbs a tree and addresses his army.

"We're going into this city together," he says, his voice carrying far. "All of the hybrids, marching together."

All of the hybrids...except the turtles, I can't help but think. Tut's eyes met mine as we were leaving, the other turtles gathered around him, the smaller children—including Calypso—standing with them. In some ways they have the hardest job—waiting to see who makes it back home, not knowing if their friends are alive or dead.

"Remember the rules of engagement," Chammy continues. "Do not fire unless fired upon!" His voice is harsh, an order from a battle-scarred veteran, but there's already some dissension in the ranks. I can see some reptilian heads gathered together, whispered discussions taking place. But they're not my people, and I can't tell them what to do. In the end, not even Chammy can. At the first shot, it's going to be like Pietro said—everyone for themselves, everyone their own commander.

No one will be in control.

I squeeze my fingers into sweaty fists and leap into the sky, rising above the canopy of the forest. Pietro and Rain left before us to get into position. Rain can pass as human, and Pietro should have no problem using his status to get access to the hospital. Langford agreed to extinguish one of their roadblocks, moving the rubble so that the delivery of two hundred hybrids to the hospital could be accomplished. I hadn't exactly liked that, either. It means Langford decides our point of entry, and if she's smart enough to put soldiers on the roofs above, they can pin us in a bottleneck easily once the fighting breaks out.

But that's out of my control—just like everything else. All I can do is rely on the information that Pietro feeds me through the radio. The air is hot and heavy, and I break out into a sweat almost immediately. I fly at the head of our army, finding the best path through the city streets from above to the steps of the hospital and Langford's soldiers waiting there.

Knowing Langford, those soldiers likely have orders to take the reptilians straight to the loading bays, where trucks undoubtedly wait to be filled. They'll likely be driven to the Marauders' home base once the trade of the vaccine is complete. Langford might dictate our point of entry, and she might think she knows how the hybrids are leaving the city, too. But she isn't counting on a healthy army with weapons under their cloaks.

"Please, please, let this work," I say again, my words going unheard into the hot air surrounding me.

Smoke rises from multiple points in the city, and I fly around and in between spires, showing the hybrids the best routes. They follow behind slowly, keeping up the pretense of being ill. The smog is thick, and it's nearly dusk, but even from here I can see them dragging their feet, heads wobbling as if too heavy for their necks.

I circle around the hospital, spotting three figures on the roof there. Rain, Melanie, and Pietro. Rain waves first, sensing my presence. The other two squint, making sure it's me before they raise their hands. I double back, eyeing the lights in the square as I do. Langford has the entrance to the square lit up with spotlights, but the center remains somewhat darkened. She's not taking any chances, either. She wants to be able to see what she's getting—sick hybrids—all while making sure Tanning can't see that he's on the raw end of this deal.

The radio squawks from in between my shoulder blades. "So far, so good," Pietro says. "Langford is standing at the entrance to the hospital."

"I see her," I say, even though he can't hear me unless I'm pressing down on the talk button. Langford is wearing all white, trying to play the part of the loving, innocent auto- crat. I smile to myself. The spotless pantsuit also makes her easy to target. It will be hard to hide herself among the dirty populace and ragged hybrids once the fighting breaks out.

"Rain says…" There's a pause from Pietro. "Still no contact with the Flock."

Chammy comes on, voice bright with anger. "Are you shitting me?"

"No contact," Pietro repeats, with no trace of emotion. "Hawk, do you want to try this without them, or what?"

I reach back, pulling the radio from in between my wings. "It'll be a lot harder without air support," I think aloud. "The more hybrids, the better."

There's a rush of static, then Pietro's voice. "Can you stall?"

"Oh, believe me," I say. "I'm very good at wasting other people's time." I mutter a quick prayer as I replace the radio, and squeeze my eyes shut before I leave the safety of the air for the unforgiving ground.

Max, please get here soon.

CHAPTER 57

I alight in front of Langdon in the well-lit streets. She's at the top of the hospital steps, white outfit glaring, her gaze cold on mine as I look up at her. A pure politician, she's got this all set up the way she wants. Her, at the top, bright and clean. Me, in the streets, dirty. Looking up. Imploring.

I hate this.

I grit my teeth and clench my fists as I climb the steps, the growing sound of the approaching reptilians echoing off the buildings. Groans and scraping feet send a shiver up my spine, but I keep it straight—and my head up—as I ascend to Langford.

She holds out a hand, stopping me. Guards flank me immediately, palms and fingers rushing over my body and checking for weapons. They step away, nodding to Langford that I'm not armed, and she motions me forward. The radio sits heavily in my wings, and I hope that both Pietro and Chammy are smart enough not to use it when I'm standing right in front of Langford.

Behind me, there are shouts of surprise and a few cries from human throats. This many hybrids in one place has the populace on edge.

"Freaks!" someone yells.

"Disease!" comes another voice, followed by the sound of a scuffle. I bite my lip, willing it to be settled quickly and quietly.

Langford flicks her wrist and one of her guards leaves my side. I hear the crack of a gunstock connecting with a skull and the sound of a body sliding to the ground. I close my eyes, praying to God or whoever that it was a human that just got knocked out, not a hybrid. I can't imagine Gila or Chammy standing idly by while reptilian blood sprinkles the streets.

The muttering drops to a low murmur as I count to ten, and the guard returns to my side. I exhale. Must have been a human, then. If the guard had gone after a hybrid there'd be a riot on our hands.

"Hawk," Langford smiles, picking up the conversation easily. She deigns to descend a couple steps to meet me. "So glad you seem to have come to your senses."

Her eyes are cold as she sweeps the crowd behind me. I can hear the reptilians, their moans of pain rising. I don't dare turn around or steal a look back. I can only hope they are convincing...and under Chammy's control.

I watch her for any hint that she smells a rat, but instead, I see something different there. Confusion. She's utterly baffled that it looks like I might actually be coming through for her.

"They came peacefully," I say, gilding the lie. "I told them you'd agreed to offer them medical care. They think they're coming to the hospital for a cure."

She laughs, a hollow sound. "Like I'd waste medicine on freaks."

My blood boils and my skin tightens, but I can't lose my control. "Okay, so...they're here," I say. "I came through on my end."

Movement catches my eye as Tanning emerges from the darkened square, moving into the well-lit street. "What's this?" he asks, warily approaching Langford, his own guards in tow.

"The solution to all our problems," she says easily, turning to him. "My pet traitor has fulfilled her end of a bargain."

"Which is?" Tanning asks, eyes skimming over me. I bristle further, hating that he's looking at me, and what plans he has in mind for my body.

"Hundreds of hybrids, primed for your use," she says, sweeping her arm to indicate the reptilians. "Hawk has led them to us in exchange for her own freedom, and that of her parents."

"I agreed with no such thing!" he erupts. "I want hybrids, not a motley crew of half-dead sewer rats."

There's a rising grumble behind me, and I leap in front of him, hopefully blocking his view—and maybe dissuading any bullets from flying in his direction. I don't need chaos...not yet.

"They're sick, yeah," I admit. "How else could I bring so many here all by myself? They're ill, and desperate for a cure. And that's exactly what you've got, so what's it to you if they have to be healed before you can begin your... work?"

I choke on the word *work,* but Tanning doesn't seem to notice. He barrels on, incensed.

"And I want Maximum Ride! That was a condition of the deal."

Langford's eyes move to mine, but I hold her gaze.

"Ah," she says with a smile. "There it is. I knew you weren't playing us straight, Hawk. What did you think you were going to do? Set your enemies upon one another?"

"What are you talking about?" Tanning demands, looking between us. "What is she saying?"

I glance over into the darkened square and catch a glimpse of Moke. He's glowing dully, his blue skin running with sweat as all his power is sucked into the infernal machine he's chained to. Heavily armed Marauders stand at all four points of the machine, on high alert.

"What she's saying," I explain to Dr. Tanning, "is that you can't always get what you want."

"Excuse me?" he asks, eyes thinning in anger. "Do you forget what I showed you? Can you remember what happens to those who don't perform as expected?"

I shudder, remembering the hand that reached for him from the pile of failed, dying hybrid experiments.

"Filth!" a human voice screams at the mob of hybrids, and I hear something sail through the air. There's a rustle in the crowd behind me, reptilian tempers rising as I stall, stall, stall.

"Infected half-breeds!" someone else yells, and glass breaks.

The growing growl of the reptilian throats rises, and I hear Chammy's voice underneath it, a low mutter, imploring. "Hold. Hold."

"I know what happens when you're unhappy," I tell Tanning. "But I can't give you Maximum Ride."

Langford pulls in a breath, her chest rising heavily beneath her white suit. I lock eyes with her: a dare. "And neither can she."

Langford's eyes flash as she realizes that I've known all along this trade wasn't going to go down. At that moment, the walkie-talkie between my wings erupts into a burst of static.

"Grab her!" Langford yells, instinctively diving for the ground as guards lunge at me. But someone else gets to me first. Strong hands wrap around my waist and I'm pulled upward in a draft of warm air as Maximum Ride announces:

"Nobody's got me, assholes. But I've got my daughter."

And that's when the world explodes.

CHAPTER 58

The first blast is a bright pink, and I hear Gazzy's triumphant yowl from the air above just before the second bomb—shocking fluorescent yellow—drops amid the humans crowding the sidewalks. People run, fleeing, not seeming to notice that there's no danger here; whatever Gazzy put in the bombs is meant to disperse them, not harm anyone. Tiny, bright fires have erupted all over, but they burn for only a few seconds before sputtering out.

No, the real danger is from the hybrids, who have heard enough. Insults have been thrown at them since the moment they arrived, and they've been holding their tempers for generations. The charade of sickness is dropped, and cloaks fly back as guns come out.

"What are they doing?" Max yells. Dropping me, she runs to the front of the hybrid mob, holding her hands out imploringly.

"Mom, wait!" I yell, catching up.

But it's too late. Years of mistreatment and banishment have fueled this moment, and the reptilians won't be stopped. I snatch the radio from between my wings, screaming into it.

"Chammy, no! Don't!" I plead, but his voice is cold and emotionless when he responds.

"Sorry, Hawk," he says. "This was never going to end well."

Max realizes this at the same time, hurtling into the air just before the bullets spray. I'm about to join her when a bullet zips right past my head, close enough that it's a *snap* instead of a *hiss*.

Too late, I remember Langford's warning. There are snipers on the buildings, and they're aiming at anything with wings.

"Max!" I scream, bolting after her through the hot air above the square. She's hovering, scanning the seething mass below as she tries to figure out where she's needed most.

"Don't hold still!" I yell, hitting her in the midsection at half speed. Her breath comes out in a grunt and she spins, ready to fight, only to see me.

"Snipers! They're aiming for wings!" I shout.

I don't have time to explain, but Max doesn't need more. She gives me a grim nod and zips up above the low-hanging haze, no doubt to let the Flock know that they're targets, too. Another bullet skims the air near me, and some feathers fly.

"Shit!"

I dive in a zigzag pattern, eyeing the buildings. On top of the hospital, Pietro, Rain, and Melanie hover low.

There's movement on top of another high-rise that catches my eye, and I head straight for it, barreling down on him. Too late, I remember that I'm armed with nothing other than my wits and a walkie-talkie.

We lock eyes, and I'm zooming toward him, arms outstretched, as he wheels the barrel of his rifle around. This guy is a pro, and I already know the math is bad; he's going to get a shot off before I reach him. But I'm moving too fast to pull up, so I bear down, wind whipping tears from my eyes and a scream from my throat.

The rifle goes flying, falling through the air. I whirl, diving after it like a stone. My fingers brush the stock and I pull up, ascending again, gun in hand. I reach the roof to find Fang standing over the stunned soldier, sweat running down his chest.

"Don't ever do that again!" He grabs my shoulders when he sees me, eyes bright with anger. "You could've died!"

"So could you!" I shout back. "And now I've got a gun."

I give him a bright smile and step backward off the building, but not before I see the smile slipping across his face.

I feel it, too. We're in a fight, battling for our lives. Things are not going to plan. The streets below are in pure chaos, hybrids fighting humans, Marauders wandering into the melee to grab reptilians and carry them—shrieking—to vans that wait on the corner, doors open. Langford is nowhere to be seen. Nothing has gone right, and just about anything could go wrong.

But my dad is smiling, and somehow...I am, too.

It's the wind in my hair and the rush of adrenaline in my veins. We might not win this fight, but damn if I'm going to run away from it.

I hit the hospital roof running, to find Rain and Melanie ducking behind a heating vent. Pietro stands at a corner, radio in one hand, binoculars in the other. I kneel next to Rain.

"Max is here," she offers with a wan smile.

"Thanks for the update, psychic friend," I say, and she gives me a thumbs-up.

Melanie gives me a weak wave, but I can see her pulse pounding a mile a minute in her throat.

"You okay?" I have to yell over a fresh barrage of gunfire, and a new explosion, this one neon green with glitter included.

She nods and motions for me to come closer so that she can be heard. "Best...night...of...my life," she manages to whisper in my ear.

"Yeah," I agree. "Mine, too."

They seem fine so I run to Pietro, who is yelling instructions into the walkie. "West alley, west alley...Chammy, do you copy? There's a whole..." He hesitates before using the word, but then seems to decide there's only one way to describe what's happening. "There's a mob coming."

He's not wrong. The alley is lit, not with the bright explosions of Gazzy's bombs—meant for distraction—but with something more insidious. The flickering light of fire.

"Roger, solid copy." Chammy's voice comes across the

radio, and the hybrid crowd below swarms to the west, their leader at the front of the charge.

"That's the one time he's responded," Pietro tells me, his mouth a flat line of disappointment. "He only hears what he wants."

"I didn't exactly think he'd heel like a dog," I admit, watching as the tide of hybrids clashes with the humans pouring out of the alleyway. "But I wasn't expecting this."

Smaller fights have broken out all over, hybrids and humans fighting in groups of two and three. Some humans are taking advantage of the chaos and sprinting for the hospital doors, as if there's still some solace to be found here. I see a bright flash from a high window of one of the buildings and sight it in my own rifle. Sure enough, one of Langford's snipers sits on a balcony, easily picking off whoever he chooses to target.

And the Flock is still out there.

I don't have to think. All I have is emotion, and a second later there's a dark red smear on the wall behind him, his rifle falling to the crowd below.

"Jesus!" Pietro says, cradling his ears. "Warn me next time!"

"Next time, you'll be the one doing the shooting," I tell him, snatching the pistol from his waistband and handing over the rifle. He refuses it, pressing the barrel back against me.

"No," he says urgently. "Hawk, listen—it's a melee down there. You can help from up here. You're a better shot than I am. But down there..." He leans over the side of the building, looking at the bloodshed below. I follow his gaze, scanning the square for a flash of blue, for Moke, who I left behind with the Marauders. I promised I would come back for him. I promised I wouldn't lose him, the way I lost Clete.

"Down there, nobody is safe," Pietro finishes.

"I know," I say, throwing one leg over the ledge. "And that's exactly why I'm going."

CHAPTER 59

Bullets are flying, screams fill the air, smoke is in my lungs, sweat running down my face—but all I can think about is Moke.

I land behind the machine, crouched on one knee, pistol at the ready. Tanning has most of his men slipping through the crowd and abducting any reptilians they can grab. The hybrids struggle with them, but the Marauders have muscle on their side, and these thugs had the best training in the world—from the Pietro family. They know how to fight, and fight to win. That means fighting dirty.

They're gouging eyeballs and slamming gun barrels into the backs of knees. Tanning doesn't need his experimental hybrids unbroken; he just needs them able to reproduce. I'm still crouched, breathing hard, as one of Tanning's men passes me, Gila thrown over his shoulder.

"You son of a bitch!" she's screaming, pounding his shoulder blades with her fists. But it's useless. He's three times her size, she's lost her gun, and her temper will only take her so far. Fortunately, she's got a weapon he knows nothing about. And it's in her mouth.

Gila draws back, revealing rows of teeth that flash brightly for a moment before sinking into his shoulder. The man shrieks and drops her, screaming and reaching for the wound. Blood pours from his back as Gila rolls to a sewer grate, her blood flowing freely from a slash in her side. She gets to her feet unsteadily, too slow to react as he draws his gun.

"Gila!" I yell, rushing toward her. But I'm too far away, and even though her poison is working through his body, he's got plenty of time to get off a shot. There's a crack and the bullet flies. I'm screaming, running for the shooter, ready to take him down.

But I don't have to. The sewer grate flies open and a dark shape emerges, curling over Gila just in time. The bullet pings off of it, ricocheting to catch the shooter in the throat. He falls, seizing from the gila monster's poison in his veins and the bullet that just opened them.

I rush to Gila's side—but Tut is already there. Tut, who Chammy told to stay behind. Because he was too slow. Because he couldn't fight. Because he was...

"Useless, right?" Tut says to me with a smile, then points to the spot on his shell where he'd taken a bullet for Gila. A shot that would've killed her bounced right off him, and she folds into his arms for a hug as he pulls her to her feet. All around us, turtle hybrids are rising from the sewer grates and using their bodies as shields for the reptilians.

"Nice," I say, but we don't have time for more; Gazzy and the Flock pass overhead once more, and we crouch low as another explosive is dropped. This one lands near the square, emitting a thick wall of smoke. It's so hazy I can't see anything except vague shapes and...the light glow of something blue.

"Perfect, thank you," I say quietly.

Tut and Gila rejoin the fight, Tut spinning to cover her from fire as I slip into the square, keeping my sights trained on the dim blue glow that I know is Moke. I creep low to the ground, assessing the situation as I approach.

There were at least two guards still on my friend the last time I had a clear look. Gazzy's smoke bomb will make it easy enough for me to sneak up on one, but what about the other? If I can pull one back quickly and quietly, I might be able to nab the second one as well. A scream erupts from the smoke, but I can't save everyone, and I promised Moke I wouldn't leave him behind.

I slip behind the machine, eyeing the back of the guard closest to me. Sweat drips into my eyes, and I swipe it away. Here in the midst of the fighting and this near the machine I can hear the whirring parts, feel the pulses of energy coming off of it. My ears ring and my teeth hum in my mouth. It feels like my bones are splintering inside of my legs. How can Moke stand this? How can the guards?

The guard nearest me is keeping a safe distance from Moke and the bright flashes of electricity that ripple over his skin. I don't know what Tanning has given Moke to boost his power, but it looks like it might be killing him. His head hangs low, his mouth gasping as he tries to breathe in the gathering smoke. His arms are pinioned to the machine with chains, his legs collapsed underneath him.

He can't stand this much longer.

And I can't take it another second.

I leap for one guard, landing a spinning kick right in the middle of his shoulder blades. He cries out in surprise as he's flung into the smoke and the melee of battle. He doesn't come back out. I raise my pistol and draw a bead on the guard across from me, but he's already got his hands up, his weapon falling from his grasp.

As badly as this battle must be going for the reptilians, it's even worse for the Marauders, I realize. They were hired to come into the city and load up docile specimens, not fight for their lives in a mob. And no matter what Tanning is paying them, it's not enough... at least, not for this guy.

"I'm done," he says, backing away.

"That's correct," a steely voice says, as a pistol emerges from the smoke. Tanning shoots the guard in the temple, the bright light of his eyes there one second and gone the next.

"Hawk," Tanning says, turning the pistol—and his gaze—to me. "What exactly do you think you're doing?"

CHAPTER 60

I step in front of Moke, my gun extended.

"This is my friend, and you can't have him," I tell Tanning.

"Fair enough." He shrugs, lowering his gun arm. "I neither need nor want him any longer. He's served his purpose."

"What?" I ask, disbelief flooding me.

"Hawk…" Moke's voice behind me is weak. "It's not worth it. *I'm* not worth it."

"Shut your face," I yell over my shoulder, eyes still trained on Tanning. "I told you I wasn't leaving you, and that's final."

"You're not going to leave him," Tanning says, bending slowly to put his gun on the ground. He lifts his arms, showing that he's no longer armed.

"This can end, here and now," he goes on, moving toward me smoothly. A scream erupts from the smoke, and he smiles. "Well, I can't stop *everything* that is happening. But this…"

He flicks one finger in between me, Moke, and himself. "This is what really matters to you, isn't it? The one thing you can't give up on?"

Everything inside of me wants to disagree with him, but what he's saying is right. "Yes," I nod, my tongue heavy in the heat, my throat dry. "Yes, I want Moke to be free."

"And you'd exchange yourself for him, right?" Tanning asks, still moving forward.

Behind me, Moke has gone silent. And I think, for the breath of a moment, that maybe—just maybe—the heat at my back has stopped radiating. From the corner of my eye, I spot a new glow forming. But this one isn't blue. It's red. And I can smell hot metal. Moke has diverted his energy, is moving it into his chains instead of into the machine.

"Yes," I say quickly, fumbling a step backward, willing Tanning to move with me.

"Yes, I'd trade myself for Moke."

"There you have it," Tanning says, still smiling, still advancing. "You promised to not leave him behind, and you don't have to. Come with me now—quietly—and this is all over. You've not broken your word, and your friend is safe and healthy."

But even Tanning can't bluff his way through that lie. "Well," he amends, the smile widening. "He's healthy enough, but I'm afraid you won't find him entirely unchanged."

"What did you do to him?" I ask, taking another step back. I can feel the heat from Moke, the hot scent of the metal. The electricity running across his skin is so strong

275

that my hair rises in a halo around my face, and I feel sparks catching in the back of my jeans.

"Oh, nothing much," Tanning says, still advancing toward me. "Just some run-of-the-mill steroids."

"Go on three," Moke whispers into my ear, and I nod that I heard him. But Tanning thinks the nod is for him.

"So you'll come?" he asks, extending a hand. "I promise you nothing but the best. The mother of my children…"

"One…" Moke breathes.

"…will have all that she requires."

"Two," he says.

"I do have a request," I say.

"What is that, my dear?" Tanning asks.

"I want you to die, right now," I say.

And then I hit the ground.

Moke breaks free from his chains with a massive lunge, the last hot links practically liquid as he charges for his tormentor. Tanning shrieks and backs away, but too late. Moke's hand, flickering with electricity, closes around Tanning's throat. Moke raises him into the air with one arm. The doctor's legs kick wildly for purchase, and his entire body seizes with electricity as a fire breaks out around his collar.

Moke's muscles glow brightly now, all his reserved energy pouring into this man who has mutated him beyond anything he was born to be. Tanning's eyes roll back into his head and Moke drops him, shaking fiery remnants of skin from his fingers. Tanning's body quivers for a moment longer, the last pulses of electricity rolling through his limbs, chasing away the life.

All around us, the smoke has started to dissipate, and the cries of anguish come more clearly now, a reminder that the battle wages on.

"Moke?" I ask, coming up behind him. I want to reach out, want to touch his shoulder in reassurance, but sparks of electricity still dance across his skin.

"Don't touch me, not yet," he whispers, falling to his knees, all energy expended. "Go," he says, eyes meeting mine before he loses consciousness. "Go and fight."

CHAPTER 61

I rush past the still-smoldering remains of Tanning as the smoke clears. With their leader gone, the Marauders have broken ranks. They're nowhere to be seen as I scan the crowd. Without Moke to power the machine, its light hum no longer fills the air as the temperature begins to fall.

But the battle is far from over. The citizens of the City of the Dead have been fed on fear and loathing through Langford's smear campaign, and they're not about to let a single hybrid walk out of here alive. I break out of the square to find a human squeezing a reptilian's throat. His eyes bulge, ready to pop out of their sockets and onto his scaled skin.

"Stop!" I scream, running to his assistance. I catch his attacker with a kick to the ribs, sending the man flying into the crowd. But that was a single struggle in the war that's being waged, and I can't save everyone.

"Humans!" Langford's voice—rough and metallic— rises out of the chaos. I spot her standing at the top of the hospital steps, megaphone in hand.

"They came in peace, only to promote a lie!" she screeches. "The hybrids would lay this entire city to waste, erase our existence, and push the world to a new future— one where they are the last living things!"

Surged on by the thought of a world without their species, the humans fight harder, gaining a second wind as their leaders' words fill the night.

"Do not let our species fade quietly!" Langford screams again, backing toward the hospital doors as a tangled mass of humans and hybrids swarms up the steps, clawing, fighting every step of the way.

"Somebody shut her up!" Pietro's voice comes from my radio, but it's thin and staticky compared to Langford's megaphone.

I press against the crowd, fighting through clumps of struggling bodies as I try to reach the hospital steps. The white flash of Langford's suit catches my eye as she drops the megaphone, pushes through the glass doors, and wraps a chain around the handles on the inside.

"She left us!" a human yells, pointing toward the hospital steps. "She's saving her own skin and leaving us to fight!"

"Traitor!" I scream, adding my voice to the growing chaos as I pump my wings and push upward, hoping to rise above the crowd. But a hand clasps onto my ankle and I'm dragged downward.

"Let go!" I screech, kicking at a woman's face. But there is blood running from her ears and her eyes are fogged over, uncomprehending. She's too far gone with the virus, and knows only to hurt those who she's been told are the enemy.

Other hands clutch at me as I kick, pumping my wings. There are too many of them, and I'm dragged to the ground. I scream, lashing at the mob around me. Hands tear at my wings and feathers fly.

"Freak!" someone yells, and stomps on my wrist. I cry out, curling into a ball. I can't fly, can't fight. They are a boiling mass around me, and all I can do is make myself smaller as they aim for any opening they can find to hurt me.

"Stop! Listen!" I try to cry out, but a boot lands in my gut and I lose my wind. Something strikes my temple and the world goes gray, my vision blurring, a high-pitched whine in my ears.

This is it. This is how I go out. Not falling from the sky like a meteor from heaven. Not with a smirk on my face and a glint in my eye. I'm going to die in the fetal position and be pulled apart by a crazed mob.

There's a sharp *crack,* and a warm spray covers my face as a body falls on top of me, blocking the fists and feet of the crowd.

"Back off!" Chammy's voice cuts through the chaos, and the weight of the dead man is shoved aside. I scramble to my feet, breathless, to see him standing with his weapon, facing down the people who tried to kill me.

He's covered in blood, his skin constantly fluctuating to follow the ripples and trickles as it runs down his body. Chammy is breathing heavily, his chest rising and falling, straining against tears in his shirt. I can see ragged strips of flesh and scratches across his torso. The humans are fighting with everything they have, right down to their teeth and nails.

"You okay?" Chammy growls, his eyes never leaving the group of humans that stare us down, hate burning in their gazes.

"Yeah," I say. "Got the wind knocked out of me, but I'm good."

"Lost a few feathers, too," he says, a smile forming as one floats past on the breeze. I pluck it from the air, examining it.

"This one isn't mine," I tell him, just as Max lands on the hospital steps and picks up Langford's megaphone.

"People of the City of the Dead!" she shouts. "You've listened to my voice once before. Hear me again now, please!"

All around us, people turn to Max with something other than fear and anger on their faces. She's got their attention, and she won't let it go. Overhead, the Flock circles, slowly angling downward as the fighting falls to a low simmer.

"Are you stupid?" Max asks, and a hoarse cry rises from the crowd.

"No!"

"What is she doing?" Chammy whispers in my ear, but I only shrug. Max knows how to handle people, and I trust her judgment.

"I didn't think you were stupid," Max goes on, spinning with her megaphone so that everyone can hear her. "But someone else did. Someone else was counting on you to be scared, and fearful. They told you lies, and you believed them. They told you who your enemy was, and to fight them."

"It's you!" A scream comes from the crowd. "Hybrids are the enemy!"

"I understand why you feel that way. I'm different, right?" A hush falls as she spreads her wings, showing them to the world. "I don't look like you. So I must be bad. I must be wrong. I must be your enemy.

"But look down at the ground," Max goes on. "Look at the blood spilled here today. It's red, all of it. Yours... and mine." She lifts the edge of her shirt to reveal a wound there, red seeping from the edges.

"I bleed, like you," she says. "I can be hurt, like you. And not just my flesh. I can feel, just like a human. I love my child, like any mother would."

One of the women who had been kicking me looks over at my wings and wipes a tear from her eye.

"Hybrids!" Max yells out, jerking half the crowd to attention. "You're not alone!"

When she says this the rest of the Flock land around her, each of them falling into place on either side of her, creating a phalanx of wings.

"You're not alone just because we're here," Max goes on. "You were never alone. Look around you. These humans can be hurt, and they can die. They can fall sick and they can be made weak. But why is that the only way you interact with them?"

Next to me, Chammy shakes his head.

"Look in their eyes," Max implores. "They're scared, too. They've been told by a higher power who to hate and who to fight, and they listened because they didn't have a choice. Who have you listened to? Do you also fight simply because that's what you've been told to do?"

"Damn it," Chammy says, starting to push through the crowd. "She's going to demotivate our entire army."

I grab his arm, pulling him back. "Yes," I say. "She is. But maybe we don't need an army anymore."

"What?" he snaps at me, his eyes burning. "How can you say that after everything you've been through?"

"Just look around," I say, turning him by the shoulders so that he can see the change that is happening. The fire of battle is gone, the hard truth of reality settling among everyone—hybrids and humans alike. There's shame in the air along with the smoke. A breeze blows through the city, dropping the temperature and cooling fevered skin. I see one man looking at his bloodied hands with disgust.

At the height of the fighting I would have put my fist through any one of these people's teeth, but Max's words have given me pause. That same mouth I was so ready to pulverize might have kissed a lover before going out to fight, or told a child they loved them.

"I've seen Max kill and fight," I tell him. "But I've also seen her love and protect. Both take strength, and there's a time for each of them."

He shakes his head, denying the tears that are rising in his eyes. "I can't forgive them for what happened to my parents."

"I'm not asking you to," I say. "It wasn't the city's fault, or the responsibility of the people who live here. They fought because someone told them they had to—the same person who threw your parents out with the garbage."

"Langford," he says, his jaw tightening.

"Langford," I agree. "Let's go pick a fight with the real enemy."

CHAPTER 62

"Mom!" I yell, pushing through the crowd to the top of the hospital steps.

Max wraps her arms around me, and even though I can feel the strength in them, she's shaking. "When I saw you get pulled down, I didn't think you would come back up," she whispers in my ear, her voice thick with tears.

"I'm okay," I say, pulling back and brushing away my own tears. "Chammy saved me."

"With my last bullet," the reptilian says, showing me his empty chamber.

"It was well spent," Fang says, holding his hand out. "I'm Hawk's father. Thank you for what you did."

Chammy shakes my dad's hand, but his eyes are on the glass doors of the hospital behind the Flock, where Langford had disappeared.

"We need in," I tell Max. "I promised Chammy he would have justice."

Max looks at the chains covering the inside of the glass doors. "Breaking in would be easy enough," she says.

"But I just got these people calmed down, and it won't take much to fire them up again."

As she speaks, the Flock is dispersing throughout the crowd, helping humans and hybrids alike to their feet, and seeing to wounds. Fang stands shoulder to shoulder with Max, shaking his head as he agrees with her.

"Your mom is right," he says. "It's not worth the risk of the mob rushing the hospital. Remember, a lot of these people are still sick. Peace is a tenuous thing, and it doesn't take much to break it."

"Besides," Max adds. "I don't think she's in there. Langford is a rat, and she'll head for her nest when she's in danger."

"You think she went to the Council building?" I ask.

"Probably," Fang agrees. "She likely has a stash of weapons there."

"Be careful!" Max shouts after me, but Chammy is already pulling me down the steps, anxious to make up for the lost time. He stops when he spies a stunned reptilian leaning against a building and trades his empty weapon for the reptilian's loaded one.

"Nice," I snipe at him as we run down the street. "What if he needs that?"

"I need it more," Chammy says tightly, his breath coming in jagged rasps.

I take to the air, leaping forward and leaving him below. My legs are tired and shaking, but my wings don't let me down. I rise above the city, watching as the knots of humans and hybrids below separate. Most of them are pulling back into their groups, humans helping humans, hybrids caring for hybrids. But occasionally I see flesh mixed with scales, and hands reaching across the invisible boundaries.

Chammy might be right. He might need that gun more.

The flash of white grabs my attention and I zero in on it. Langford is moving through back alleys, making her way to the Council building—just like Max and Fang had predicted. I circle as she enters through a loading dock, the early rays of the rising sun illuminating her like a spotlight. She glances up before disappearing inside, her glare landing directly on me. I veer back to Chammy and land just as he's clearing the front steps, winded and gasping.

"She's inside," I say. "But you need a minute, and we need a plan."

"She dies, that's the plan," he says. "And I don't need a minute."

But his ragged breath says otherwise, and I encourage him to lean against the wall for a second.

"There's no point running in there with nothing on your side other than your temper," I say. "She wouldn't have left this building empty, and she spotted me before. She'll be expecting us, and there will be guards inside still loyal to her, maybe even other Council members."

"I'm ready," he says, straightening up and checking that his weapon is fully loaded. "What have you got on you?"

I hold up my empty hands. "I left my rifle with Pietro, lost my gun and radio when the mob came after me. I'm going in with my wits."

"Then you're not going in at all," he argues. "This is my fight, not yours."

"Maybe, but you need me," I say. "I know this building, and where Langford will likely be. You cover me if you want, but I'm going in."

And with that, I push open the front door.

CHAPTER 63

It's cool inside and oddly calm. Chammy drips blood and I leave behind a few stray feathers as we make our way across the lobby.

"Disgusting," he says under his breath as he takes in the nicely decorated walls, the overstuffed furniture, and the glass-paneled fireplace. "I lived in a dank cave my whole life, and humans have this?"

"Not every human," I tell him. "There were plenty of kids on the streets when I was an orphan, and they weren't all hybrids. This is how people like Langford live, ignoring the suffering around them."

I head for the elevator bank quietly, easing around the corner, on the alert for any guards. But it's eerily silent, so quiet I can hear Chammy's breathing behind me. It's short and shallow, with a hint of a gurgle. He's injured, and badly. But I know he won't back down. Not now. Not with his goal in sight.

I press the button on the elevator bank and feel the

whoosh of air pushing through the cracks of the doors as the car descends.

"Get ready," I say under my breath, just as the elevator dings.

The doors separate and two guards rush for us. I duck low, taking one out at the knees. We roll together into the hall, his legs tripping up his buddy. Chammy drops onto the second guard, rendering him unconscious with a quick jab to the temple.

My opponent doesn't go down so easily. He gains his feet just as I latch on to his back, wrapping my legs around his waist from behind, and my arms around his throat. He cries out and throws himself backward, crushing me against the wall. My wings creak and pop under the pressure, but I'm not letting go. I can feel the guard's pulse under my touch as he presses back against me, his air running out. He falls forward, trying to dislodge me, but I hang on. He goes slack just as his skin turns purple, and I release him.

Chammy pulls me up and we pile into the elevator. I push the button for the top floor and take a second to stretch my wings. They're ragged in patches and bloody in spots, but it doesn't feel like anything is broken. In the mirror wall of the elevator I can see Chammy's skin mottle and change, reflecting the brown whorled interior, and the streaks of blood still running freely down his face.

"I got this," he says, meeting my eyes in the mirror.

"You better," I tell him, as the doors slide open at the top floor.

CHAPTER 64

We step out into the hall to find a Council member standing at the end, blocking the double doors and holding a gun.

"Stop!" he cries out. "Stop right there or I'll shoot."

"Me, too," Chammy says, extending his gun. "And with better aim."

It's true. The guy is shaking all over, and his weapon moves erratically—first pointing at me, and then at Chammy. I wrack my brains, trying to remember his name. Unfortunately, all I can recall is that I thought of him as Worse Breath. That's not helpful right now.

"Listen," I tell him, moving forward. "It's over. Langford played a game, and she lost. You know she was going to disband the Council, right?"

"What?" he asks, sweat running behind his glasses. "No, she would never do that. She's a good leader."

"Is she?" I ask, taking another step. "I've been in meetings with you...Holden." *There it is! Thank god!* "I've seen how you react to some of her statements," I go on.

"You don't always agree with Langford, or her stance on hybrids."

"No." He shakes his head, and the gun bobs with it. "But that doesn't mean I'm letting you kill her."

"You're trying to do the right thing," I say. "But you're doing it for the wrong person."

"She's scum, man," Chammy says, following close behind me, gun still centered on Holden. "And I'm going to take her out. If you're in my way, you go down, too."

Holden's eyes flick to me, real fear in them. This is the hybrid he's been warned about: the bloodthirsty kind that doesn't hold back.

"I can't stop him," I tell Holden. "But you can stop Langford. She's—"

I don't get to finish. There's a loud *crack,* and Chammy yells, dropping his gun. Holden screams at the same time, looking in amazement at the destruction he caused by pulling a trigger. Chammy's weapon is ruined, a warped piece of metal…and his hand isn't in any better shape. Blood pours from the wound as he staggers, holding the stump of his arm. Enraged, he knows only one thing.

He is going to get what he wants.

With a loud bellow, he runs straight for Holden, who fires again. But this time the bullet goes high, and Chammy hits him full force, knocking the double doors of the Council room open as they both roll into it, grappling with each other.

"Chammy!" I yell, following. There's a broad streak of

blood and I slip, grabbing the doorframe for balance just as a bullet flies where my head was a second ago.

"You bitch!" I scream, catching sight of Langford and an open safe just behind the meeting table. Fang was right—she did have a gun stashed here. She took a shot at me, a shot to kill.

And now it's pointed right at Chammy.

CHAPTER 65

"Get up!" she screams, and Chammy comes to his feet slowly, eyes on Langford's weapon. On the floor, Holden moans, one hand still clutching his gun. I edge toward him, but Langford isn't falling for it. She spins the gun to face me.

"Don't even think about it," she sneers, and I come to a halt.

"Holden!" she snaps, and the Council member comes to his feet, cradling one arm at an awkward angle. "Keep your gun on her!" she says, her weapon pointing at Chammy now, who glares at her with fire in his eyes.

This close, there's no denying the resemblance. Even Langford seems taken aback by what she sees. The sharp jawline and aquiline nose can't be ignored, but it's the eyes that tell the story. Anyone can see the hate burning inside both of them, twin spires emanating from a shared fire.

Even though he's dripping blood, Chammy steps toward her. "I know what you did," he says, his voice low and threatening. "I know what happened to my parents."

"Parents?" Holden asks, eyes meeting mine. "What's he talking about?"

"She created him," I tell Holden, who shakes his head in disbelief. "Chammy and all the rest of the reptilians."

"That's not true," Langford says sharply, but there's a tremor in her voice.

"It is!" I argue. "Just look at them! She used her own DNA to—"

"Enough!" Langford shouts. "What I did or didn't do is in the past, and can't be undone."

"No," Chammy agrees. "But I'm here now, and your past is catching up to you."

She laughs, the sound ringing out loud and clear while the gun remains steady on the reptilian. "You're here, certainly," she says. "Bleeding all over my carpet. Shall I just wait you out? Let you drain while I watch?"

A growl escapes him and he moves closer, but Langford raises the gun to point at his head.

"Or do you prefer a quicker death?" she asks. Chammy stalls out, his eyes cutting to mine for the first time. A breeze whips through the room, snapping the tarp that covers the broken window where Max and Fang leaped to their freedom. From below, the muted sounds of a gathered crowd rise to our ears.

"They're not fighting for you anymore," I tell her. "Do you hear that? That's the sound of hybrids and humans coming together. They saw you make a run for it back at the square. You've lost their confidence, and pissed off more than a few of them. You've got two enemies up here, but down there are a lot more. You're trapped and you know it."

Her eyes flicker for a second, and I push my advantage.

"What are you going to do?" I ask. "The city isn't behind you anymore."

"The city will listen to the Council," she snaps at me. "People need guidance in trying times. They want rules to follow. I gave them that."

"You gave them lies!" I seethe, turning to Holden. "The virus didn't come from hybrids," I say. "Langford just wanted the city divided and the Council distracted while she made a grab for power. She was going to disband you and take over as a dictator!"

Something flashes in Holden's eyes, and I realize he's listening to me, just like the crowd listened to Max at the square.

"She's a liar, Holden," I tell him. "She sent the people into the forest to clean up the mess she created a generation ago when she threw hybrid experiments out with the trash. People died because of her, the very people she was supposed to protect."

Holden's gun lowers, and he turns to Langford. "Is this true?"

"No, of course not!" she sputters, edging toward the door as he brings his gun up—to point it at her.

"Holden!" she cries. "How dare you?"

"How dare *you*?" Chammy explodes, the last of his energy bellowing forth in rage. "You've cheated and lied, destroyed and manipulated. My parents died because of you!"

"I gave your parents life!" Langford snaps, her wrath seeping out, no longer worried about control or image. "I created their damn ugly skins, grew them, tended to them. And when the plug was pulled I was told to get rid of them, by whatever means necessary. And so I did," she finishes, gaze going to Holden. "Some people do what their superiors tell them."

"They were your children!" Chammy seethes.

"They were experiments!" she shouts back, gun wavering as she screams. "They were a bunch of cells in a dish, bastardized life that grew into hideous forms. I sent them to the sewers, where they belonged!"

Chammy screams and lunges for her, just as Langford gets a shot off. He hits her full force and her arm flies upward, sending the bullet into the ceiling. Holden screams as the lights go out, sparks flying from the broken tiles overhead. The emergency lights come on, the white strobe flashing just in time for me to see Langford and Chammy fall out the broken window—together.

CHAPTER 66

There's no time to think.

I dive. The canvas whips at my face, and then I'm in the open air, plummeting. I tuck my wings close to my body, streamlining myself as much as possible. I'm a missile plunging for the ground, aiming at the struggling mass of Langford and Chammy as they fall.

Droplets of Chammy's blood fly into my face as I dive, pulling nearer to the two of them. They fight even as they fall, Langford screaming and scratching for Chammy's eyes, his arms tight around her waist as he crushes her.

I grab him from behind, snaking an arm under his shoulders. I can't speak, can't breathe. The air is rushing past me too quickly to be pulled into my lungs. I can only hope Chammy understands what I'm about to do.

I unfurl my wings and we pull up, hard. Chammy lets go of Langford at the last moment. She clutches at him furiously, but his bloody scales provide no purchase. He slips through her grasp just as I pump my wings.

The hybrids rise, and the human falls.

CHAPTER 67

Days later, fires still burn.

The square has been cleared, the Marauders' weapon dismantled for parts. The Flock found huge quantities of vaccine loaded into the vans that Tanning brought, hoping to trade them for hybrid bodies to experiment on. What remained of the Council met with the Flock and determined that one crate of vaccine would go to the city's scientists, so that they could figure out how to make enough for the entire population.

The rest of the vaccine was portioned out evenly among hybrids and humans.

But still, there were voices of dissent, memories that didn't fade as quickly as the bloodstains in the street. A few hundred humans had relocated to the east side of the city, declaring it a no-hybrid zone. They left before the vaccine had been distributed, and gunshots could be heard from that side of town both day and night as the virus burned through them and fighting broke out.

"We have to get some vaccine over to them," Max is

saying, raising her voice above the snapping of the tarp. Holden had promised to get the window of the meeting room fixed. But it hasn't happened yet. I guess there are bigger problems than broken glass in a city that is still healing.

"I don't see why you're so interested in helping people who'd just as soon see you dead," Chammy argues. His arm is in a sling, and he winces as he readjusts himself at the table. His missing hand hurts both his body and his pride, but he'd jumped at the chance to be on the new Council and refuses to miss a single meeting.

"Max is right," Moke speaks up from his seat—a safe distance from the others. Spirals of electricity still ripple from his skin, and he'll need to leave the room for a discharge soon, before he becomes a danger to those around him. But for now he's here and provides a good counterpoint to Chammy's need for revenge.

"Giving these people more reasons to hate us will only be fuel for their flames," Moke goes on. "If we air-drop some medicine in, they might have to finally acknowledge that we're not the enemy, that we only want to help them."

"Or they'll destroy it, suspecting that we only mean to poison them," Chammy says gloomily.

"Then that's their choice," I speak up. "We can't make them do anything, but we can give them the option of saving themselves."

"And with the progress being made on duplicating the vaccine, if they destroy what we give them, it won't be much of a waste," Max adds. "I call for a vote—who agrees to distribute vaccine to the humans occupying what they call the no-hybrid zone?"

Hands go up around the table—mine, Moke's, Holden's, a few women who had been on the Council before, Max and Fang. Chammy is the last holdout. He looks around the room, and sighs, finally raising his stump.

"At least no one can accuse me of lending them a hand," he jokes, and a chorus of laughter rings out around the table. Just then, there's a hesitant knock at the door, and Pietro sticks his head in.

"Hawk?" he asks, scanning the room for me. "You'd better come quick."

CHAPTER 68

Melanie lies in her bed, sickly white with blue-tinged lips.

"Hawk." She smiles when she sees me, her skin stretched thin. "I'm sorry to pull you away, I know the Council has a lot of work to do right now."

Just like her, to apologize about dying.

"Shut your face," I say, choking back tears as I sit next to her on the bed. "And save your breath."

"We're a little past that," she says, wheezing. The door quietly clicks closed behind us, and I silently thank Pietro for leaving us alone as Melanie's eyes drift shut.

Her cool hand reaches out for mine and we link fingers. I can't think of anything to say, and I know there's nothing I can do except watch her struggle to breathe.

"Thank you so much," she says, eventually, her eyes flickering open. "You've made the last few days of my life the most interesting ones yet."

"You can say a lot of things about me, but I'm never boring," I tell her, and she manages a smile.

"To see you flying that night, above the city," her eyes slide shut again, remembering. "Among the fire and the smoke and the bullets, all that bloodshed and anger and there was you, rising above it all, fighting it out in the skies. It must be so amazing up there. So free."

"Want to find out for yourself?" I ask, standing up.

Her eyes fly open, one last spark lighting in them. "Really?"

"It's the least I can do," I say. "Hell, it's the only thing I can do."

We get to the roof and I wrap my arms around her waist. She's thin as a stick and light as a bird, her breaths coming in short, shallow gasps as we stand on the edge of the building.

"Ready?" I ask into her ear.

She nods, too breathless to say more. I pump my wings and we rise, her body like a child's underneath me as we skim the tops of buildings, her hospital gown fluttering around us. I take her to all my favorite places—pointing out the old McCallum home where I used to live, and Pietro's Hope for Opes center. Every time I circle back to the hospital to touch down, she squeezes my arm and begs to stay aloft a little longer.

I take a pass over the forest, showing her the lake and pointing out the thin stream of hybrids that still trickles into the city from the edges. Chammy told his people that a better life awaited them in the city, but a few have been slow to realize that the tide has turned in their favor, and the city that once hated them now stands ready to welcome them. It looks like the last few holdouts have come to their senses. I spot Tut leading a group...slowly.

I wheel back for the hospital, and this time she doesn't argue. When I touch down on the rooftop, I realize why. She died somewhere over the forest, with the wind in her hair and green trees below her. She died in my arms.

But I can hope at least that she died happy.

CHAPTER 69

"You really think it's safe?" Calypso asks me for the twenty thousandth time, eyeing me suspiciously as she shrugs her shoulders and unveils her antennas.

"Kiddo, it's safe," Moke reassures her.

Rain reaches for Calypso's antennas, brushing them with her fingers as if they were gossamer strands of hair. "We wouldn't even think of letting you come to the ceremony if we thought for one second you could be hurt," she tells her.

"Yeah, dingbat," I say, giving her an affectionate nudge. "And if I can walk around like this"—I unfurl my wings, lush and glorious now that all the feathers have come back in—"then I don't think you have much to worry about."

"And I can't exactly hide what I am," Moke agrees, holding up a finger to illustrate as a spark dances around the tip. "Nobody has given me any trouble on the streets all winter. I know it's hard to believe, but I think they've finally accepted us."

"Well, not everyone," I say, bitterly. "There's still the no-hybrid zone."

"But heavily depleted," Moke argues, and it's true.

After we air-dropped them some medicine and food, a few of the humans who had chosen to flee the center of the city came skulking back. More showed up during a long, hard winter, half-starved and shaking. They were given care and food with no questions asked. I even saw one man being spoon-fed by a hybrid, his demeanor softening with every bite.

Still, there were a handful of stalwart humans who refused to move into the future, refused to see hybrids standing alongside their species, shoulder to shoulder.

"Some people just need someone to hate," Rain says quietly, and I nod that I understand.

"Are you guys ready?" Pietro asks, walking in from the hallway. "The whole city has shown up, and Max and Holden are ready to start."

We hustle downstairs, Calypso's hand in mine. Her antennas bounce as we walk out into the spring sunlight, but no one stares.

I leave Calypso with Moke and Rain in the front seats that had been reserved for them and march up the Council building steps to take my place next to Max and Holden. Pietro and Chammy flank them on the other side, along with the rest of the Council members. Max steps up to the podium and speaks confidently into the mic.

"Humans and hybrids, welcome," she says, and a wave of clapping and cheering greets her words.

"People love her," Pietro whispers in my ear.

"So do hybrids," I tell him, with a wink.

"It's been a long, hard winter," Max goes on. "We've all lost something. Some of us lost loved ones, some of us lost hope. But we held on. We kept going. Together, we became more than we could ever be apart. We became something more, something stronger, and we've created a new city."

She takes a breath as applause breaks out again.

"This city used to be covered with smoke from the dope factories, and Opes clogged the streets. Everywhere you went there was someone who would kill you for what you had. It was called the City of the Dead, because even those who were alive had little to live for.

"That has changed," Max goes on. "And we need a new name for this city, a name that says not only who we were, but who we are together. We've made it to this day, through fire and through heat, through cold and through winter, through starvation and sickness. We made it to this day, because—human or hybrid—we are survivors."

She steps down from the podium, and a wave of cheering breaks out. Calypso joins in, her antennas bobbing as she jumps up and down in the front row.

Holden walks to the podium and adjusts the mic.

"As the new head of the Council, I declare that we are no longer the City of the Dead," he says, and the crowd hushes as they await to hear the new name of their home.

"We are now the City of Survivors!" Holden exclaims, and the loudest wave of applause yet breaks loose, sweeping across the crowd. Humans and hybrids alike cheer as Holden makes a show of unlocking the front doors of the Council building.

That's my cue. I clear my throat, and Pietro squeezes my hand as I make my way to the podium.

"This building used to be just for the Council," I say. "The elites sat high above the people and made decisions that affected everyone. No more," I shout, banging my hand on the podium. "From now on, if you have an issue or concern, you can bring it to the Council—hybrid or human. Bring your problems to us, and I promise you, we will listen, and help find a solution."

There's another wave of cheering as Calypso breaks free from the crowd and runs for me, arms open. I sweep her up and she leans her head against my shoulder, her antennas snaking around her and tickling my neck. I make my way back to her seat and share it with her, settling her onto my lap. There's a gasp from the human behind me as Ridley wings over the crowd, spots me, and settles onto my shoulder.

Holden takes the mic again and begins to explain new policies and procedures for the City of Survivors, but I'm not listening anymore. All I can see is the smile on Calypso's face as she looks at the human behind me and wiggles her fingers in hello.

The woman laughs, and Calypso settles into my lap, her fingers finding mine. "So what do we do now?" she asks, as Ridley nuzzles my ear.

"Either we go looking for trouble, or we let it find us," I tell her, and she scrunches her nose.

"It'll find you, Hawk," she declares. "It always does."

I can't argue against that, but for now I'm happy to sit here in the spring breeze with one of my orphans, my hawk on my shoulder and surrounded by those I know I can trust. I can see how a person could get used to this.

But I can also see how it might get boring....

Turn the page to start reading James Patterson's next incredible thriller:

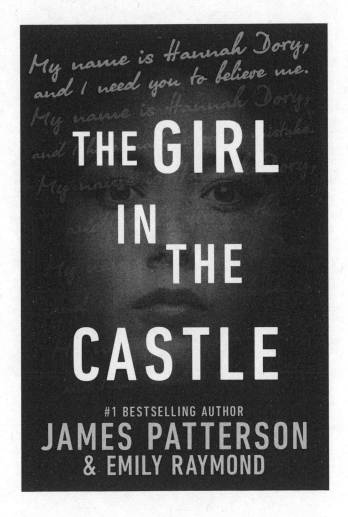

My name is Hannah Dory, and I need you to believe me.
My name is Hannah Dory,
and I ... ...istake.
My na...

THE GIRL IN THE CASTLE

#1 BESTSELLING AUTHOR

JAMES PATTERSON

& EMILY RAYMOND

AVAILABLE NOW!

CHAPTER 1

It starts with a girl, half naked and screaming.

Even though it's midtown Manhattan, in January, the girl is wearing only a thin white T-shirt over a black lace bra. She slaps at the air like she's fighting an enemy only she can see.

A gangly teen, halfway through his first-ever shift at the Gap, watches her nervously through the window. Every other New Yorker just clutches their phone or their Starbucks cup and pretends not to see her.

Maybe they really don't.

She lets out a tortured cry that strangles in her throat, and then she crumples to her knees. "How do we get out of the castle?" she wails. "They're going to kill us all!"

A police car speeds up to the curb and two officers step out. "Are you hurt?" the first asks. DUNTHORPE, his name tag reads.

The girl's answer is more wordless screaming.

"We need you to calm down, miss," his partner, Haines, says.

"Are you hurt?" Dunthorpe asks again. He thinks he's seen this girl around the neighborhood. Maybe she's one of the shoplifters or the dopeheads—or maybe she's just some scared, crazy kid. Either way, he can't just let her stand here and scream bloody murder.

When Dunthorpe moves toward her, she drops to her hands

and knees and starts crawling away. Haines tries to grab her, but the minute he touches her back, she spins around at the same time her right foot flies out, smashing into his chest. Haines loses his balance and falls backward, cursing. The girl stands up and tries to run, but she stumbles over her backpack and goes down on all fours again.

"Help me!" she screams. "Don't let them take me! Call off the guards! They'll kill me!"

As Dunthorpe moves toward her with one hand on his Taser, she launches herself forward and hits him in the face with a closed fist. He reels backward, roaring in surprise, as Haines springs into action and gets her into a headlock.

Dunthorpe rubs his cheekbone and says, "Call the ambulance."

"But the little bitch hit you."

Dunthorpe's cheek smarts. "That'll be our secret."

"You sure you don't want to book her?" Haines's arm tightens around the girl's neck and her knees buckle. Quick as a snake, Haines gets behind her, grabs her hands, and cuffs them behind her back.

"I'm sure," Dunthorpe says.

The girl keeps quiet until the ambulance comes, and then she starts screaming again. "Don't let them take me!" she yells to the passersby as the two cops and an EMT wrestle her onto the gurney. "I have to save Mary. Oh, my sweet Mary!"

Strapped down, the girl wails over the sound of the ambulance siren.

"You can't take me! I need to save Mary! No, no, you can't take me!"

But of course, they can take her wherever they want to.

Half an hour later, the ambulance pulls up to the hospital, where a small but powerfully built nurse stands with her hands on her hips, waiting.

Arriving at the exact same time—but on foot, and voluntarily— is a handsome young man of nineteen or so. "Excuse me," he says, peering at the nurse's badge, "are you Amy Navarre? My name's Jordan Hassan, and I think I'm supposed to shadow you—"

"You'll have to wait," Nurse Amy says curtly as the ambulance doors open.

Jordan Hassan shuts his mouth quick. He takes a step to the side as the EMTs slide a metal gurney out of the back. Strapped onto it is a girl, probably right about his age, with a dirty, tear-streaked face. She's wearing a T-shirt and pair of boots but little else.

The nurse, who he's pretty sure is supposed to be his supervisor for his class-credit internship this semester, walks toward the girl. "You can take the straps away," she says to the EMT.

"I wouldn't—" he begins.

The nurse looks at the girl. "It's okay," she says.

Jordan's not sure if she's reassuring the EMT or the girl. In any case, the EMT removes the restraints, and the nurse gently helps the girl off the stretcher. Jordan watches as the girl shuffles toward the entrance.

As the doors slide open automatically, she feints left and bolts right.

She's coming straight for him.

Acting on reflex, Jordan catches her around the waist. She strains against his arms, surprisingly strong. Then she twists her head around and pleads, "Please—please—let me go! My sister needs me!"

"Keep hold of her!" Nurse Amy shouts.

Jordan has no idea what to do or who to listen to.

"I'm *begging* you," the girl says, even as Amy advances, radioing security. Even as one of the girl's sharp elbows jams into his solar plexus. Jordan gasps as air shoots out of his lungs.

"Just let me go," the girl says, quieter now. "*Please*. I need your help."

Jordan's grip loosens—he can't hold her much longer, and he doesn't want to, either. But then two uniformed men come running outside, and they grab the girl's arms and drag her into the hospital, and all the while she's fighting.

Nurse Amy and Jordan follow them into a small room off the lobby. The guards get the girl into a geri chair and strap her down, and Jordan watches as Nurse Amy prepares a syringe.

"Your first day, huh?" she says to Jordan, her face looking suddenly worn. "Well, welcome to Belman Psych. We call this a B-52. It's five milligrams of Haldol and two milligrams of Ativan, and we don't use it unless it's necessary for the safety of patient and staff." She injects it intramuscularly, then follows it up with an injection of diphenhydramine. "Don't worry. It'll quiet her down."

But it's not like in the movies, when the patient just slumps forward, drooling and unconscious. The girl's still yelling and pulling against her restraints. It looks like she's being tortured.

"Give it a few minutes," Amy says to Jordan.

Then she touches the patient's hair, carefully brushing it away from her gnashing teeth. "You're home, sweet Hannah. You're home."

DELIA F. BELMAN MEMORIAL
PSYCHIATRIC HOSPITAL
INTAKE & EVALUATION

PATIENT INFORMATION

Name: Hannah Doe

Date of Birth: 1/14/2005

Date Service Provided: 1/17/23

FUNCTIONING ON ADMISSION

ORIENTATION: Confusion w/r/t to time,
place, identity; pt believes herself to
be in a castle, possibly as a captive

APPEARANCE/PERSONAL HYGIENE: Pt presents
disheveled, dirty, with clothing missing.
Underweight. Superficial contusions and
excoriations on legs and arms

PSYCHOSIS: Pt experiencing auditory and
visual hallucinations

MOOD: Angry, upset, incoherent, uncooperative

LABORATORY RESULTS: Lab evaluation within normal limits. Toxicology report negative, and pt does not have history of substance abuse.

NOTES: After a breakdown on 44th St., pt was brought by ambulance at 9:34 a.m., mildly hypothermic from cold exposure. She attempted escape before being admitted. She was unable to answer orienting questions and insisted security staff wanted to kill her and her sister. Tried to attack security guard. We were unable to complete intake interview due to her delusional state; we will conduct further evaluation tomorrow if she is coherent.

Chapter 2

*M*y name is Hannah Dory. I am eighteen in the year of our Lord
1347, and God forgive me, I am about to do something extraordinarily stupid.

I crossed myself, stood up, and threw a heavy cape over my
shoulders.

"Hannah!" cried my sister, Mary. "Where are you going?
Mother won't like—"

I didn't wait to hear the rest of the sentence. I marched down
the narrow, frozen lane toward the village square, my jaw clenched
and my hands balled into fists.

It was deepest winter, and there was misery everywhere I
looked. A boy with hollow cheeks sat crying in a doorway of a
thatch-roofed hovel, while a thin, mangy dog nosed in a nearby
refuse heap for scraps. Another child—a filthy little girl—watched
the dog with desperate eyes, waiting to steal whatever it scavenged.

I had nothing to give them. Our own food was all but gone.
We'd killed and cooked our last hen weeks ago, eating every bit of
her but the feathers.

My hands clutched over my stomach. There was nothing in
it now—nothing, that is, but grief and rage. Just last night, I'd
watched my little brother Belin die.

Mother hadn't known I was awake, but I was. I saw him take his last awful, gasping breath in her arms. He'd been only seven, and now his tiny, emaciated body lay under a moth-eaten blanket in the back of a gravedigger's cart. Soon he'd be put in the ground next to his twin, Borin, the first of them to come into the world and the first one to leave it.

My name is Hannah Dory. I have lost two brothers to hunger, and I will not lose anyone else. I am going to fight.

Have you ever felt a beloved hand grow cold in yours? If not, then I don't expect you to understand.

"Blackbird, Blackbird," crazy old Zenna said as she saw me hurrying by. She winked her one remaining eye at me. "Stop and give us a song."

She called me Blackbird for my midnight hair and my habit of singing through a day's work. She didn't know that my brothers had died—that I'd rather scream than sing. I bowed to her quickly, then hastened on.

"Another day, then," she called after me.

If we live another one, I thought bitterly.

Mary caught up with me a moment later, breathless and flushed. "Mother wants you at the spindle—I keep over-twisting the yarn."

"What use is spinning when we're starving?" I practically hissed. "We'd do better to *eat* the bloody wool."

Mary's face crumpled, and I instantly regretted my harsh tone. "I'm sorry, my sweet," I said, pulling her against my chest in a quick embrace. "I know Mother wants us to keep our hands busy. But I have…an errand."

"Can I come?" Her bright blue eyes were suddenly hopeful.

My Mary, my shadow: she was four years younger than me and four times as sweet, and I loved her more than anyone else in the world.

"Not today. Go back home," I said gently. "And take care of Mother and little Conn." *The last brother we have.*

I could tell she didn't want to. But unlike me, Mary was a good girl, and she did what she was told.

Down the hill, past the cobbler's and the bakehouse and the weaver's hut I went. I didn't stop until I came to the heavy wooden doors of the village church. They were shut tight, but I yanked them open and stumbled inside. It was no warmer in the nave, but at least there was no wind to run its cold fingers down my neck. A rat skittered into the corner of the bell tower as I grabbed the frayed rope and pulled.

The church bell rang out across our village, once, twice—ten times. I pulled until my arms screamed with effort, and then I turned and went back outside.

Summoned by the sound of the bell, the people of my village stood shivering in the churchyard.

"Only the priest rings the bell, Hannah," scolded Maraulf, the weaver.

"Father Alderton's been dead a week now," I said. "So I don't think he'll be complaining."

"God rest his soul," said pretty Ryia, bowing her head and folding her hands over her large belly. She'd have a baby in her arms soon, God willing.

Father Alderton had been a good man, and at my father's

request, he'd even given me a bit of schooling and taught me to read. He'd never beaten me or told me I was going to hell for my stubbornness, the way the priest before him had.

Now I just hoped God was taking better care of Father Alderton's soul than He had the priest's earthly remains. Wolves had dug up the old man's body from the graveyard and dragged it into the woods. Thomas the swineherd, searching the forest floor for kindling, had found the old man's bloody, severed foot.

Do you see what I mean? This winter, even the predators are starving.

"What's the ringing for?" said Merrick, Maraulf's red-cheeked, oafish grown son. "Why did you call us here?"

I brushed my tangled hair from my forehead and stood up as tall as I could.

My name is Hannah Dory, and I am about to save us—or get us all killed.

I jabbed my hand in the direction of the graveyard. "Tomorrow, my little brother, Belin, will be taken there to join his twin," I yelled. "He was weak from months of cold and hunger, and he couldn't fight the fever when it came for him. Our mother knew this, and so she lied to him: she told him that he should sleep, and that he would be better in the morning. But in the morning, he was *dead*." Tears had begun to stream down my cheeks, and I angrily wiped them away. "But maybe my mother was right. Maybe Belin *is* better, because he's not suffering anymore. And maybe death is the only way to escape our torment. Who among us has not buried someone this winter?" I heard low murmurs: they all had lost fathers, children, sisters. Fever, hunger, the bloody flux—they were killing us, one by miserable one. "How much longer until there are more of us *under* the ground than above it?"

"Winter is always a hard season," said Morris, the wheelwright, stupidly.

"This one's the worst I've ever known," said ancient Zenna, who'd managed to stagger her way toward us. "Death himself has settled in our village, hasn't he?" She let out a strangled-sounding cackle. "He tells me he finds it very much to his liking."

"Hush, you old witch," said Maraulf roughly, and she jabbed him in the foot with her walking stick.

"Drunken softsword," she replied with a sly smile.

"Be quiet and listen to me!" I said. "I know what we need to do."

"We must pray harder," said the wheelwright.

"Yes, we could ask God for help," I said viciously. "But my mother and I tried that for the twins, and all it got us was sore throats and dead boys." I lifted my skirt and climbed to the top of the churchyard's stone fence. "I propose that we take matters into our own hands."

From that height, when I shielded my eyes and squinted, I could see the thing that had haunted my dreams ever since Borin first took sick.

The baron's castle. It loomed on the horizon like a squat, black mountain, and it was full of everything we lacked.

"I know how to get food. Maybe medicine, too," I said.

"Oh, get down from there before you fall," Serell, the cooper, said. "You're mad."

Of course they doubted me: I was the girl who always had a fanciful story to tell or a rosy song to sing, my voice as sweet as a lark's.

But that was the old Hannah. The new one was as sharp and cold as a knife.

"Baron Jorian died in battle last summer," I said. "And his son, Joachim, is young and untested. Now is our time to act."

"And what would you have us do?" scoffed Maraulf. "Knock on the castle doors, ask for scraps, and hope he's kind enough to give us some?"

"We shouldn't ask for anything," I said. "We should *take* it!"

Zenna began her crazed cackle again. Her eye, cloudy with mucus, rolled around in delight. "Death finds this notion very interesting indeed."

Suddenly I felt like telling her to shut up. "Maybe I'm asking you to risk your lives," I said, gazing down at the hungry, desperate villagers. "But what are lives like ours worth, anyway?"

No one spoke. No one wanted to be the first one to say *Nothing. Our lives are worth nothing at all.*

ABOUT THE AUTHORS

For his prodigious imagination and championship of literacy in America, **James Patterson** was awarded the 2019 National Humanities Medal, and he has also received the Literarian Award for Outstanding Service to the American Literary Community from the National Book Foundation. He holds the Guinness World Record for the most #1 *New York Times* bestsellers, including *Confessions of a Murder Suspect* and the Maximum Ride and Witch & Wizard series, and his books have sold more than 400 million copies worldwide. A tireless champion of the power of books and reading, Patterson created a children's book imprint, JIMMY Patterson, whose mission is simple: "We want every kid who finishes a JIMMY Book to say, 'PLEASE GIVE ME ANOTHER BOOK.'" He has donated more than three million books to students and soldiers and funds over four hundred Teacher and Writer Education Scholarships at twenty-one colleges and universities. He also supports 40,000 school libraries and has donated millions of dollars to independent bookstores.

Patterson invests proceeds from the sales of JIMMY Patterson Books in pro-reading initiatives.

Mindy McGinnis is an Edgar Award–winning novelist who writes across multiple genres, including post-apocalyptic, historical, thriller, contemporary, mystery, and fantasy.

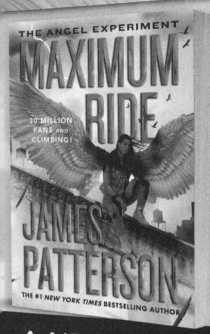

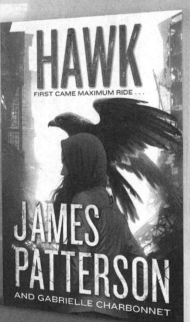
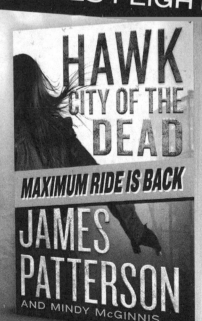

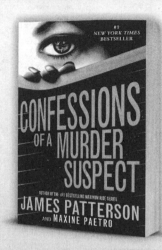

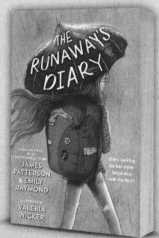
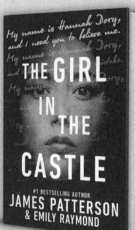